DON PENDLETON'S MACK BOLAN

PAYBACK

D1039017

A GOLD EAGLE BOOK FROM

W**O**RLDWIDE.

TORONTO • NEW YORK • LONDON
AMSTERDAM • PARIS • SYDNEY • HAMBURG
STOCKHOLM • ATHENS • TOKYO • MILAN
MADRID • WARSAW • BUDAPEST • AUCKLAND

Recycling programs
for this product may
not exist in your area.

First edition September 2014

ISBN-13: 978-0-373-61571-1

Special thanks and acknowledgment to
Michael A. Black for his contribution to this work.

PAYBACK

Printed in U.S.A.

I am concerned for the security of our great nation; not so much because of any threat from without, but because of the insidious forces working from within.

—General Douglas MacArthur,
1880–1964

I don't care who the enemy is. I will always defend this nation and her people to my last breath.

—Mack Bolan

PROLOGUE

The South American jungle,
five years ago

The undergrowth rustled in the darkness about twenty yards ahead. Mack Bolan, aka the Executioner, raised his fist to signal the rest of the squad to halt. The heavy foliage had made the movement almost imperceptible, but he was certain he'd seen something through his night-vision goggles. Exactly what, he wasn't sure. An animal, perhaps? They were in the jungle, after all. Or could it have been a man? Was someone up there waiting for them? Their nighttime insertion by truck along the twisting, mountainous road and the subsequent mile-long hike had been treacherous and lengthy, but supposedly assured the element of surprise. It should have been impossible for anyone to shadow or precede them. Unless they were expected.

Bolan kept his eyes on the area ahead. There was no more movement, but it was still one more tiny crack in the ops plan that he'd been given.

The Executioner didn't feel totally at ease with this mission. Even its tag name, Operation Cat's Cradle, bothered him. He remembered the childhood game of looping string around your fingers. He also remembered the Kurt Vonnegut novel by the same name, with the repeating refrain, "See the cat? See the cradle?" Like characters in the book, Bolan never thought the configuration resembled a cat or a cradle.

Things hadn't seemed quite right at the onset of this op, either. Maybe it was the degree of absolute assurance the Colombians had given them during the briefing. An overweight army colonel who looked as if he'd never missed a meal had smiled throughout the presentation, explaining first in Spanish for Captain Carlos Cepeda and his men, and then making a deferential show of adding a sentence in English for the benefit of Bolan and the two DEA agents, how perfectly crafted and secret the operation planning had been. "*Un plano muy perfecto.* A perfect plan," he'd said. "Nothing can possibly go wrong."

Bolan knew better. Something could always go wrong. Murphy's Law had taught him that: If anything can go wrong, it will. This wasn't the soldier's kind of mission, and how he'd let Hal Brognola talk him into wet-nursing this Colombian army special ops team on some namby-pamby extraction detail was beyond him. If it weren't for the two DEA agents, Chris Avelia and German Salamanca, who'd been helping the Colombian army locate the De la Noval cartel for the past ten months, Bolan would've declined. Avelia had assisted the soldier in a previous mission and he had come to like the kid.

The temperature had dropped a few degrees from the overwhelming heat of the day, but the humidity was still like a wet blanket. Bolan felt the sweat running down his sides and neck. And there was no letup from the ubiquitous mosquitoes. They buzzed constantly in his ears, occasionally landing on a patch of bare skin and stabbing his flesh. He felt itchy in several places. The soldier had told the rest of his team to keep their sleeves rolled down. It was hotter, but meant less exposure to the environment.

He heard someone approach his position from the rear, and crouch. Captain Cepeda and Chris Avelia moved up beside him.

"*¿Qué pasa?*" Cepeda whispered.

Even though Bolan spoke Spanish, he let Avelia translate for him.

"Movement up ahead," Bolan replied, once again surveying the area through his night-vision goggles, while the two men did the same. The hanging overgrowth was so thick and the trail so obscure that the flat, two-dimensional image through the green-tinted lenses yielded little. "I see nothing," Cepeda said in his limited English.

"I don't either, now," Bolan told him, flipping the reticules back up on his forehead to recover his depth perception. "Could De la Noval know we're coming?"

Avelia fell into step, translating each man's words into the appropriate language.

"Impossible. Even my men didn't know until we departed."

"How far are we from the Cathedral?" Bolan asked.

That was the code name for Vincente De la Noval's isolated mansion. From the surveillance photos the satellites had sent back, the place looked more like a fortress than a church. It was so isolated and so large that De la Noval purportedly felt safe enough to let his guard down to party until he dropped. The special informant had told the Colombian government that this was scheduled to be one of those "heavy party weekends."

Cepeda checked the readings on his GPS monitor and puckered his mouth. "*Quizás quinientos metros, no más.*"

PERHAPS FIVE HUNDRED YARDS, no more. That was according to Cepeda.

Bolan paused to take another compass reading and orient himself on his map. He never liked to totally rely on GPS systems. Murphy's Law liked to tinker with them, too. The squad was moving parallel to the solitary access road leading up to the main gate of the huge house. It was purported to be surrounded by a twelve-foot-high, chain-link fence, and the main entrance was covered by an armed guard at all times.

The rest of the twenty-five-man squad was bunching up behind them now, and Bolan knew that wasn't good.

"Have the men spread out and wait," he said to Avelia. "I'll move up and take a look."

The DEA agent nodded and whispered in Spanish to Cepeda. They talked for a moment and then one by one the team began to melt into the darkness, although their noise discipline needed some work.

Avelia grinned at Bolan and whispered, "I'm sure glad you're here leading us, my friend." The kid's grin was infectious. Technically, Bolan was there in an "advisory capacity only," but he felt a kinship with this group of Colombian soldiers. The Colombians and the DEA had been tracking drug kingpin Vincente De la Noval and his brother, Jesús, for the better part of three years, and this was the closest they'd come to closing the noose, thanks to an informant inside the drug lord's ranks.

When he'd heard that, Bolan couldn't help but recall his own past war against organized crime, and decided they could use a helping hand. Hopefully, their dedication would be rewarded this night.

He finished moving though the undergrowth, and peered through a shelf of drooping fronds. The mansion lay about a hundred yards away. The shrubbery had been extensively cleared and trimmed to form a buffer zone devoid of cover or concealment leading to the fence. Between the fence and the house was perhaps another fifty yards of lush, well manicured grass. The huge mansion was dark except for a few sparse lights in the first level. No noise. No movement. And no guard at the gate. Maybe he'd left his post to take a leak or to have a smoke.

Bolan listened intently for any noises and sniffed the air for telltale odors.

Nothing so far, he thought, but there wasn't much of a breeze, either.

Then he saw a spot of red and used his night-vision goggles again to get a clearer look. A man in jeans and a T-shirt and a woman dressed to kill in a short, revealing dress were locked in a standing embrace about twenty feet from the guard shack. An AK-47 with a collapsible stock was slung carelessly over the man's left shoulder, the muzzle pointing toward the ground.

The woman laughed as he brought a cigarette to her lips. She inhaled deeply, causing the tip to glow again. Instead of exhaling, she held her breath, and pressed the cigarette to the man's lips now. They were smoking a joint. Another flash appeared, as he inhaled. She slowly blew out her breath and the man smiled. They whispered together and then kissed before they made their way toward the darkened shadows by the house.

A sentry high on marijuana and on his way to getting laid, Bolan thought. Not a bad scenario leading up to a raid. But he wondered again at the accuracy of the intel they'd received. De la Noval was supposedly a strict disciplinarian, to the point of using deadly force on those he considered untrustworthy. This night he seemed to be running a pretty loose ship, considering that the sentry appeared to be leaving his post to collect seven minutes of heaven.

Of course, this lapse could help facilitate their mission, another aspect of which floated in the "trouble" section of Bolan's mind. The Colombian colonel had given Cepeda and his men explicit instructions that the drug kingpin be taken alive, at all costs. Bolan naturally took that with a grain of salt, as he did all orders given by higher-ups who liked to lead from behind a desk. Following an order that would hamper those in the field wasn't how Bolan liked to operate, but he was, after all, just there observing. And if the drug lord could be captured, it would put a serious crimp in the cartel's operations, not to mention enhance the potential for future intel.

The De la Noval cartel was rumored to be expanding its operation to Mexico. Bolan knew he and the DEA agents were there to make sure that the drug lord was captured alive and extradited to the United States, preferably on the same plane as he and the other Americans.

The brush rustled about twenty feet to the soldier's right. Bolan pivoted with his M-4 to face the threat.

A small deer scurried through the underbrush as a jaguar leaped from a nearby tree, narrowly missing it. The cat glanced toward Bolan and then disappeared into the jungle, as well.

Guess we're not the only hunters out tonight, he thought, as he turned and crept back toward Cepeda and his men. Once there he briefed them on what he'd observed.

"That movement I saw looks like it was a jaguar trying to get some dinner."

"*Bueno*," the captain said. "We have the advantage of surprise. We must move. *Ahora.*"

Bolan nodded, still feeling slightly uneasy, but shook

it off. Cepeda sent two of his men forward to cut a hole in the fence, one doing the cutting and one providing cover. They accomplished the task in short order and the rest of the team moved up. The area between the fence and the house was a long stretch, perhaps forty or fifty yards devoid of cover. It was, in effect, a perfect kill zone. They'd have to cross that section fast. The only saving grace was that there was an uphill grade, probably to allow drainage for tropical rains. The slight incline could provide them a modicum of cover, but was a double-edged sword: they'd be making an uphill trek, and this was no treadmill in some plush gym.

Avelia crawled forward and stopped next to Bolan. "I can't say I like this setup much."

The soldier surveyed the expanse again. "Me, either. This will be the trickiest part."

Avelia grinned and Bolan caught a flash of the kid's white teeth in the ambient moonlight. The sweat dripped off his camo-blackened face like dark tears.

"Let's just hope our element of surprise holds up," Bolan whispered, and gave Avelia a thumbs-up.

The DEA agent nodded.

As Bolan had suggested earlier, Cepeda sent two of his men forward across the expanse to take up secure positions under the overhanging balconies of the mansion. Once they'd ensconced themselves there, the rest of the team began moving through the fence line. The next step would be to secure the entrances, and then hit the house using stun grenades and 30 mm rounds containing a high concentration of pepper gas. Once they had the premises and all occupants secure, they'd call for their extraction.

But first we have to take the house, Bolan thought. He looked at Cepeda, who motioned for his men to move toward the planned positions to secure the front and sides of the mansion. They had just started their quick trot toward the structure when the darkness suddenly evaporated as spotlights from various positions flooded the grounds with light. Several bursts of staccato gunfire pierced the night, and a voice came over some loudspeakers, in Spanish, followed by accented English.

"*Buenos días, mis amigos*," the voice said. "*Mis amigos americanos también*." A guttural laugh pierced the air as more gunfire erupted. "Did you think I would not be expecting you?" The speakers emitted another hard laugh.

Bolan flattened himself on the ground just as a line of shots tore up the sod a few feet in front of him. He saw a series of muzzle-flashes on the upper levels of the mansion, then more from the side of the big house. More shots echoed in the night as he saw a group of at least ten men running from the rear of the building toward the fence line.

They're moving to flank us, Bolan thought.

He twisted to fire a burst at the running figures. Several of them twisted and fell as they ran. More shots rang out, sending Bolan to the ground again, but the problem was there was no real cover. Cepeda swore and rose, firing his M-4 on full-auto. Bolan started to reach up to pull the man down when more hostile rounds zipped over their position. Cepeda cried out in pain and gasped as he fell. Bolan loosed a burst and checked the captain. The round had hit him in the neck, and blood gushed from the bullet hole.

"Got it," Avelia said as he slapped a combat dressing over the wound. He applied pressure with his left hand as he fired his rifle with his right.

"Conserve your ammo," Bolan said, as he shot a quick, 3-round burst.

Avelia nodded and ceased his aimless firing, but the rest of Cepeda's men looked to be in danger of losing their combat discipline.

"We've got to get out of this kill zone," Bolan yelled. "Lay down suppressing fire so we can move up."

"*Mis amigos*," the voice on the loudspeaker yelled through the cacophony of gunfire. "Let me introduce you to my little friend."

A few seconds later a man appeared on the balcony holding an M-16 with an M-203 grenade launcher attached under the barrel. The man cut loose, and Bolan caught a brief glimpse of the incoming projectile. He barely had enough time to flatten out before the explosion ripped the night apart. Bolan knew the shrapnel would most likely explode up and out, so he worried less about the explosion than he did the concussive wave. It swept over their position like an invisible tsunami.

His hearing gone, Bolan struggled to take a breath. Through the hazy cloud of settling dirt he could see the figure on the balcony readying the M-203 once again. Another grenade would just about finish them. The man had to be taken out.

As Bolan raised his weapon, the man's head suddenly jerked back in a cloud of mist, and he disappeared from sight. The Executioner narrowed his gaze as a new group seemed to appear out of nowhere on their right flank, moving forward and firing over the heads of the prone Colombian soldiers. De la Noval's men, who'd been trying to outflank them, suddenly collapsed to the ground. Several of the new combatants rushed past them. Some paused, kneeling next to the stunned soldiers, pulling them back toward the fence line.

Bolan felt someone grab his shoulders and drag him back. The man was big, and strong, too. His face had a chiseled, rugged cast, and his upper lip was decorated by a dark Fu Manchu mustache. They stopped in a depression, and the man dragging him raised his radio and spoke into it. Bolan's hearing had not yet returned, but he could tell his rescuer was directing some sort of assault on the mansion.

Who the hell were these guys? he wondered.

The guy with the Fu Manchu turned toward Bolan and said something. The Executioner still could not hear, but was able to partially read his lips: *We're Americans. Here to assist.*

Beyond them the mansion shook with a series of explosions and its interior erupted in yellow flames. The big guy with the Fu Manchu got up and raced toward the burning building with the speed of a fullback running in for a touchdown, the muzzle of his weapon barking flame. Bolan felt his senses returning. He glanced around and saw that Cepeda had been laid next to him. Bolan reached over and placed his palm on the dressing to apply pressure. It was already sodden with the captain's blood.

Sounds of another explosion ripped through the night. More flames shot out of the mansion, and Bolan saw the new group of men, their saviors, pumping rounds into the burning structure. The cavalry had arrived, and they weren't taking any prisoners. No one was getting out of there alive. As his hearing slowly returned, Bolan was suddenly cognizant of the syncopated beating of helicopter rotors in the distance.

CHAPTER ONE

Present Day
Five hundred feet above northern Mexico

Thoughts of the old, failed mission in Colombia, Operation Cat's Cradle, floated through Bolan's mind as he studied the grim faces of his special ops team. Cat's Cradle had been a debacle—a setup turned into a deadly ambush. He'd later found out that they'd been betrayed by the Colombian army colonel who had given them the mission briefing. The man had tipped the De la Noval cartel to the exact time and approach of the raid. The rescue had come courtesy of an Agency team that had been independently dispatched to take out Vincente De la Noval. Bolan never found out who they were or got a chance to thank them, but such was the world of black ops. A person rarely got a look at the whole picture.

In the darkness he could make out the tops of the trees below as the helicopter surged forward. He had the utmost confidence in the pilot, though. He and Jack Grimaldi had been here many times before. The rest of the group was new to him, but the men had seemed professional and competent during the briefing. Hal Brognola had asked Bolan to step in and act as squad leader after the original team leader had unexpectedly fallen ill. It was a rescue mission just south of the border. Bolan and Grimaldi had been in the area wrapping up another mission when the big Fed had called them via satellite phone. Bolan put the call on speaker.

"Striker, you remember Chris Avelia, right?"

"Sure," Bolan said. "Good man. Still with the DEA?"

"Yeah. He's working undercover in Mexico and managed to infiltrate one of the major cartels down there."

"Which one?"

"Jesús De la Noval," Brognola said. "Brother of the guy you hit in Colombia a couple of years ago. Remember?"

"I tried my best to forget that one," Bolan said. "Chris was with me on that debacle, as I recall."

"Yeah, well, after Vincente De la Noval's untimely demise, his younger brother, Jesús, moved things north. He set up a pretty good base of operations in northern Mexico."

"And Chris managed to infiltrate it?" Bolan asked. He knew full well the dangers of working undercover, especially in something as brutal as the Mexican drug cartels.

"He did. De la Noval wasn't only moving drugs into the U.S., he's become one of the major weapons dealers for the Mexican mafia. Avelia was working on something big, but missed his check-in, and DEA's worried he's been compromised."

"What was supposed to be going down?" Bolan asked.

"I'm not sure yet, but I'm working on it."

"How long since they heard from him?"

"Forty-eight hours and counting."

The Executioner knew that meant they had to move fast. Brognola gave them the rest of it: the special ops team the government had assembled, the sudden illness of the team leader, the need to act swiftly. "The

President asked if Stony Man had anybody in the area, and—"

"I'm in," Bolan said, looking at Grimaldi, who nodded. "Jack, too."

"Any chance you could arrange to have *Dragonslayer* transported down here?" Grimaldi asked. "Otherwise, I'll settle for a fully outfitted Black Hawk with no markings."

After a moment of silence, Brognola said, "Thanks, guys."

"Thank us when it's over," Bolan replied.

That had been little more than six hours ago. Just time enough for Bolan and Grimaldi to rendezvous with the special ops team and review the plan. Satellite photos of De la Noval's headquarters looked eerily similar to his brother's estate—perimeter fence, large house, expansive grounds surrounding the place, one main access road. If the more arid terrain were replaced for the tropical one, it was Colombia all over again. And if he was holding Chris Avelia prisoner, De la Noval had to know someone would be coming sooner or later. Sooner would be better for the mission and for the DEA agent.

The plan this time was more dynamic: sweep over the compound, fast-rope to the ground, then hit the house with a quick assault. They all had body armor, M-4s, extra magazines, night-vision goggles, and enough pre-set C-4 shaped charges that locked doors weren't going to slow them. Hit them hard. In and out. Their main goal was to rescue the hostage.

It bothered Bolan that he hadn't had much time to get to know his team's capabilities, but they had supposedly been practicing for this raid as a backup plan for weeks, in the eventuality that they might have to go in at some point in the future. Now that future had arrived, but at least they were prepared. That was a bit of a plus. All of them had seen combat, he'd been told, in various operations in the sandbox and in Afghanistan, and Bolan felt confident they could get the job done. The fast descent from above would give them a bit of surprise, as well. He heard Grimaldi's voice over his helmet's comm set. "Uh-oh. I don't like the looks of this."

Bolan immediately got up and moved toward the cockpit. Through the windshield the soldier saw something rustling against the darkened sky in the distance. He flipped down the visor for his night-vision goggles. Three helicopters, UH-60s from the looks of them, were leaving the area.

What the hell were birds like that doing down here? Bolan wondered.

Something else caught his eye: a thin trail of dark smoke drifting upward over the trees.

Grimaldi was right. Something was off. He turned back to his team and pressed the button to activate his throat mike.

"Something's up. We saw three helicopters in the vicinity of the target. There's a smoke trail, too. I'll need three volunteers to fast-rope down with me to do a recon."

All the men raised their hands and Bolan grinned. No shortage of motivation in this group. He chose three at random, motioning them forward, and squatted as he unfolded the paper map of the target.

"I'll be Red One," he said, then tapped each man consecutively. "You're Red Two, Three and Four. We'll drop in here." He pointed to a spot near the corner of big house. "Red Two and I will go left, Red Three and Four right. Move and cover. Remember our primary mission is hostage rescue. We take down any hostiles in our way and search. But it looks like the mission's been compromised." He glanced up at the rest of the group. "You all hook up and be ready to deploy should we need help. Be ready. We'll determine the status of the situation and then either proceed or evacuate."

The team members nodded.

Bolan turned back toward Grimaldi. "You getting this?'

"Loud and clear," the pilot said. "Just show me where you want to be dropped off."

The Executioner's uneasiness increased as Grimaldi took the helicopter in for a preliminary fly-by. Normally, they wouldn't have risked announcing their presence, but the smoke and the departing choppers were a game-changer. Besides, Bolan doubted that De la Noval would have the firepower to take out a Black Hawk. The smoke was emanating from what appeared to be several small fires inside the mansion itself. Yellow flames licked at shattered windows and broken doors. The infrared night-vision goggles showed two prone bodies by the front gate. Several more were scattered over the expansive yard leading to the house. From the lack of movement and the twisted positioning, they appeared to be casualties. The place had already been hit by some kind of tactical assault. Bolan told Grimaldi to keep the chopper in a hover, and he and the other three team members hooked the nylon ropes through their D-rings and backed out of the open doors.

Zipping downward, Bolan didn't brake until he was almost to the ground. Once his feet were on solid earth, he unclipped the D-ring and kept his M-4 in the ready position as he advanced. His peripheral vision told him his teammates had made it down safely. They split up, each moving through the darkened yard with practiced ease.

Thoughts of the failed Cat's Cradle mission flitted through Bolan's mind. The similarities of this setup and the one in Colombia screamed for caution. Same general compound design, same trek through an expansive yard, same last name of the bad guy. From what he'd heard, younger brother Jesús was even more treacherous than Vincente had ever been.

The flickering light from the fires made Bolan's night-vision goggles practically useless, but nothing seemed to move in the flat, greenish tincture in front of him. No adversaries presented themselves. He kept an eye out for trip wires, scanning the grounds as he went, but it turned out to be a cakewalk. When he got to the side of the building, he saw why.

Two more bodies were sprawled inside the open patio doors. The interior walls burned with yellow flames, and a slew of bullet-riddled corpses littered the floor. The smell of burning flesh mingled with the scent of burned wood and gunpowder.

Bolan pressed his throat mike. "Red Three and Four, check for survivors outside. Watch out for booby traps. Red Two, you're inside with me."

Three acknowledgments came over the radio. Bolan stepped inside and tried to move forward, but the thick smoke obscured his vision and made it difficult to breathe. He kept moving quickly, scanning the faces of the dead men. Most had numerous body wounds, but each had been dealt at least one shot to the head, as well. Execution style. Whoever did this had a take-no-prisoners mentality.

A large bamboo cage sat in the middle of the big lounge area. The thick bars looked strong enough to house a tiger, but the pair of chain shackles was obviously designed to fit a man. The cage was empty. Bolan saw splashes of blood on the solid metal floor. An assortment of knives, bludgeons and what appeared to be a fireplace poker lay next to the cage. The sharp edge of the poker was blackened, as if it'd been heated in a flame. A lot of unpleasant thoughts flashed through Bolan's mind. He scanned the rest of the room. None of the nearby bodies appeared to be that of Chris Avelia.

Covering as much of the house as they could, Bolan found no one alive. He pushed into what appeared to be the master bedroom, seeing that several of the bodies in there were young, scantily dressed women. Hookers, probably, judging from their clothes. They, too, had been dealt execution-style gunshots to the head. Bolan felt the smoke beginning to gag him. He coughed as he said into his throat mike, "Sitrep. Respond in sequence. Any sign of Avelia?"

"Red One, Red Two." The transmission was punctuated by a cough. "Nothing here. No one alive. No hostage, far as I can tell."

"Red Three here," another voice said. "No survivors out here. Red Four's with me."

"Roger that. Any of them look like Jesús De la Noval?"

"Hard to say."

Bolan could taste the smoke in his mouth and paused to cough again, and then spit. The heat, smoke and stench were nearly unbearable. "Let's get out of here."

He used the muzzle of his M-4 to smash the glass of the nearest window, and climbed through. The cool clarity of the night air seemed like heaven. He took a few tentative breaths as he moved farther from the inferno, then drew in some deeper ones. When his chest felt clear, he pressed the throat mike and told his men to move to the landing zone, adding, "You copy that, Jack?"

"Roger that," Grimaldi's voice said. "One pickup on the way."

Bolan turned and saw his team trotting toward De la Noval's helipad. He told them to check it and secure it before touchdown.

The three men replied in the affirmative.

Bolan turned and took one more look at the mansion, which was now almost fully engulfed in flames. Although he hadn't taken the time to check each body, none appeared to have been Chris Avelia's. That didn't mean that Chris had survived, only that they hadn't found him.

An empty target house…and an empty tiger cage.

Was this another example of bad intel? Then he remembered those departing choppers.

Maybe somebody else had beaten them to the punch.

South Tucson, Arizona

JOHN LASSITER TRACED his fingers over his Fu Manchu mustache as he watched the men off-loading the cargo in the dark field next to the road. He took inventory: one beat-to-hell drug cartel informant, ten suitcases filled with portraits of good old Benjamin Franklin, and a couple more filled with Mexican brown heroin. Lassiter didn't care about the drugs, other than they were part of his instructions. The instructions, which had come in their customary fashion—a text from "GOD," always from an unknown number—included the recovery of the weapons that were supposed to be delivered to De la Noval, as well. Lassiter knew GOD was the code name for Anthony Godfrey, formerly of the Agency and now a civilian go-between.

This wasn't his first transaction with the drug lord. It was, however, supposed to be his last, but somehow De la Noval had slipped away. Lassiter recalled way too many missions where they ended up arming one side in a conflict, only to face down the road the same firepower he'd delivered, and keeping weapons of this level of sophistication out of the cartel's hands seemed like a good idea. But it wasn't his place to set policy or make those kinds of decisions. As always, he only followed orders. He'd been doing that his whole life. Guys like Benedict called the shots, and got rich along with the guys producing the goods, like Godfrey.

One of Lassiter's men was using a forklift to remove the heavy stack of crates from the helicopter for transfer to the trailer. It would be one well-packed semi, that was for sure. He glanced at his watch. Everything was on schedule. Another fifteen minutes and they'd be able to take the copters back.

Not a bad haul, he thought, although a couple things bothered him slightly. Not nailing Jesús De la Noval for one thing. Killing those women for another. He sighed. It wasn't like they were neophytes or anything. Sure, they were hookers, but they were still civilians in a war zone. Collateral damage. Hanging out with scum like De la Noval, they had to know that death was their sorority sister. But Lassiter still felt bad about killing them.

The women had deserved better, even if it was all about the orders. Collateral damage wasn't something new to him. Still, it was beginning to bother him more and more. He knew he'd see their twisted faces and hear their piercing screams in his dreams for many nights to come. They'd have plenty of company there.

And then there was the captive. The idea of turning over the semiconscious, beaten-to-a-pulp, barely alive informant to the Wolves wasn't a pleasant thought, either, although the guy had looked so bad that death would probably be a relief. But he had been involved with the cartel and was getting what he deserved. Just like the Afghan traitors in Afghanistan, the ones who'd tried to play both sides of the fence. Still, Lassiter couldn't help but think about the fate awaiting this poor bastard. Better to put a bullet in the guy's brain now and spare him any further suffering. But his orders had been explicit in that regard, too. Bring the man back alive; turn him over to the Wolves. They were troubling orders, but orders just the same.

A lot of things had begun to bother Lassiter lately. Maybe it was time to get out.

Morris, his second in command, came jogging up to him and saluted. "The cargo's been successfully off-loaded, sir."

Lassiter thought about telling him to can the salute, but the kid was new to wetworks and fresh from military service in his last deployment. Lassiter had been right there once, just like him. Loyal to a fault and totally by the book. Before he got officially "killed in action" a few years ago, that was. He grinned. Shit, why should any of this matter to "a dead man"? He told Morris to relax, adding, "Don't call me 'sir' and don't salute me. I work for a living, remember?"

Morris nodded tentatively.

"What's the status of the prisoner?" Lassiter asked.

"He's pretty banged up, si—"

Good, Lassiter thought. The kid's learning. "Go on."

"I had Marquis give him some first aid. He's slipping in and out of consciousness." Morris paused, and then added, "Those two motorcycle guys want to take him and the stuff now."

"So give him to them. Our orders are to hold on to the rest until tomorrow."

Morris hesitated again.

"Is there a problem?" Lassiter asked.

"The prisoner." Morris blew out an audible breath. "He mumbled something like 'not part of cartel.' I'm wondering if maybe he's a Mexican Fed. Undercover or something."

"People say a lot of things when they're desperate."

Lassiter's cell phone vibrated with an incoming text, but this one wasn't from Unknown. It was from Ellen.

Are you there?

He glanced at his watch: 0222. He'd assumed she'd be sleeping. Maybe she was just anxious to see him, to talk to him, among other things. He smiled as he texted her back: You're up early. Or should I say late?

Been waiting for you. Are you back?

I am.

I need to see you ASAP

He texted her back: Busy now.
It's important, she replied.

Ok forty mikes. The regular?

Yes. ASAP, her return text said. Very important.

Ok. Be there with bells on.

Lassiter turned to Morris. "I've got to go meet someone. Secure the Mexican brown and the money in my
car, return the choppers and take the van back to base.
I'll tag up with you at 0700 tomorrow for debrief."

"What about the prisoner, sir?" Morris asked.

Lassiter shrugged. Could the guy possibly be a Fed?
Godfrey would have told him if that was the case. So
the poor bastard was probably lying through his teeth.
If he had any left. He was practically half-dead, anyway,
and he'd made his own bed. Now it was time to die in it.

"Give him to them."

"But what if he's really one of the good guys?"

"You do this long enough, Morris," Lassiter said,
"you'll learn one thing. There are no good guys."

Morris nodded, turned and left. Lassiter watched him
walk away, knowing his doubt still lingered. Could the
prisoner be telling the truth? Could he be a Fed? But
why would they send them with explicit orders to grab
the guy from De la Noval, only to have him turned over
to the motorcycle goons? If the guy really was a Fed,
Benedict or Godfrey would have known. They'd only
said the guy had been playing both sides of the fence.
More than likely he was somebody's low-level snitch
who probably knew a few of the players higher up. The
guy looked Mexican, too. Maybe he was one of their
crooked cops. It was hard to tell. Besides, keeping a
prisoner wasn't something Lassiter had the desire or
the facilities to do. Better to get rid of him sooner rather
than later. More collateral damage.

Lassiter's cell vibrated again.

Are you coming?

On the way, he texted back.

As soon as I make the call, he thought, and punched in the number. As he listened to the ringing, he took a deep breath as he pictured her beautiful face and body moving toward him in a translucent glow of the motel's small lamps. It would be the perfect ending to a semi-successful mission.

Fairfax County, Virginia

ANTHONY GODFREY SET down the disposable cell phone and ground his teeth as he poured more of the amber liquid into his glass. He was careful that none of the liquid spilled on his desk, which was made of high quality teak and imported from Europe, a remnant of the court of King Louis XVI. The whiskey tasted smooth going down, but left just enough of a burn to remind him that everything, as Lassiter said, had not gone according to plan. Jesús De la Noval had slipped away before being terminated, but hopefully he would not find resurrection like his namesake.

But Godfrey would cross that bridge when he came to it. If he came to it. One thing he'd learned during his years as a deputy assistant secretary of state was not to worry about the intangibles. Just deal with them if and when they came up. He tried to let that philosophy carry over to his civilian mind-set now that he'd left government service and taken over the family business, GDF Industries, after the death of his father.

Don't sweat the small stuff, he could almost hear the old man saying. It had served them both well in the long run.

Godfrey sipped some more of the whiskey, savored it and swallowed. He needed to call the future president of the United States, even if it was five-twenty in the morning. Smiling, he picked up his own cell phone, scrolled to the number for Brent Hutchcraft and pressed the selection button. The senator answered after the third ring, sounding wide-awake and cheerful, but then again Hutchcraft made it a point to go for a three-mile run every morning, rain or shine.

"Tony," Hutchcraft said. "What are you doing up so early? Or is it more of a late night?" This guy was as cool as dry ice.

"How did you know it was me?" Godfrey asked.

"You're using the same disposable number that comes up as GOD on my phone," Hutchcraft said. "Who else would have such audacity?"

Godfrey forced a laugh. Best to sound courteous, deferential and matter-of-fact, just in case someone out there was listening. He didn't think anyone was, and if they were, he'd most likely already know about it, but the secret of survival was to adhere to security procedures at all times, until they became second nature.

"I was hoping I'd catch you before your morning jog," Godfrey said. "Want to grab some breakfast?"

This was their customary code for calling a meeting.

"I'm on a diet of egg whites and a protein shake this week," Hutchcraft said. "The D.C. Triathlon's coming up in three weeks. Besides, I'm announcing this week, and how would it look if some reporter saw me having breakfast with the ghost of Alfred Hitchcock?"

Godfrey bristled at Hutchcraft's comparison of him to the deceased filmmaker, although he did recognize that the resemblance was striking. He said nothing.

Hutchcraft chuckled. "Sorry. How about you, me and Dirk in a game of racquetball at the club at three?"

Godfrey said he'd have his secretary make the reservation, and wished Hutchcraft well on his training run. Why the man sought to punish himself to such a degree by entering triathlons at the age of forty-four was beyond Godfrey. Still, image and looking fit were a big part of running for president.

After he'd clicked off he reached for the disposable cell phone to place his last call of the night. He punched in the number and Animal answered with his usual belligerent, "What?" Godfrey hated dealing with this motorcycle moron, but sometimes life left a person little choice. And Godfrey was, for the most part, used to lowlifes and ignorant bastards. He'd dealt with enough politicians.

"It's me," he said. "Just checking to see if the package arrived."

"Yeah," Animal replied. "But I ain't getting much. He's pretty beat up already. Plus I ain't seen no Benjamins, or no guns and roses, neither."

Godfrey considered that. It meant that Lassiter still had the money, the weapons and the heroin, which was just as he'd said in his report. Godfrey was big on confirmation. He'd learned that during his tenure in the State Department and the Agency during the cold war. Trust, but verify, as many times as you could, until you were certain. Turning all the goodies over to Animal prematurely wasn't in the cards.

The DEA man was a different story. The quicker they found out what he knew, and to whom he'd told it, the better. As far as Avelia being worked over, Del la Noval had to have done some preliminary interrogation before the strike team intervened. Maybe that's how he'd figured the team's imminent arrival and realized it was safer to boogie. That guy Jesús was as crafty as an alley cat, but it was a moot point now. Godfrey would deal with that loose end later. The bird in the hand had to be eliminated.

"Get whatever you can find out and dispose of him," Godfrey said. "But do it in a judicious manner." He wondered seconds later if a guy like Animal would know what *judicious* meant.

"Yeah, yeah, I know how to deal with a snitch. What about the goodies?"

The "goodies" meant the drugs, along with the twenty Stinger missiles, two-hundred M-72 LAWs, fifty Barrett sniper rifles, five-hundred M-4 rifles, accompanying ammunition, assorted grenades, starlight scopes, claymore mines, and five hundred level-four body armor flak jackets that were supposed to be delivered to De la Noval for a cool ten million dollars. Instead, the drug lord got a shipment of full-metal jackets, courtesy of Lassiter and his group.

"That should proceed as planned."

"So we're still on for tomorrow night then?" Animal asked.

"Most assuredly," Godfrey said. "I'll get hold of you tomorrow." He pressed the end button without waiting for a reply or acknowledgment. He needed to make sure Benedict's cleanup wet team was set to take care of this one. Looking out the window, he watched the nascent sky changing from pink to a gray, almost colorless hue that he knew would inevitably turn to a robin's egg blue. The monuments and landmarks of the nation's capital still had that faintly orange glow. Hutchcraft was probably out running in the Virginia woods near his house, enjoying the crisp morning air.

Well, goody goody for him, Godfrey thought. And goody goody for me.

He had more worlds to conquer.

CHAPTER TWO

Stony Man Farm, Virginia

Bolan watched as Hal Brognola poured himself a cup of coffee. The big Fed took a sip, shook his head with a disgusted expression and asked Bolan if he wanted a cup. It was closing in on 6:00 a.m., and Bolan had barely slept on the plane ride from Mexico to Stony Man Farm.

"No, thanks," he said. "I want to hit the sack for a few and then the range later on."

"The range? I figured you'd want to sleep for a week after your abrupt trip south of the border."

Bolan shrugged. "Have to keep in practice. We didn't fire a shot down there."

Part of the reason he was in the office Brognola sometimes used when he was at Stony Man Farm was to give his old friend the briefing so he could, in turn, brief the President. The other part was to get some answers. Bolan wished he had better news. He'd given Brognola a partial sitrep by sat phone on the flight back. Sleep had proved elusive after that, and even Grimaldi's attempts at humor as he piloted the plane hadn't shaken the darkness from Bolan's introspection.

"No sign of Avelia, eh?" Brognola said as he set the cup on his desk. His face showed the fatigue and creases of little or no sleep, so Bolan knew he was in good company.

"Like I said on the phone, somebody beat us there. They hit the place hard, left a bunch of bodies and an empty tiger cage that I assume they'd been using to hold Chris."

"A tiger cage?" Brognola shook his head. "I thought those things went out a couple of wars ago."

"Evidently not," Bolan said. "It looks like they tortured him, too."

The big Fed winced. "Damn. No sign of Jesús De la Noval, either?"

"As far as we could tell," Bolan said. "We checked as many bodies as best we could, and didn't see him. But at that point I figured, since things had already gone to hell in a handbasket, there was no sense sticking around waiting for company."

Brognola nodded. He picked up the coffee cup and took another sip. "Ah, Aaron outdid himself making this batch. You could run a deuce-and-a-half on it. I knew I should have declined his offer to make a fresh pot of coffee before he headed back to the computer room."

Even Brognola's attempts to lighten the mood talking about Aaron Kurtzman's legendarily terrible coffee did little to lift Bolan's spirits. The big Fed seemed to sense that. "I'm sorry we missed finding Chris. Do you think there's any chance he may still be alive?"

The fact the tiger cage had been empty, except for the shackles, meant that Avelia had most probably been there, but had then been removed at some point prior to Bolan's arrival. Too much time had elapsed between the discovery of his capture and the rescue mission. Somebody had messed up on this one. Badly.

"It's hard to say," Bolan said. "Did you find out what Chris was working on?"

"Not a lead in sight, but Aaron's keeping at it."

Bolan shook his head. "They hung him out to dry."

"Yeah." The sadness was evident on Brognola's tired face. "That's obvious."

"A couple more things are obvious," the soldier said, holding up two fingers. He tapped the first one. "They should've pulled him sooner. Or had a react team on standby in the area. Whoever was in charge of putting him in there undercover dropped the ball as far as scheduling the rescue, and needs to be fired." He clenched his fingers into a fist. "Or worse."

"Damn straight," Brognola said.

"And," Bolan continued, "somebody who knew we were going in there had advance notice and sent in another team to beat us to the punch. I don't know if they got Chris, but it's a likely probability."

"You think maybe Jesús De la Noval took Avelia?" Brognola asked.

"Run with a prisoner he knew was a federal agent? Not likely."

Brognola compressed his lips, and then nodded. "Yeah, I agree." He stared at Bolan as an uneasy silence descended over them. The higher-ups in the federal government never liked to admit they'd made a mistake when an operative ended up compromised, especially in cases where the screwup caused a loss of life. They both knew there would be substantial hand-wringing and finger-pointing as everyone struggled to avoid culpability. But that didn't change the facts: Chris Avelia hadn't been properly protected and was most likely now in enemy hands, or dead.

Finally, Brognola said, "There was a leak somewhere along the line. I'll see what I can find out about that, and get back to you. And I'll make sure that the President knows, as well."

Bolan nodded. He knew his friend would do his best in that regard. "Have Aaron check into something else, too. Jack and I saw some helicopters leaving as we approached. It's doubtful they belonged to De la Noval. They looked like old surplus U.S. military. They had to have transported the team that hit the compound before we arrived. Maybe he can track them down."

"We'll get right on that, too," Brognola said. "Anything else I need to brief the President on?"

"Just that Chris is a good man. Tell him I'm not about to stop looking until I find him. He'd better not, either."

Brognola's expression grew sadder and he nodded. At this point the chance Chris Avelia would be found alive was slim to none. Once Bolan knew for sure, his mission would shift from one of rescue to revenge, or as he called it, moral justice.

Tucson, Arizona

THE LIAISON WITH Ellen at their usual spot, the Holiday Inn, was turning out to be anything but the romantic interlude that Lassiter had anticipated. In fact, it was having just the opposite effect on him. The first thing she did was have him take off his shirt, which he took as a good sign. Then he noticed the bed. It was covered with fresh towels. What was that about?

They'd been meeting there for the better part of a year, ever since Dr. Allan Lawrence had brought her in to assist with the GEM Program. Lawrence had introduced her as "Dr. Campbell," and said, "I've brought her west from D.C. She was my finest student at Johns Hopkins."

Lassiter couldn't care less about that. One look at the young, twenty-something blonde, with oval glasses and a knockout figure even in a lab coat, and he was smitten. He didn't hesitate at all when they'd moved to the private examination room and she'd told him to strip down for his physical.

"I'm ready to check anything you want," he said with a smile. "Demonstrations can be arranged also."

She'd smiled, too. Briefly. Just a hint of perfect white teeth flashing behind an almost shy expression. But she wasn't smiling now. The blue eyes looked deadly serious…and sad.

"We need to do this now?" Lassiter said as he reclined on the rather hard motel bed and extended his bare arm toward her. He used his other hand to fluff up the pillow. "I've only got about two hours, you know."

She shot him one of her piercing glances as she tied a rubber ligature around his massive biceps.

"Is this going to hurt?" he asked, trying to sound playful. Getting an IV right now was probably the last thing on his mind. What the hell had gotten into her that this took precedence over them enjoying each other's bodies for a while?

"I'll try to be gentle," she said as she wiped the inner aspect of his right elbow with an alcohol swab. Her dainty fingers looked glossy in the thin, latex gloves. Those were a bit of surprise, too. If she was worried she was going to catch something, it was way too late at this point in their relationship.

"What's with the gloves?" he asked.

"John, please," she said, looking around. "I need something to hang this bag on."

He glanced toward the door. "Too bad this isn't one of those old bed-and-breakfast places. They'd probably have a coat rack handy."

She reached into her medical bag and pulled out a

catheter. He barely felt the needle slide into his distended vein. A few drops of blood fell out of the shunt before she attached it to the IV line, secured the hookup with some tape and then straightened, holding the plastic plasma bag over him.

"Hook it on the mirror over that." He pointed toward a dresser adjacent to the bed. "Use one of the coat hangers."

She looked, and then told him to hold the bag as she went to the small closet and tried to pull one of the thick metal hangers from the clothes rack. They were secured by a circular design that kept patrons from stealing them. Swearing, she turned to him with a frustrated look.

Lassiter was already off the bed and moving toward her. She started to protest, but he held the IV bag above his head as he walked. When he was next to her he asked, "Need some assistance, milady?"

Ellen bit her lower lip, then reached up and took the bag. "Do you think you can pull one of those off without disturbing the hookup?"

He grinned. "Does a bear shit in the woods?"

"John, be careful. Don't bend your arm. I'm serious."

He kept his right arm straight as he grabbed the hanger. The fingers of his left hand curled around the thick, circular metal. For a moment the muscles in both his arms flexed like gigantic pythons awakening. He bent the circular clasp, freed it from the rod and handed the hangar to her. "How's that?"

"Fine," she said. "Thank you. Now go back and lie down."

"Don't I get a kiss as a reward?" He leaned close to her, his lips brushing hers.

She kissed him softly, but with a gentle urgency, and he once again sensed that something was off.

"What's going on?" he asked.

"Go lie down. Let me get this hung." Still holding the IV bag, she guided him toward the bed and waited while he resumed his position of repose. Then she slipped the tab of the IV bag over the bent portion of the hanger and looped it over the corner of the mirror.

Lassiter watched the steady drip of clear liquid as it fell from the transparent bag into the plastic line attached to the adapter.

"What is that stuff?" he asked. "More GEM goodies?"

She blinked, holding her eyes closed a second or two longer than she should have, and then smiled. "It's a combination of antibiotics and some other medications."

"Antibiotics?" He grinned. "Afraid I picked up an STD south of the border?" When she didn't smile back, he added, "For the record, I didn't."

"I want to beef up your immune system a bit." She patted his arm gently, ending with an affectionate squeeze.

"What's going on?" he asked. "Really?"

She gazed at him, her blue eyes misty, then looked away quickly.

He grabbed her arm, harder than he intended, and she jerked. Lassiter immediately released her and ran his left fingers softly over her cheek.

"Sorry." He waited a couple of beats, and then added, "Tell me."

"I'm not sure yet." Ellen leaned down and kissed him on the lips, keeping her chin on his shoulder, her face out of his sight. "Let the medicine do its work."

This whole scene was starting to resemble one from some kind of crazy movie.

"Do its work?" He pulled her back so he could look at her face. Streams of tears had found their way down both her cheeks.

"Hey," he said. "What's wrong?"

"I want you to know that I need to run more tests. I don't know everything for certain."

"What exactly are you saying?"

She looked away, wiped at her cheek, peeled off her latex glove and turned back toward him, her expression caring, but severe. She opened her mouth, but no sound came out.

"Ellen?"

"John," she said, regaining control, "I don't know for sure yet, but I'm afraid you could be sick." Despite her almost professional demeanor her words came out choppy, truncated, like a ball bouncing unevenly down some steps. "From the GEM treatments."

"Sick?" he asked. That couldn't be. He felt great. Strong, powerful, never better. "What are you talking about? I feel fine."

"Like I said, I've got to run more tests." She wiped at her eyes. "But depending on how things go, we might have to start an aggressive treatment plan."

"Huh?"

She went into another rambling discourse with terms he didn't understand, about having to do more tests and it being too early to assume anything, least of all a prognosis, but he barely heard her words. Only three of them reverberated inside his skull, over and over again.

Aggressive treatment plan.

What the hell was going on?

Washington, D.C.

THE RUBBER BALL bounced off the far wall, struck the floor and then sailed toward Senator Brent Hutchcraft. He deftly swung his racket, sending the ball back toward the far wall again. Gregory Benedict, assistant director of the CIA, stepped in and slammed the ball as it shot back toward them. Now it was Anthony Godfrey's turn, and he purposely let the ball zoom past him.

"Aww, come on, Tony," Hutchcraft said. "You weren't even trying."

"Too much on my mind," Godfrey said. The ball bounced against the rear wall in a lazy loop and Godfrey grabbed it. "We've got a lot to discuss. Why don't we get some steam?"

The steam room was Godfrey's favorite place in the club. He'd reserved it for the three of them. The accompanying attire, bath towels and nudity, assured him that no one in the room would be wearing a wire, and any attempts to bug the place would be fruitless. Not that he was worried about Hutchcraft and Benedict. They were both in as deep as he was, and had infinitely more to lose, but he hadn't survived twenty-five years in the Washington, D.C., political rat race without exercising due caution. Plus, it worked both ways. His associates took a measure of comfort in these precautions for the same reasons. To assure that they weren't disturbed, Godfrey had one of the senator's security detail standing by at the door to the steam room. The guy was as big as a house, plus he was packing a SIG Sauer .357 semiauto pistol. Godfrey looked at the hulk as he held the door open for them.

It pays to have friends in high places, Godfrey thought with a smile on his face. And in low ones, as well.

Wisps of steam hung in the air. The locker room attendant had sprayed a dash of eucalyptus in the air, just as Godfrey had requested. He moved to the tiled bench, adjusted his towel and sat. Hutchcraft, obviously proud of his physique, and how he was keeping in shape despite being in his mid-forties, tossed his towel on the bench with careless abandon and sat beside him. Benedict, always guarded and cautious, glanced around nervously and then sat across from them, his back to the wall. The man moved with an almost reptilian precision.

"Okay, Tony," Hutchcraft said. "You called this little tête-à-tête. Suppose you lead off."

"Last night's activity was a mixed bag," Godfrey said. "As you'd previously advised, the White House did authorize a rescue mission to extract Avelia." He looked at Benedict. "Luckily, your strike team arrived first and snatched the target, along with the intended cash and drugs."

Benedict nodded. "As expected."

"And the weapons our less-than-reputable friend thought he was purchasing?" Hutchcraft asked.

"Safe and to be delivered to my Arizona warehouse facility tonight," Godfrey said.

Hutchcraft smiled. "Ah, I love it when a plan comes together. So what's the bad news?"

"Avelia was delivered to our motorcycle friends in such bad shape that they weren't able to get much out of him. We don't know how much he found out and who he told."

"But I'm working on that," Benedict said.

Hutchcraft frowned. "I assume that loose end has now been terminated."

Godfrey nodded. "As of this morning. But we're

going to have to brace for the fallout concerning the death of a federal agent."

"Brace for what?" Benedict said. "He'll just go down as another unfortunate casualty to our long, ongoing and unsuccessful war on drugs."

"I might even find some purchase in the debates." Hutchcraft's voice assumed a deeper tenor. "Mr. President, please explain the reason you didn't pull this young man out of harm's way before he was discovered and murdered." A smile stretched the corners of his mouth. "As Harry Truman used to say, the buck stops at the top."

"Careful," Benedict said. "There's always a risk if you shit too close to where you eat."

Hutchcraft looked almost wounded. "Please, spare me your scatological metaphors. I'm going out to dinner later."

Godfrey didn't want this to develop into a debate between the two of them. Hutchcraft had his sights set on becoming president, and if that happened, Benedict was the heir apparent to finally take over as director of the CIA. Both of them were so laser focused on their goals that they often lost sight of the big picture.

"Gentlemen," Godfrey reminded them, "the devil is, as they say, in the details."

"Very true," Hutchcraft said, exhaling a long breath.

The temperature felt as if it was edging up into the unbearable range. That was another reason Godfrey liked this place. The longer you stayed, the more of a chore superfluous conversation became. It was like conversing in hell itself.

Hutchcraft stood, went to the shower head and doused himself with a jet of cool water. When he sat again, Godfrey saw the man was ready to talk facts. No more bullshitting.

"What about Jesús?" he asked. "You said the little bastard got away?"

"That's what I was told." Godfrey felt like going to the shower for a cool rinse himself, but decided to wait.

"I thought you sent Lassiter?" Hutchcraft said. "Didn't you say he was one those GEMs you keep bragging about?"

"He is," Benedict interjected. His mouth twisted in a frown. "He was the prototype."

"Another triumph for SNPT Laboratories, a division of GDF Industries," Hutchcraft said, affecting a deeply resonant tone. He wiped a handful of sweat off his forehead and flung the droplets toward the heating unit. "Well, don't forget I was the one who steered the funding for that particular special program GDF's way."

"Before you start handing out cigars as the proud father," Benedict said, "you should know he's become something of a liability lately. He needs to be dealt with."

"Oh?" Hutchcraft said. "What's that story?"

Godfrey fidgeted. "It's too complex to go into here. Suffice it to say, he's outlived his usefulness. But that could work in our favor, as well."

"How?" Benedict snorted. The heat was getting to him, too.

"Is your cleanup team ready to intercept the shipment tonight?" Godfrey asked.

"Of course."

Godfrey cracked a smile. He could taste his own sweat now. It felt as if the steam was parboiling him. "With Jesús De la Noval on the loose, and angry at the overnight attack on his compound, it'll seem logical that he's behind the little retaliatory strike involving the shipment and the motorcycle whackos."

Hutchcraft blew out another long breath. "I see your logic, Tony. But how does this benefit us?"

Godfrey rubbed his index finger and thumb together. "I've got another buyer lined up for the shipment. We simply take it away from the intended recipients, the Wolves, and then turn it around in a sale to our new interested party."

"And who might that be?" Benedict asked."

"Our old friend Dimitri Chakhkiev," Godfrey said.

"That Russian son of a bitch?" Hutchcraft said. "I trust him about as far as I can throw him."

"You'd better get used to dealing with him," Benedict said. "If you want to be president, that is. Word is he's on the Russian leader's favorite persons list for building the new Russia."

Godfrey had about all he could stand of the heat and his two companions. He stood and pulled the cord, giving himself a cool rinse, then reached for the door handle. "If we have no other pertinent business to discuss, I suggest we vacate this hellhole and wait until Greg receives verification that his cleanup team has taken care of Lassiter and his boys."

"I'm expecting a call from Artie on that later tonight," Benedict said. And it's called a wet team, remember?"

"Whatever." Godfrey started to pull on the door.

"You never did explain to me why you're so anxious to get rid of Lassiter," Hutchcraft said.

The senator was still laid out naked on his towel as if posing for some male nudie magazine. "I thought he was one of our best and brightest. Except for having been declared KIA a few years ago, that is."

"He's a walking dead man." Godfrey looked at Benedict. "You explain it to him. I'm done here."

He pulled the door the rest of the way open and stepped out of the oppressive heat.

CHAPTER THREE

Stony Man Farm, Virginia

Bolan crouched behind the remnants of a shot-up old Buick. In its day the car had probably been the apple of its owner's eye. Now the front and back windows were pocked with bullet holes, as were the doors and fenders. He dropped the magazine in his Beretta 93R and tapped in a fresh one. The selector switch was set in 3-round-burst mode. Grimaldi was doing the same with his SIG Sauer P-221. He glanced at Bolan and nodded.

Behind them something clicked, and Bolan moved along the doors and extended his gun hand around the rear post panel. Downrange, two lifelike images flashed in front of a window: a man holding a woman before him. Bolan acquired a quick sight picture and double-tapped two rounds into the assailant's face, then he sprinted to the next cover point, a solid metal mailbox.

Grimaldi was firing at the building as Bolan moved, then the soldier laid down some suppressing fire so his partner could move, as well. He'd set the Beretta to full-auto, firing at the building. Another target swung into a doorway: a man pointing a rifle. Bolan sent a 3-round burst into the target. Grimaldi was firing now, too, taking his place by the mailbox as Bolan moved to the next cover point, an old utility truck on the other side of the street. The Stony Man pilot joined him seconds later, huffing and puffing.

"Ready?" Bolan asked.

"I was born that way," Grimaldi said.

They moved in unison again, one man laying down suppressing cover fire as the other ran. Two more hostile targets appeared, more men holding handguns. Bolan took out the first one, Grimaldi the second.

Three more buildings to go.

This portion was known as the Gauntlet. No cover—just a straight, shoot-on-the-run Hogan's Alley, with targets popping up along the way.

Bolan went first, taking three strides before his first target appeared: a woman pushing a baby carriage. He held his fire. Seconds later another target popped up next to the woman. This one was definitely hostile: another man with a shotgun. Bolan put two rounds into the target, Mozambique style.

Another pair of targets popped up, both adversarial, both easily dispatched.

Three more running steps and Bolan reached the end of the course. He turned and watched his partner negotiate the same turf.

Grimaldi whirled as the first target popped around a corner: a wild looking guy extending a large semi-auto pistol. The pilot put two bullets through the target. Another one popped out, this one holding a sawed-off shotgun. Two shots from Grimaldi, both "lethal." Three more strides and he'd be done, as well.

Yet another target popped up, holding a gun. Grimaldi whirled, almost with casual indifference, and plugged the aggressor between the eyes, just as a final target appeared from around a corner. The pilot's arm was already extended and he squeezed the trigger just as the bright blue of the target's uniform and the silver image of the police badge became apparent. The round had gone through the cop's heart, right next to his shield.

Grimaldi stopped, lowered his weapon and swore.

A voice came over the loudspeaker in a rebuking tone. "Shame, shame, shame, Jack. You shot a good guy."

Grimaldi's frown deepened as he decocked his pistol and slipped it back into his holster. He peeled off his ear protectors and goggles as he walked to Bolan.

"Damn. It's been a long time since I messed up that bad."

"Better to do it here," Bolan said, "than out in the field." He took off his protectors in turn, and they walked back through the course, assessing their shot patterns.

"Man, how do you stay right on with every shot?" Grimaldi asked. "I haven't seen such small patterns since Jimmy Stewart outshot Dan Duryea in *Winchester '73*."

Bolan grinned at his friend's movie reference. The guy loved old Westerns.

Grimaldi shook his head again. "It really bothers me when I shoot a good guy."

"Let's go through it again," Bolan said.

"Are you serious?"

He nodded, reaching into his pocket and taking out his sound suppressor. "With these."

Grimaldi tapped his ear protectors. "What for? We've got ears."

Bolan lined up the fine threads of the suppressor with the end of the barrel on the Beretta. "The weight of the suppressor can throw off your aim. Plus it can affect your ability to get a good sight picture."

Grimaldi shrugged. "Isn't that why we have laser sights?"

"Laser sights can malfunction," Bolan said. "Batteries can go dead. Right?"

Grimaldi nodded.

"Come on," Bolan said, giving his friend's shoulder a slap.

The pilot heaved a reluctant sigh and began screwing on his sound suppressor as he followed Bolan back toward the beginning of the Hogan's Alley course.

Bolan's cell phone vibrated in his pocket. He pulled it out and looked at the incoming text. It was from Brognola.

Come by the office ASAP.

"What's up?" Grimaldi asked, leaning over to try to get a look at the LCD screen.

"Hal wants to see us right away."

"What do you know?" the pilot said as he put the sound suppressor back into his pocket. "Saved by the bell."

Pima County, Arizona

IN THE STERILE environment of the state-of-the-art laboratory in the GDF Laboratory, Dr. Ellen Campbell leaned intently over her microscope as she placed the second slide tray under the lens.

"You look tired, my dear," Dr. Allan Lawrence said as he entered and stopped by her table. His long gray hair was pulled back in a ponytail, and his light blue eyes focused on her in their customary, probing fashion. "Haven't you been sleeping well?"

She smiled as warmly as she could manage. "I've got a lot on my mind lately."

Lawrence made a tsking sound and moved across the lab to the nude, muscular man on the steel table. Trang was the latest and most successful candidate in Dr. Lawrence's GEM program. So many failures, so few successes…and yet John Lassiter had been one of those successes. If you could call him that. When she'd gone to Dr. Lawrence weeks ago with the somewhat puzzling results from her latest tests, he'd pooh-poohed her findings, patting her arm like a condescending favorite uncle. "Nothing out of the ordinary," he'd said. "Typical fluctuations well within the parameters."

Only now she knew they weren't.

Campbell went back to studying the slide showing the breakdown of the cells she'd taken from Lassiter's blood sample of the previous night, or more accurately, early that morning. The correction did little to alter what was grimly obvious: inflammatory myopathies leading to oncosis. She switched to another slide. Same effect, only in a more advanced stage of pyknosis. Something was causing them to break down at a progressive rate. The nuclei were dissolving into the cytoplasm. Karyorrhexis. She straightened and looked across the lab as Lawrence, her mentor and surrogate father figure, injected a syringeful of the AAV-IGF-X5 into Trang's arm.

Lawrence had wooed her from her research studies at Johns Hopkins by promising her a chance to make a real difference. That had been seven years ago, and he'd fulfilled his promise in spades. Not only did he take her under his wing and give her total access to the fantastic, governmentally financed research projects that he'd already begun, but he welcomed her input as an equal partner.

Back then she was thrilled, but intimidated. Deep down she knew she could never be Lawrence's equal. His peer, maybe, but she soon discovered his work, his outlook, was too cutting edge. He was unafraid to take risks, boldly cut swaths through regulations and restrictions, forging a new frontier in genetic enhancement, but ultimately, at the expense of the test subject's safety.

"We're this close to curing major diseases like M.S., Alzheimer's, cancer," Lawrence had said. "We'll take the bold step—administration of dystrophin—to the next level."

It had sounded wonderful, and his promise to give a new hope to so many made her look the other way as he explained the necessity of going from experimentation on mice and guinea pigs to human volunteers. She'd balked, until he'd reassured her once again.

"All the advancements, all the great leaders in medical science—Pasteur, Currie, Fleming—all saw the necessity of putting their theories to the ultimate test. The human test."

Her reticence lingered, however, until he assured her that nothing could go wrong. "That's why I need you in the program," he said. "As a safeguard. You could be a distaff Daedalus to my impulsive Icarus."

She was flattered by his allusion to Greek mythology, giving her, by implication, the more dominant role. He'd sounded so idealistic, so brilliant, how could anything possibly go wrong? And that was, she reflected, how she first got involved in the supersecret governmentally funded research called the Genetically Enhanced Male—GEM—project. What she'd originally thought would be a quest to eradicate disease soon was transformed into the quest for a super soldier. Human volunteers were no problem. Most experienced violent side effects and were quickly dropped from the program, faceless young men who came and went. Then she met John Lassiter, and everything changed.

Now, instead of the allusion to Daedalus, she likened her experience more to Pandora.

She watched as Trang grimaced slightly when Lawrence depressed the plunger, and wondered if the risks of what they were doing had been fully explained to him. She thought about the slides. She thought about John. All these ramifications, albeit unexpected and sudden, certainly hadn't been explained to *him*.

"Doctor," Campbell said, "I need to talk to you."

Lawrence glanced at her briefly, then turned back to Trang. He was Asian, but the enhancements had begun to give his face a more brutish cast. The high cheekbones had begun to expand, as had his mandible.

John's face hadn't shown the same degree of distortion, she thought. That had to mean that Lawrence was using a higher dosage. She had to tell him about her new findings immediately.

"Doctor, I really do need to talk to you," she repeated.

He looked toward her, his ponytail flipping over the collar of his lab coat. When she'd first seen him she'd thought he resembled a tall, handsome Einstein. Now, she wasn't so sure.

Trang gritted his teeth. "Feels cold. Like you're injecting ice into my veins."

Lawrence patted his shoulder with a gentle assurance. "That will pass soon."

The door opened and Mickey Potter entered. The man made her think of a human weasel, with his thick tufts of dark hair slicked back, and his small, feral-looking teeth that slanted back into his mouth. He smiled and Campbell wanted to gag.

"Phone call, Doctor," Potter said.

"What? Can't you see I'm busy?" Lawrence seemed genuinely irritated.

"Artie sent me." Potter's lips peeled back from the disgusting teeth. "It's Washington. Greg Benedict."

Lawrence shot him a sharp glance, then turned to Ellen. "Monitor Trang's vitals until I get back," he said, as he set the now empty syringe on the metal tray and followed Potter out of the lab.

Campbell approached Trang and looked over the telemetry. Heart rate 56, blood pressure 120/70, respiration 9...everything seemed normal. Trang's dark eyes stared at her. His body exuded a sharp, almost pungent odor, like pure testosterone. She didn't like being alone with him, although she knew he wouldn't try anything. She had only to scream or hit the red safety button and the security forces would be in the lab in seconds.

His piercing stare continued, and the thought of the security guards gave her little reassurance. Trang was progressing at such an accelerated rate that he'd soon equal John's abilities. Maybe even surpass them. Plus, with John's current affliction, who knew how long it would be before he'd begin to feel the degenerative effects? She forced a lips-only smile to reassure Trang, and said, "I have to check something over there," as she moved back to the microscope.

Looking down, she transferred another slide to the shelf and adjusted the focus. These cells showed something new: karyolysis. The nuclei were breaking into fragments. That could mean an acceleration was imminent. But what was causing it? And why was it showing up now?

"Doc, I don't feel so good," Trang said.

She went back to him. "What is it, exactly?"

He frowned and shrugged. "I just feel, like, all flushed or something."

Campbell patted his shoulder. "That's perfectly normal. Lie back and try to relax. It should pass soon."

He reclined on the padded table, the huge muscles flexing under skin that looked as thin as paper.

"What's causing it?" he asked. "Is it the strength serum?"

"It's probably the vector spreading the serum to your cells throughout your body," she said.

"Vector? What's that?"

"Think of it as a sort of dye," she said, not wanting to use the term virus, even though the AAV—adeno-associated virus—had been tested as non-pathogenic. "It's a special medication that spreads to each cell."

"Man, it sure feels weird. Like I'm one of the X-Men or something." Trang's face showed a forced smile. "This ain't gonna turn me into a mutant or anything, is it?"

Campbell patted his arm again and said something reassuring to calm him, but her own mind was racing. A mutant.

Something clicked in her brain and she rechecked all three slides. It was as if the cells were being affected by a new, lethal virus. The AAV had been thought to be safe, in its original form, but that was seven years ago. What if the virus, through the repeated injections John received, virtually one after each mission, had caused his immune system to attack the carrier? What if the AAV had mutated in some way, and was now causing the necrosis?

It's got to be the vector, she thought. That has to be the answer. It's killing him.

Stony Man Farm, Virginia

BROGNOLA'S FACE LOOKED even more haggard and drawn than it had twelve hours earlier when Bolan had last talked to him. It was obvious he hadn't slept or rested in quite a while. He motioned Bolan and Grimaldi to two chairs in front of his desk. They sat and waited while the big Fed refilled his coffee cup.

"You look like you're running on caffeine and adrenaline," Grimaldi said. "You had any sleep in the last day and a half?"

"Sleep?" Brognola asked. "What's that?" He made an attempt at a smile, but it failed to reach his eyes. After taking a sip of coffee he took his seat, then blew out a long breath. "You want the bad news first?"

"That's usually the best way," Bolan said. "We didn't think you called us here to talk about the weather."

Brognola set the cup on his desk and closed his eyes, squeezing the bridge of his nose between his thumb and forefinger. "They found Chris Avelia. He's dead."

Bolan had been expecting that news. He gave Brognola a few seconds, then asked, "Where and how?"

"Arizona, just outside South Tucson, near the Tohono O'odham Indian Reservation. He was dumped alongside the highway with a bullet through his head." The big Fed compressed his lips, then added, "It looks like he was tortured, too."

"Who caught the investigation?" Bolan asked.

"You name it," Brognola said. "It was first reported to the Pima County Sheriff's Department. As soon as they found out who the victim was, the FBI got involved, not to mention the DEA sending somebody, as well as the ATF. Avelia was supposedly investigating a pending arms deal. There're rumblings that even the Agency was involved."

Bolan nodded. Dealing with so many organizations would make it both trickier and easier. He'd have to have a rock-solid cover story to get through the door by using Justice Department credentials. Once he was in, the Feds could eliminate a lot of the legwork for him, if they shared information. That was always a problem, and not playing catch-up on this one was imperative. Still, with so many agencies involved, his Justice Department cover story would make it look as if there was one more federal agency wanting a piece of the pie. It was something all bureaucrats could relate to in spades and would probably attract little attention. "Any good news come with this?" Grimaldi asked.

"Yeah," Brognola said. "Aaron was able to trace home base for those helicopters you guys saw."

"Where?" Bolan asked.

"South Tucson area, outside city limits. The helicopters are registered to Rigello Transport and Tours, an outfit that does helicopter tours of the Grand Canyon and other choice places. It also buys up a lot of old military hardware that it tunes up and rebuilds for Hollywood productions."

"And they rented the copters out on the same night as the raid?"

Brognola nodded. "As far as we could tell, they're the only game in that region that could have. Aaron hacked into their accounting system, but all we could come up with was some company named Bannerside Productions periodically renting two old Black Hawks and a Hind. They did so on the same day as the raid and returned them the following day."

"Did Aaron find anything on Bannerside Productions?" Bolan asked.

Brognola shook his head. "Nothing yet. It seems to be a front. He's working on it."

"What's the background of this Rigello Transport?"

"Now this is where things get a little bit more interesting." Brognola picked up his coffee cup and took another sip. "Aaron checked their financials. The business was started about four years ago by Joe Rigello and his brother, Dean. Where they got the capital for such a big investment is a mystery. Before that, they owned a small motorcycle repair shop in South Tucson."

"Motorcycles," Bolan said. "Any gang affiliations?"

Brognola smiled. "It seems that one of them, Dean, was particularly close to a less-than-reputable motorcycle gang called the Aryan Wolves. The club supposedly is nothing more than a social-athletic organization, but it's listed by the G was a one-percenter club. In other words, they're into all the standard hard-core gangster activities like drugs, guns and, this close to Mexico, human trafficking."

"Having a fleet of copters would make smuggling a bunch of drugs and illegals across the border pretty damn easy," Grimaldi stated.

"Too easy. I found out the Wolves were rumored to be connected to De la Noval's group. He supplied them with brown heroin, and they would get him whatever firepower his little heart desired. That's what Avelia was purportedly working on. He was trying to find out who was supplying the Wolves with guns to sell. And there's a new wrinkle."

Bolan and Grimaldi both looked at Brognola.

"Our old buddy Dimitri Chakhkiev is supposedly coming to the U.S."

"Chakhkiev?" Grimaldi said. "Where have I heard that name before?"

"Russian arms dealer," Bolan said. "He used to be KBG before the Soviet Union broke up. Now he's dipping his fingers into every little conflict he can, from Africa to Chechnya to the Middle East."

"Maybe he's planning on doing a little sightseeing," Grimaldi said with a grin. "The Statue of Liberty, the Grand Canyon, Vegas…"

"Any idea what Chakhkiev is up to?" Bolan asked.

Brognola shrugged. "We have no idea yet, but it's got to be something to do with an arms deal."

Bolan stood. "I've heard enough. Jack, how soon can you get the Learjet at Andrews ready for a trip to Arizona?"

Grimaldi shrugged. "How long does it take to put in some gas and file a flight plan?"

"Call and put things in motion then," Bolan said. "Hal, you'd better square things with the Air Force base."

"Arrangements have already been made. And it's already been fueled, Jack," he added drily.

"Did I mention that I have to unpack from our last trip first?" Grimaldi said, shooting Bolan a smile, which he transformed into a fake yawn. "Not to mention repacking for this one. And according to FAA rules, I can't fly until I've had at least eight hours sleep. How about we shoot for first thing in the morning? After all, we'll gain three hours flying out West anyway."

"Fine," Bolan said. "Make it 5:00 a.m. I'm going to the gym."

"Want some company?" Grimaldi asked. "I'd be glad to hold the heavy bag for you."

Bolan shook his head. "Thanks, but I need some time alone."

Pima County, Arizona

A couple things bothered John Lassiter as he rode shotgun in the blue van while Morris drove south under the dark canopy of twinkling stars set against the velvet of the moonlit sky. One was the informant they'd turned over earlier. The other was what Ellen had said. He tried to put all that out of his mind and concentrate on the mission. They were in the middle of nowhere on a lonely stretch of Arizona highway. The semi, laden with the cache of weapons, was three car lengths behind them. Lassiter had the suitcases with the money and the Mexican brown in the van with him. GOD had texted telling them to meet the Wolves to get their payoff money for the heroin, make that exchange, and then drive the weapons and the cash to the warehouse at GDF Industries. Then they'd collect their money and proceed to some much needed R and R.

The stuff about the tests that Ellen had mentioned still lingered in his mind, still bothered him. Was she right? Was he really sick?

But hell, he felt fine. During their liaison last night, which had lasted longer than he'd anticipated, Lassiter had dropped and done twenty-five one-arm push-ups with each arm as if it was nothing. She'd watched him with marveling approval and said she had to run more tests, and not to worry until she'd confirmed a few things. From his experience, doctors, especially women doctors, always made things out to be worse than they really were.

"I don't think we're too far from Wally's Waterworld," Morris said. "I grew up around here. The park closed about twelve years ago."

Lassiter nodded. He remembered the place. He'd

used the abandoned park from time to time as a staging area for raids into Mexico and Central America.

One of the Wolves escorting them pulled up alongside Lassiter's window and motioned for him to lower it. The percussive rumbling of the Harley nearly drowned out the biker's words, but Lassiter could still make them out: "Take the next right."

Up ahead he saw a dirt road that intersected with the highway.

Lassiter used his radio to relay their turnoff to the semi. "You guys pull over, but stay on the main highway. Set up sentry positions," he added. "Morris and I will make the exchange down that road, then come back to meet you. Remember, our orders are to take the semi to the GDF facility outside South Tucson afterward."

He waited until his guys in the Peterbilt truck gave him a "Roger that."

The lead biker swerved onto the dirt road and glanced back to make sure the van was following. Lassiter didn't fully trust the bikers, but he had dealt with them enough times to know this was how they operated. Besides, he had his insurance. He nudged the Beretta 93R on his hip for reassurance and rubbed his fingers over the plastic grip of his M-4. He usually left the rifle in the van on these high desert transactions, but there was no way he was going in unarmed. The van jolted as the wheels left the pavement and hit the dirt surface of the side road. The other Harley swung in behind them.

While Lassiter didn't care about turning over the drugs to the motorcycle idiots, having the weapons along at this point, albeit back on the highway, didn't seem like a prudent move. Of course, he reminded himself, that wasn't his call. Or his concern. He was just following orders. It had to be Godfrey's bright idea, his master plan. He'd been using the Wolves motorcycle gang to transport weapons south of the border for the past year, in exchange for the drugs and money to run their secret, dirty little operations. The deal with De la Noval, set up through the bikers, had been the largest they'd attempted. So large, the Wolves said, they'd have to use helicopters to transport it in. A handy little excuse for dropping Lassiter and his team on the unsuspecting drug lord and his cronies.

They were expecting a large cache of weapons, after all. And that's what they got. Lassiter smiled. He and Morris had gone perhaps half a mile, with the headlights of the van illuminating the cloudy wake of dust the lead motorcycle was raising, when Lassiter spotted a group of motorcycles parked in a smoothed-out circular patch perhaps a hundred yards distant. A headlight flashed momentarily, and he assumed it was a signal. They came to a stop, and Lassiter waited for the dust to settle before he stepped out.

The terrain was typically barren. Short sprouts of cactus and sage speckled the undulating landscape, which stretched away into the darkness.

Four bikers were leaning on their hogs, each wearing the distinctive burning crosses with the white wolf's head in the center. The one closest to them pushed off his seat and sauntered forward.

"About damn time you got here," he said.

Lassiter could see the biker was missing a few important teeth. The guy was maybe six-three and had no shirt on under his leather vest. His fat belly jiggled as he walked.

"You got the stuff?" he asked.

"Yeah," Lassiter said. "You got the money?"

The biker rolled his tongue over his gap-toothed grin. "First we test it."

"Be my guest," Lassiter said. "But then we count."

The biker spit onto the ground off to his side. At least he knew enough not to get near Lassiter's boots.

"Do that again and I'll break your neck," Lassiter said in a calm, but firm voice.

The biker tried to smile, but his bravado was obviously shaken.

Morris brought the suitcase from the rear of the van. The biker held out his hands.

"You got something for us?" Lassiter said.

The biker frowned and then snapped his fingers. One of the other guys got off his motorcycle and undid some bungee cords fastening a suitcase to the rear seat. He walked forward holding the bag.

The third biker stepped up with a small, clear plastic case about the size of a matchbox. It contained three small tubes. He reached into his pocket and came up with a Buck knife, which he flipped open. The blade shone in the moonlight.

"Well, open the motherfucker," the lead biker said.

Morris looked to Lassiter, who nodded.

After Morris unzipped the suitcase, he lifted the lid. It was full of neatly wrapped, bricklike blocks sealed in plastic.

The biker with the knife reached for one.

"Take one from the bottom," the first biker told him.

"Show us the money first, asshole," Lassiter said.

The gap-toothed biker glared at him momentarily, but Lassiter knew it was all bluff. If this idiot had any sense at all, he'd know when to rein in his tough-guy act.

Gap-tooth motioned for the second man to open the

suitcase. It was full of rubber-banded hundred dollar bills.

"Make sure there are no flash rolls," Lassiter said.

Morris grinned as he moved forward. Suddenly, his body made an uncontrollable jerking motion and his hands went to his chest. By the time Lassiter heard the sound of the report he was already dropping to the ground.

Gap-tooth and his friends weren't so lucky. They looked around and started to draw their weapons, but more shots sounded. One by one they went down, in rapid succession.

Two snipers, Lassiter estimated. The shots had come in too quickly to be from one weapon. The snipers were using night-vision scopes, he figured.

He rolled over, wedging himself into the dirt so he could get to Morris.

His hands found the kid's neck. No pulse. He swiveled the head toward him. Open, dead eyes stared back.

At least it'd been quick, Lassiter thought. The bullet had hit him in the back and exited the front. A massive tear in Morris's shirt indicated a big exit wound. It had been made by a large-caliber round. Lassiter brought the radio to his mouth and said, "Condition red. We're under fire here, over."

No response.

That probably meant that whoever it was had already taken out his two men with the semi.

Another shot ripped the dirt a few feet from Lassiter's head.

You missed, asshole, he thought. That was your first mistake.

He reached into the pocket of his cargo pants and grabbed the cylindrical object there. He rolled onto his back as his fingers found the plunger, and he closed his eyes.

He felt the pop and then heard the rushing release. Seconds later the popping sound told him the Starlite flare had ignited high overhead, and he rolled to his feet, running all-out toward the expanse of low hills to the west. From the trajectory of the rounds, that had to be where the snipers were. And if his luck held out, they were temporarily blinded by the star-light, star-bright flash.

For once, he hoped his adversaries had been using night-vision goggles.

As he passed the van, he paused to rip open the passenger door and pull out the M-4. If he was going to have a chance, he'd have to settle it rifle to rifle. Snapping off the safety, Lassiter continued his run. Ahead of him something moved.

Your second mistake, asshole, he thought as he brought his M-4 up and fired.

The shadowy figure jerked in the fading light of the descending flare. His spotter next to him obviously panicked and turned to flee. Lassiter's second shot got him squarely in the back.

Time to zigzag, Lassiter thought as he made an abrupt right turn. If he was setting up the ambush, that's where he would be. The light from the flare was almost totally diminished now, but perhaps a hundred feet ahead he saw two more men moving in the darkness. He flipped the selector switch to full-auto and sprayed their position. They did a pell-mell dance of death before falling.

Lassiter got to their location and flattened out, grabbing the elongated barrel of the Barrett sniper rifle. It had a mounted night-vision scope. The spotter had a set of goggles on his face. Lassiter aimed the Barrett toward the black silhouette of the semi and used the goggles to survey the area. Three figures moved by the truck. A van had pulled in behind it. Someone had been tailing them, but who?

Better take care of these three before I worry about that, he thought as he braced the butt of the Barrett against his right shoulder. The scope gave him a telephoto green image of the three men. One of them was frantically talking on a cell phone. The second held a radio to his mouth, and as Lassiter's hearing began to return, a radio on one of the dead men next to him crackled.

"Al, what's going on?" the voice on the radio said. "Did you get them?"

Lassiter lined up the man's chest in the crosshairs, then squeezed the trigger. The jolt was hardly perceptible as the big, .50-caliber shell popped out of the ejection port. He lined up the crosshairs on the second man, the one with the cell phone.

Squeeze, boom, pop. His ears automatically went into audio-occlusion due to the concussion of the blast.

Lassiter swiveled the barrel to the third man and repeated the action.

Squeeze, boom, pop. He immediately got up and sprinted toward the semi, circling and pausing periodically to check for any more hostiles. Everything looked pacific in the tranquil green field of display. When he got to the scene, he checked his fallen men first. All dead.

It looked as if they'd been caught off guard. They probably thought the real action was unfolding down the dirt road. The hostiles were all dead, too, and Lassiter dragged the bodies to the side of the road and quickly went through their pockets, but found nothing in the way of IDs. He did a cursory search of their van as well, again finding nothing in the way of traceable identifiers. This was beginning to take on all the earmarks of a Company operation. He did find a GSP with this location blinking. Somebody had planted a tracker on either the semi or his van.

But who? And why? Although the why might take a bit of figuring, he already had a good idea about the who.

All that would have to wait a bit longer, he thought. He had a mess that he had to clean up.

CHAPTER FOUR

Bolan watched as the mountainous terrain of the dry Arizona landscape became gradually bisected with ribbons of highway that intersected with small clusters of buildings and finally with larger towns and cities. As they neared Tucson, the expanse of buildings and civilization grew denser, but Bolan wondered what it had looked like back in the day, when the first settlers edged westward, facing the adversity of the savage land. The tops of some of the mountains, he noticed, were blackened from the summer's wildfires. He'd spent more years than he cared to remember putting out wildfires of a different type.

Grimaldi banked the plane and began calling the airport to report their approach. When they'd been cleared for landing he swiveled toward Bolan, who sat in the copilot's seat, and grinned.

"See? Aren't you glad we waited until morning before we took off?" he asked.

Bolan said nothing as he watched the ground gradually getting closer and closer.

Grimaldi spoke again to the control tower and slowed the Learjet's descent a bit more.

They were at perhaps five hundred feet now, going over a shopping center and a ball field. When they touched down about thirty seconds later it was as easy as a limousine making a lane change on a freeway.

"And how's that for the epitome of smoothness?" he asked.

"Careful," Bolan said. "Don't strain your arm patting yourself on the back."

Grimaldi snorted a laugh as he radioed for instructions on proceeding to the appropriate location. Then he turned to Bolan as he steered the plane. "Well, at least I got you to talk. You hardly said two words during the whole trip."

"I was just thinking how screwed up things have gotten with this one already."

"That isn't our fault."

"No, but it means we've inherited a can of worms, as the saying goes."

Grimaldi taxied the jet toward the section of private aircraft hangers. A man wearing a vest with brightly colored orange stripes directed them to proceed to the right, where an open hangar awaited.

"So what's our first move?" Grimaldi asked. "After we secure this baby and our gear, of course."

Bolan had been thinking about how to proceed, and there seemed to be only one course open to them at the moment. "We're going to see a couple guys about a chopper."

"Hot damn," Grimaldi said. "One of my favorite things to do."

RIGELLO TRANSPORT AND Tours was on the edge of town in what appeared to be an unincorporated part of the county, about half a mile beyond the city limits sign for South Tucson. The business itself had a dirt parking lot that gradually gave way to an expanse of asphalt and a long driveway. Three brick buildings with tinted windows were adjacent to the paved lot, and beyond that

Bolan could see an extensive area holding neat rows of dilapidated aircraft, trucks, cars and motorcycles.

As they drove by, Bolan noticed a large metallic sign on the front that read Rigello Transport & Tours. By Appointment Only. The big junkyard out back was surrounded by a seven-foot-high cyclone fence topped with three strands of barbed wire, and an additional hand-painted sign on the front gates said, To Hell with the Dog. Beware of the Owneres.

"Obviously, we're about to come into contact with a couple of real Rhodes Scholars," Grimaldi said, looking at the misspelling through the passenger window.

He and Bolan had rented a black Escalade with tinted windows, and the air-conditioning was going full blast as the dark SUV sat idling in the late afternoon heat. They'd also opted to wear dark suits, white shirts, ties and sunglasses to fit the role of federal agents.

"We look like refuges from a *Men in Black* movie," Grimaldi said.

Bolan was studying the layout, figuring where the points of entry and egress were, estimating the approximate locations of the bathrooms by the vent pipes on the roof, and trying to get a feel for the place. He also was watchful for any human activities, but there were none visible.

"Not really a hotbed of commercial activity, is it?" Grimaldi asked, leaning back in the passenger seat. He took off the nondescript baseball cap and began fanning some of the cold air pouring from the vents toward himself.

"Go try the door," Bolan said.

"Why me?" Grimaldi winced as he looked outside. "It's gotta be a hundred and five degrees out there."

"But it's a dry heat." Bolan grinned as he stopped the Escalade.

Grimaldi heaved a sigh and opened the door. He stepped out and slipped on his suit jacket, pantomiming some heavy panting as he said, "Dry or not, it's damned hot." He fanned himself with his open palm as he walked slowly to the front door and twisted the knob. The door opened.

The pilot turned toward Bolan with a wide grin, waved and went inside. Bolan pulled into a parking space nearest the door and followed him.

The room was divided into two sections, with a solid rear door leading somewhere. A pair of opaque, plastic shells, about the size of small coffeepots, was affixed to opposite walls, no doubt housing cameras. Their positioning would give a clear view of the entire space 3x to anyone monitoring them.

The office area was rather small, tucked behind the crudely built wooden counter that served as the divider. Metal shelving units behind the counter held stacks of dusty boxes. Crumpled bags from various fast-food restaurants and half-crushed foam coffee cups littered the floor around a small, overflowing garbage can. The place smelled of smoked cigarettes, half-eaten burgers and body odor. A trace of booze lingered in the air as well, like a slightly noticeable aftershave.

A lone figure sat at a small gray desk that held a tattered notebook, a telephone and a calendar.

Grimaldi was already engaged in conversation with him.

"What do you mean, you're closed?" he asked. "The front door was open."

"That don't mean nothing," the man said. He was a short, gray-bearded guy with an aquiline nose and a handkerchief tied over the front of his head, giving way to a long ponytail in back. His light blue T-shirt was stretched tightly over a belly that indicated a rather flabby, out-of-shape body. Huge rings of sweat radiated from each armpit. He wore a holstered Glock on his right side.

"I'm doing office work at moment. You want to make an appointment, call that number and leave a message." From the way he spoke Bolan could tell he was missing some teeth in front. The man pointed to a handwritten notice on the wall.

"Actually," Bolan said, breaking into the conversation, "we won't take much of your time." He held up an official-looking credential identifying him as Special Agent Matthew Cooper of the Justice Department. "We need to talk to you about some helicopters you rented."

The man behind the counter cocked his head back and regarded both of them. His mouth gaped slightly, and his lips twisted into what might have passed for a smile in more pleasant surroundings.

"What exactly are you looking for?" he asked.

Bolan stepped to the counter and took out his notebook as Grimaldi walked to the windows on the opposite end of the room.

"May I have your name, sir?" Bolan asked.

The man's eyes shifted from him to Grimaldi, then back again.

"I'm Joe Rigello."

"It'd be easier if you just showed him your driver's license," Grimaldi said from the windows.

Before Rigello could reply, the Stony Man pilot cried, "Hey, that wouldn't be a genuine CH-47 you got out back there, would it?"

Rigello's eyes went back to him. "Yep. You familiar with Chinooks?"

"Hell, yes," he said with a wide grin. "Flown many a mission in them in my time."

"You're a pilot, huh?" Rigello said.

"Show me your ID," Bolan said, holding out his hand.

Rigello reached into his pocket and took out a brown leather wallet, one side of which looked as sodden as the underarms of his T-shirt. He dug through it, removed his driver's license and gave it to Bolan.

"And do my eyes deceive me," Grimaldi said, his voice imbued with artificial awe, "or is that a genuine Huey Cobra, teeth and all?"

Rigello laughed. "It is. Only without the rockets and minigun."

"Too bad," Grimaldi said, grinning back. "Old UH-60s? People want to take tours in those things? They must like sitting on hard surfaces."

"Looks like you know your helicopters, mister," Rigello said. "But yeah, we do a lot of work with movie companies. They're gonna be making another one of them 'Nam movies pretty soon."

"No kidding?" Grimaldi moved closer to the counter. "You a pilot?"

"Naw." He shook his head. "I just fix 'em. My brother, Dean, is the pilot."

"Could you use another one?" Grimaldi flashed him a wide smile. "I love to fly."

Rigello grinned back, showing his missing front teeth.

It was beginning to sound like a war buddy reunion, Bolan thought. He cleared his throat.

Rigello's eyes drifted to him as Bolan handed the ID back. "What did you guys say you wanted again?"

"Information," Bolan said. "The names of the people who rented those three helicopters last Tuesday."

Rigello ran his tongue over his upper lip and shook his head. "Tuesday?"

"Give or take a day or two," Bolan said. "They might have rented them before that, but they definitely used them on Tuesday."

Rigello licked his lips again and gave a little shake of his head. "Don't sound familiar."

"Sometimes it's hard to remember back that far," Bolan said. "Do you mind if we take a quick look at your books?"

The rear door suddenly opened and a larger, younger version of the man behind the counter came storming in. His face was thinner, but he had the same aquiline nose. This guy's beard was jet-black, and his hair was pulled back in a similar looking ponytail style. He was also wearing a Glock in a pancake holster.

"Yeah, we do mind," the new guy said. "Unless you got a warrant."

He turned to Joe Rigello and said, "What did I tell you about keeping your trap shut?"

Bolan studied the man. From his remarks, it was obvious he had been both watching and listening to the conversation from the next room.

"I'm Special Agent Matthew Cooper, Justice Department," Bolan said. "This is my partn—"

"I don't give a shit *who* you are," the man said. "We don't got to show you nothing concerning our business 'less you got a warrant." He thumped his chest with his fist. "I *know* the law."

"No need to get hostile, pal." Grimaldi strolled over with an ingratiating grin stretched across his face. "Me and your brother here were just talking about helicopters when you interrupted. Uh, at least I'm assuming that you and Joe are related."

"That's my brother, Dean," Joe blurted.

Dean Rigello shot him another look of disdain. "Shut up."

He turned the look toward Bolan. "Get outta here and don't come back unless you got a warrant."

"We'll look into getting one," Bolan said, then turned to exit the building, followed by Grimaldi.

"You do that. We run a respectable business here and got nothing to hide."

"Then what are you afraid of?" Grimaldi asked.

Dean's head swiveled toward him. "Nothing. I ain't afraid of nothing."

"Is that so?" the pilot said.

"Yeah." Rigello's lips twisted into a sneer. "I just don't like cops, is all. I'm a civil libertarian."

"You know—" Grimaldi looked at Bolan, then back to Rigello "—that reminds me of that old saying, two weeks ago I couldn't even spell *civil libertarian,* and now I are one."

The sneer deepened on Dean Rigello's hawkish face.

Back in the Escalade, Grimaldi made a clucking sound and said, "That went really well."

"I don't know, you and Joe seemed to be getting on, one chopper enthusiast to another."

"Yeah, but it looks like our boy Dean's running things." The pilot directed the air vent toward himself again. "Got any bright ideas about our next move?"

"Maybe," Bolan said, glancing at his watch. It was 1:54 p.m. He considered their options and decided that time was definitely not on their side. They had to go into accelerated information-gathering mode, and that meant stretching the rules a bit, as needed. He put the Escalade in gear and drove away slowly. "I think perhaps a little heart-to-heart talk with our boy Dean is in order."

"Especially since he holds the law and his libertarian principles in such high regard." Grimaldi smiled. "So what do you think? Hard or soft?"

Bolan considered the question, and then said, "Well, we're pressed for time. I was thinking perhaps the deep blue goodbye."

Grimaldi nodded. "Good choice."

AFTER SLIPPING a clear plastic covering over the license plates of the Escalade, changing the numerals, they spent half an hour finding an old, suitable, sleazy no-tell motel in a semisecluded spot along the stretch of highway. It was only a quarter-mile drive from the Rigello Transport and Tours establishment. The motel, aptly named the Desert Shadows Motel, was laid out in a T-shape, with a dilapidated, but high wooden fence surrounding the rear portion. The fence was obviously intended to shield vehicles from the view of the highway. Wearing his sunglasses and a baseball cap, Grimaldi went in and rented a room for "a four-hour nap," with a possible extension. He asked for and got one of the rooms on the fenced-in side.

"I'd like to inspect the room before I rent it," he said.

The clerk stared at him through the heavy sheet of smudged Plexiglas that separated his booth from the customer portion of the front counter, and then shoved a key with a plastic tag attached through the slot at the bottom. "Be my guest." The guy looked like a human version of a Gila monster—no neck, just a massive head set on top of a pair of narrow shoulders. He moved with a lizardlike precision, too. "Just give me your ID until you bring the key back, and pay."

Grimaldi pulled out an authentic-looking driver's license for one Irving Grim out of Los Angeles, California, and tossed it into the slotted portion. He then walked briskly out of the office and went through a small passageway that separated the motel office from the rooms. The tag on the key had a 9 emblazoned on it, although the white lettering was virtually worn off.

The pilot opened the door and surveyed the interior. A dilapidated double bed took up most of one side. A beat-up wooden table with a phone sat off to the left, and at the foot of the bed was another table with an old-fashioned television on top. An odd-looking box was attached to the side of the set, with a coin slot on the top. A hand-printed sign taped to the box read: Adult Movies for Rent. 25 Cents for Three Minutes. Quarters Available in Office.

Grimaldi went to the bathroom and checked the shower area. It had a bathtub that butted up against a vanity sink and toilet. After pulling back the shower curtain, he twisted the hot water faucet as high as it would go and held his hand under the flow. The water started to get hot after about ten seconds and then got very hot, almost scalding, after about twenty.

Passable, he thought.

He shut the water off, relocked the room and walked back to the office. The Gila monster clerk was waiting.

"Like it?" he asked.

"A regular Taj Mahal," Grimaldi said.

The clerk gave him a quizzical look as he recorded the information on an index card and shoved the fake ID back through the slot. The guy looked about as interested as a man halfway through an intense reading of the city phone book as he said, "Don't do no damage to the room and be out in four, unless you call and say you want to stay longer, in which case it'll cost you forty more."

Grimaldi nodded, keeping his head down in typical "guilty" fashion. He hadn't noticed any cameras on the way in, but figured he'd play his part, anyway.

"Say," he said with a grin as he passed a five under the glass. "Can you give me some quarters?"

The clerk smirked. "They come in rolls of ten dollars."

Grimaldi raised his eyebrow, took another five out of his wallet and tossed it down.

The clerk picked up both bills, held each up to the light to check the watermarks, and then dropped a paper roll of coins into the slot. "Enjoy yourself."

"I intend to," Grimaldi said as he turned and left. He paused at the door and held up the roll. "There aren't any quarter-sized washers in this, are there?"

The lizard's lips peeled back from his teeth into what he probably thought passed for a grin.

The Escalade was waiting outside and Bolan was now in the passenger seat, dressed in his combat blacksuit. He had his Beretta 93R in a low-slung drop-holster on his right leg, and the Espada knife clipped inside his left pants pocket.

"I was right all along," Grimaldi said, getting behind the wheel. "Now we really do look like the men in black."

"At least one of us does," Bolan said.

AFTER GRIMALDI CHANGED into his set of black fatigues, they left the Desert Shadows Motel and drove back to the vicinity of the helicopter place and parked. Balancing a pair of high-powered binoculars on the top of the steering wheel of the Escalade, Grimaldi asked, "So how do you propose getting our buddy Dean to come out and play?"

They were a few hundred feet down the block from Rigello Transport and Tours. Bolan glanced at his watch. It was 4:40. He raised his high-powered binoculars to his eyes and adjusted the focus.

"It's getting close to the dinner hour," he said, "and from the looks of their office, I'd say neither of the Rigellos is very skilled in the culinary arts."

"Yeah," Grimaldi said, "their wastebasket made it look like they were the sole source of support of several of the burger joints up the block."

"So it's just a question of seeing which one goes to pick up the takeout."

Grimaldi snorted. "My guess it'll be Joe. I don't think Dean likes being the gofer."

"I think you're right." Bolan saw the front gate of the yard swing open, and a dilapidated old pickup pulled out and made a right turn onto the highway. "Take a look."

Grimaldi raised his binoculars, then smiled. "I'll bet old toothless Joe is heading over to get their daily dose of coronary-bypass specials."

"I'd say that's an affirmative. And he was nice enough to leave the gate open for us. Let's roll."

Grimaldi slammed the Escalade into gear and peeled away from the curb. Bolan glanced around quickly. No passing police cars were in the area despite the moderately heavy traffic flow. Grimaldi slowed as he approached the driveway to the Rigello facility and drove through the open gateway, pulling to an abrupt stop. Bolan hopped out and went around the back of the SUV as the Stony Man pilot pulled forward in a sweeping U-turn.

Bolan headed straight for the back door of the building, scanning the eaves for any cameras. He saw one on each end of the building, facing the expansive junkyard of miscellaneous machinery. Bolan slipped on some thin, black leather gloves as he approached the entry. He twisted the knob and found that the door was unlocked. Stepping inside with a decisive movement, he surveyed the office area. It was empty. Sounds of a flushing toilet and running water came from a small room to the left.

Looks like the timing couldn't be better, Bolan thought.

He left the exit door slightly ajar and took up a position next to the bathroom door. It opened seconds later and Dean Rigello came out. Bolan stepped around and delivered a quick left hook to the man's solar plexus, and then followed with a chopping right cross directly behind his left ear. Rigello grunted with each blow, and then his eyes rolled back in his head as he started to crumple.

Bolan grabbed the collar of the man's T-shirt and lowered him facedown to the floor, then reached into his pants pocket and removed a plastic riot cuff and a black nylon hood. After securing Rigello's hands behind his back, he checked the man's carotid pulse. It was steady and strong. After ascertaining Rigello was still out, Bolan slipped the black nylon hood over the unconscious man's head, and moved to the array of camera monitors on the desk. The Escalade was on one of them. Bolan quickly located the master control box sitting on a shelf under the monitors. He disconnected the cables to the camera system and pulled the box from the shelf.

Rigello emitted a soft moan.

It was time to get moving.

Bolan stepped over to the prone man, adjusted him into a sitting position, then lifted him to his feet. The limpness of the man's body indicated that he was out of it. Bolan slung Rigello over his right shoulder like a sack of potatoes. He then grabbed the camera control box and strode toward the exit. He made one last check for any more cameras or telltale signs of his brief visit and, satisfied there was none, nudged the door with the toe of his boot and pushed it open. The Escalade was idling a few feet away. Bolan heard the click of the door locks and walked to the SUV. He set down the camera monitor control box momentarily and opened the right rear door of the vehicle.

"Taxi?" Grimaldi asked with a wide grin.

Jamming Rigello onto the spacious seat, Bolan tossed the control box onto the floor and got in himself. Once he was inside the Escalade peeled out of the yard. Bolan took two more plastic riot cuffs from his pocket and secured Rigello's feet and knees together. From the sonorous breathing, he could tell the man was still out cold.

Neither of them spoke as Grimaldi drove at a moderate rate back to the Desert Shadows Motel and turned into the parking lot. There were two cars in spaces on the front side. Grimaldi drove around the back to their rented room. The area was devoid of other vehicles. He parked in his slot, got out and felt for the key. After unlocking the door, he held it open as Bolan got out quickly and carried Rigello into the room.

Grimaldi shut the door behind them and smirked as he secured the flimsy safety lock. "That gives us about as much protection as a silk nightgown," he whispered.

Bolan took out his Espada knife. He paused to check Rigello's pulse again, then cut the plastic straps securing the man's legs and ankles. Grimaldi shot Bolan a questioning look, and the soldier nodded. After an exaggerated grimace, Grimaldi removed Rigello's boots and pants. The man wasn't wearing any underwear. Bolan slipped the blade of the knife under the T-shirt. They then refastened his ankles and knees with more riot cuffs, carried him to the bathroom and set him gently in the tub.

When Bolan came back into the room a moment after Grimaldi, he saw the pilot dropping quarters into the slot on the adult movie box. Grimaldi picked up the remote and flipped the TV on. He handed the remote to Bolan, who hit the mute button. On the screen a blond woman and several men seemed to be engaged in some sort of superfluous conversation.

"Hey, I wish we could watch this one," Grimaldi said. "It looks like it has a great plot."

Bolan's mouth tugged into a half grin and he motioned toward the bathroom. It was time to begin.

Neither Bolan nor Grimaldi subscribed to torture due to their personal code of honor, but the code didn't prevent them from using the threat or pretense of such acts when the situation required it. That was what the Deep Blue Goodbye was all about. Bolan had gotten the idea for the technique from an old John D. MacDonald novel he'd found at the Farm and read, and they'd used it numerous times. It was all about making the subject of the interrogation believe that he was in danger and out of options.

Bolan leaned halfway out the bathroom door and pressed the remote to turn the volume on the television set to a distractingly suitable level. A series of forced moans and groans flooded the small motel room. He looked at Grimaldi and nodded.

Grimaldi glanced down at the still slumbering Dean Rigello and pulled out the water faucet. It was already adjusted to the hottest position, but he knew from his previous test that the water would take a moment to warm up. He pulled up the stopper to start the shower, and adjusted the nozzle to spray over Rigello's legs and side. The man grunted and tried to move. The grunts turned to a panicked sounding moan and finally he emitted a low scream.

Grimaldi shut off the water.

Bolan leaned over, placing his right hand on Rigello's shoulder, and spoke in a soft voice.

"How you doing, Dean?"

"Who...who are you?" Rigello asked in a quavering voice. "Whaddya want?"

"Information," Bolan said.

"Huh? What is this?" Rigello's head was still covered with the black nylon hood, so his voice was somewhat muffled, but he nonetheless managed to recover a modicum of arrogance and bravado. "You guys don't know who you're messing with."

Bolan nodded to Grimaldi, who pulled out the faucet again, giving Rigello a quick blast of the hot water once more.

The man grunted and squirmed as Bolan held him down, preventing him from thrashing around and possibly injuring himself.

"Information, Dean," Bolan repeated.

"Fuck you."

Grimaldi applied two more short bursts of the hot water.

Rigello grunted each time. When he spoke again, the bravado had given way to a more plaintive tone. "Please. You guys can't do this."

Grimaldi gave him one more shot of hot spray.

"We can," Bolan said. "And we will." He waited a

few more seconds, then continued, knowing Rigello was in such an anxious state that he would probably believe anything he was told. "We've had you prisoner for twenty-four hours, Dean, checking on and verifying things. Twenty-four hours."

"What? No way." Rigello groaned. "I got friends. Lots of friends. They'll be looking for me."

"They won't find you," Boland said. "We're practically in Mexico now. All we have to do is find a suitable place under a cactus for you."

"No," Rigello said. "Please don't kill me."

"That'll depend on you," Bolan said. "Information."

Rigello took a deep breath, then asked, "Whatcha want?"

"Who do you work for?"

"What? Me and my broth—"

Grimaldi gave him another dose of hot water.

Rigello swore. "Okay, okay. The Wolves, man."

"The Aryan Wolves?"

"Yeah," Rigello said. "And when they get wind of this they're gonna be real pissed."

"They launder their drug money through your company?" Bolan asked.

When Rigello didn't answer immediately, he added, "I'm about through wasting my time with you, Dean. Want me to take this up to the next level?"

When Rigello still didn't speak, Grimaldi used a rough voice to say, "We've got a Gila monster in the next room. And he's agitated."

"All right, all right. Yeah, yeah, we do that. We launder their money."

"So what else do you do for them?"

"Huh?"

"What else?" Bolan asked. "Fly anything south of the border?"

Rigello hesitated, then said, "Yeah, sometimes."

"Like what?"

The black nylon hood shook. "Look, I been saying too much already. I can't—"

Grimaldi pulled the faucet again. "How's the water?"

Rigello grunted. "Okay, no more. I'll tell ya. Sometimes, when they asked me, I'll fly 'em down to a landing spot in Mexico. Drop something off, I don't know what, pick something up. I don't know what that is, either."

It sounded like what Bolan had expected. This little charade was nearing its conclusion.

"What about last Tuesday?" Bolan asked. "You fly them down south?"

Rigello didn't answer immediately, and when he did a sliver of confidence came back into his voice. "Hey, I know who you guys are. You're them two Feds from the Justice Department, ain't ya?"

Bolan heaved an audible sigh. "Dean, do you really think some federal agents would conduct an interrogation like this?"

"Let's give him the Deep Blue Goodbye and be rid of him," Grimaldi said.

"Deep Blue what?" Rigello asked.

"The Gila monster," the pilot said. "Once they bite you, they never let go."

The black hood bobbled like a buoy on rough water. "Hey, no, please. I won't say nothing. Honest."

"Last Tuesday," Bolan said. "Tell us about it."

"Animal," Rigello said, "he's the chief honcho of the Wolves. He calls me up and says a guy's coming and to get three choppers. He wants them fueled up and ready to go. I say, want me to fly one of 'em? He says, no, the dude's got his own pilots. All we have to do is make sure they're gassed up. This dude shows up with three other guys, looked like ex-military or something, and they take the choppers. They used the name Bannerside Productions as a cover. They brought them back the next day. Paid us cash, and that was that." Rigello wiggled a bit in the tub. "I just do what they tell me to do, that's all. Honest."

"Did the guy who rented the choppers have a name?" Bolan asked. "Besides Bannerside Productions?"

"Animal called him Artie or something."

"What's Artie's last name?" Bolan asked.

"I dunno."

"Have another blast of scalding water," Grimaldi said, putting his hand on the faucet.

"No, please, no more." Rigello began to sob. It sounded like hiccups inside the nylon hood. "I don't know. Honest. I'd tell ya if I did. I don't know."

Bolan looked at Grimaldi, who shrugged and wiggled his open hand, palm down.

"You been lying to us, Dean?" Grimaldi asked.

"No, no. I ain't. I swear on my mother's grave."

Grimaldi shrugged again and got up from his seat on the edge of the tub.

Bolan took his Espada knife and sliced off the plastic ties around Rigello's wrists and knees. He left the one fastened around the man's feet. Grimaldi was already walking toward the door.

The Executioner leaned close to Rigello and whispered, "Give me one good reason why I should let you live."

Rigello moved slightly but made no motion to remove the nylon hood. "Because I told you what you wanted?"

Bolan waited a few seconds, cut the last plastic tie around Rigello's feet and said, "Stay there. Don't move."

He then backed out of the bathroom, turned and strode to the door. Grimaldi already had the Escalade out of the parking space, engine running. Bolan hopped in the passenger side and they took off. Grimaldi's grin was wide as he turned the corner from the parking lot and drove onto the highway.

"A Gila monster?" Bolan asked. "Where'd that come from?"

"Hey, whatever works," the pilot said. He clucked sympathetically. "I'll bet those grease burgers Joe brings back are going to be pretty cold by the time Dean gets enough gumption to put on his pants and get the hell out of there."

"Maybe he'll decide to stay and watch the rest of the movie."

"Yeah, well, he's going to need a lot more quarters," Grimaldi said, as he accelerated down the highway. "I only fed it enough to keep it running for about five more minutes, and I kept the rest of the roll."

They'd driven a few blocks when Bolan noticed Grimaldi stare again at the rearview mirror.

"Something wrong?" Bolan asked.

"Maybe," he said. "Seems like we picked up a tail coming out of the motel, and from the looks of them, I think it's the cops."

CHAPTER FIVE

Fairfax County, Virginia

Anthony Godfrey slammed his fist on the desktop. "What the hell's going on out there?"

Greg Benedict, who sat across from him, winced slightly. "Like I said, it was a little slipup."

Godfrey felt the flush burning upward from the base of his neck. The two of them were alone in his plush, well-furnished corporate office. "It doesn't sound so *little* to me. I thought you had your best cleanup team on it?"

"I did. Apparently they weren't up to the job." Benedict pinched the bridge of his nose and then shook his head. "Lassiter was too good for them."

"Too good? The son of a bitch is dying, for Christ's sake."

"Yeah," Benedict said, "but apparently not quickly enough. I wonder if he was tipped?"

"Tipped? By whom?"

Benedict blew out a long breath. "I'm not sure. Maybe we have a leak somewhere. Have you run security checks on the staff at GDF Industries and the lab lately?"

Godfrey felt a surge of rage. The very idea that *he* was somehow responsible for this screw-up? It was preposterous. "All my people have been screened. What about *yours?*"

"I'm in the process of rechecking my own staff." Benedict stopped rubbing his nose and looked up. "All I'm saying is we need to double-check everything and everyone. Make sure we're secure. Make sure there are no leaks. No whistle-blowers."

Godfrey considered this momentarily. It wouldn't do any harm to run some new security checks. It was always a good thing, even if he found nothing. He nodded and then said, "You mentioned you wanted to talk about something else?"

"The latest rumbling is that I'm going to get called before this new congressional committee next week. Especially when it comes out that we've lost another federal agent along the border."

"That couldn't be helped. He knew way too much. Just be glad we intercepted and canceled him before he could report back to D.C."

"Canceled." Benedict grinned. "Like a stamp."

Godfrey allowed himself a rare laugh. "If only the rest of it would have gone that smoothly. We're still nowhere with finding the damn shipment."

"Any ideas on that?"

Godfrey frowned. "We can only assume that Lassiter hid it somewhere in the desert. The GPS tracking system was disabled. The last known location was somewhere outside South Tucson, where the meeting with the Wolves was supposed to go down. I heard from Artie, by the way. The motorcycle idiots are very perturbed about their men getting wasted."

"That also couldn't be helped." Benedict smirked. "Besides, wasting a few of those lowlifes was a public service. I thought you wanted to blame the whole thing on a retaliation by the De la Noval Cartel?"

"I'm in the process of doing just that. But we still have the little matter of the missing shipment to deal with. Chakhkiev has gotten one of his transport ships coming up from Cuba to Mexico as we speak. I assured him the shipment would be ready for pick-up."

"What? Like you don't have enough surplus weapons to whip up another batch?" Benedict grinned.

"That might work for the damn M-4s and the Barretts, but I have to cross my t's and dot my i's when it comes to the damn stinger missiles. You got any idea how closely the current administration is going over my inventory records?" Godfrey frowned. "They're out to get me, and if I have a big discrepancy I can't explain, they just might."

"What's a couple of million to a company pulling in a billion dollars a year?"

"They get suspicious they'll put the IRS on my ass," Godfrey said.

"All the more reason for both of us to make sure that we have President Hutchcraft sitting in the Oval Office next time around." Benedict raised an eyebrow. "Brent's press conference is this afternoon, isn't it?"

"Yes." Godfrey bit his lower lip. "It's better if he doesn't hear about this latest development until after that. We don't want to throw him off his game. He'll shit when he hears about those missing Stingers." He cursed and shook his head. "I don't know what I'm going to do about that."

"Just cook the books like you usually do," Benedict said. "Anyway, in a related matter, what's the latest on our newest GEM candidate?"

"Trang?" Godfrey sat back and smiled. "That's probably the only bright spot in this otherwise bleak picture of late. Artie says he's doing great."

"Good. We're probably going to need him sooner rather than later. If I were you, I'd tell Dr. Lawrence to speed things up. I don't want to lose another wet team going after Lassiter."

"Neither do I. But we have to find the slick bastard first."

"As well as the shipment," Benedict said.

"That's the main reason I'm flying out to Arizona to get a firsthand look at things. After I meet with Chakhkiev, of course."

Benedict smiled ruefully. "Well, give that Russian son of a bitch my best regards."

"I will," Godfrey replied, matching his partner's cynical smile with one of his own. "Among other things."

Pima County, Arizona

"JUSTICE DEPARTMENT LIAISON Officer?" Sergeant Sergio Valdez said as he looked at Bolan's identification. "How come I never heard of that?"

The cop looked to be pushing forty, but he was in fairly good shape, judging from the powerful, corded forearms that sprang from his tan uniform shirt. A pair of chevrons decorated the sleeves under the county sheriff police patch. "What the hell's the Justice Department doing nosing around in this neck of the woods, Cooper?"

They were in a small interview room, after having been pulled over on a traffic stop shortly after leaving the motel. Three of the four walls were cinder block and devoid of decorations. The fourth, which faced them, reflected their images on a mirrorlike surface, only Bolan knew it was no mirror. It was the opaque side of a pane of one-way glass. He also noticed several miniature microphones positioned at various points within the room.

Special Agent Audrey Callahan was standing next to Valdez, while Bolan and Grimaldi were seated behind a small table. They had shown their Justice Department badges and identifications at the stop, and been asked to accompany the police to the station for verification and further investigation.

"Especially armed with these," Callahan said, pointing to Grimaldi's SIG Sauer P-221 and then Bolan's Beretta 93R. "I didn't even think they made that model anymore."

"They don't," Bolan said. "That's why I'm pretty fond of this one."

"So tell us again what you're doing out here, Special Agent—" Valdez looked down at Bolan's Justice Department ID again.

"Cooper," he said. "Matt Cooper."

Bolan was always as respectful as he could be to local law enforcement, although he usually liked to circumvent any association with them if possible. He operated outside the box, and rules and regulations usually slowed him down way too much. In this case, however, he had figured on making a connection with them regarding Chris Avelia's death investigation, sooner or later. He'd just figured on later. And having the FBI involved certainly wasn't expected, either. The Bureau was all about following the rules. This raised the strong possibility he'd have to use a wild card he hadn't wished to play yet.

"I told you," Bolan said. "We're here conducting a special investigation."

"What kind of investigation?" Valdez asked.

"We're looking into the death of a federal agent."

"Oh, really?" Callahan said. "Who was the agent?"

"Chris Avelia," Bolan stated.

Valdez and Callahan exchanged glances. A uniformed deputy opened the door, grinning. When he saw the quartet inside the small office, the grin faded immediately.

"What did you find, Mitchell?" Valdez asked.

"We found Dean Rigello in that motel room." The deputy tried to keep his expression serious, but the corners of his mouth kept edging up into a smile as he spoke. "He was half-naked, pulling on his pants, and there was a porno movie playing on the TV."

Valdez frowned. "What did he have to say?"

"Nothing. You know what an assho—" He paused and his eyes glanced toward Callahan. "I mean, what an idiot he is. All he would say was he wanted a ride back to the chopper shop. I did find these in the bathroom, though." He held up the three severed plastic ties.

Valdez took them, glanced over at Bolan and Grimaldi, then dismissed the deputy. He turned back to the Stony Man warriors and held up the ties. "Care to explain these?"

"Those were probably there from the last occupants," Grimaldi said. "And whatever consenting adults want to do behind closed doors is fine with us."

The sergeant tossed the ties onto the table and leaned forward, his face jutting toward Grimaldi. "I got a low tolerance for smart-asses."

Before Grimaldi could answer, Bolan jumped in. "How do you know we were in the room with Rigello?"

Valdez turned toward him. "We've been watching him. We saw you there earlier, and then your quick trip the second time."

"We were debating whether to interrupt the party when you guys abruptly left," Callahan said. "What were you interrogating him about?"

That fits, Bolan thought. The Feds were customarily cautious when making a move. If the Deep Blue Goodbye had lasted a little longer, there might have to be a bit more creative explaining to do. As it was, with Dean Rigello either too reticent or too embarrassed to complain, Callahan and Valdez didn't have anything other than some suspicions. At least Bolan knew who was calling the shots here.

He looked up at Callahan. "Why did you have Rigello under surveillance?"

She smiled but said nothing.

"Well," Valdez said, crossing his arms, "it seems you picked the right guy to interrogate. The closemouthed kind. He give you anything?"

"Hey, we're not those kind of guys," Grimaldi said with a grin. "And I'm curious. Don't detectives wear civilian clothes instead of uniforms out here?"

Valdez's eyes narrowed as he shot Grimaldi a look that said he was not amused. "It just so happens I'm working patrol on my day off today."

"Look," Bolan said, "we're all on the same side here. Don't tell me you've never met with one of your snitches in an unorthodox place."

"You rented the room using a false name," Callahan said, leaning forward, her arms on the table.

"Would you want that sleazy place showing up on your credit card history?" Grimaldi said. "Not that I'd ever ask a gorgeous babe like you to pay for a room like that."

Callahan's face remained stony. "And what about that

phony plastic shield you had over the license plates?"
Valdez asked.

Grimaldi shrugged. "It's a rental."

Valdez snorted and turned to the FBI agent. "I don't
like these guys. I know B.S. when I smell it. Something's not right here."

"What's not right," Bolan said, "is that we're all sitting here jaw-jacking and Chris Avelia's murderers are
still out there. Look, we gave you a phone number you
could call to check us out. Did you call it?"

"Yeah," Valdez said. "But that doesn't mean I have
to believe it." Both he and Callahan looked down at
Bolan. Not liking the physical disadvantage of being
seated while they were standing, Bolan stood. He now
towered over Valdez, who was a squat, but solid five-
nine, although Callahan was almost tall enough to look
Bolan in the eye.

"What can you tell us about Chris's murder?"

Callahan and Valdez exchanged one longer look, and
then the sergeant moved toward the door. "You brief
them. I'll get the report."

Grimaldi stood and made a show of stretching.
"That's mighty neighborly of you, amigo. I heard you
Westerners were very hospitable people."

Valdez paused at the door to flash Grimaldi another
look of displeasure before he went out.

"Still working on that sequel to *How to Win Friends
and Influence People?*" Bolan said with a grin.

"Who are you guys, really?" Callahan asked. "I've
never seen special agents from Justice act like you two."

"Yep, that's us," Grimaldi said, flashing what he
termed one of his two-hundred-watt smiles. "We're your
very special, special agents."

Callahan's nostrils flared slightly and she canted her

head. "I'll bet you're both real legends in your own minds."

"Why don't we quit trading barbs and start sharing information?" Bolan asked, signaling Grimaldi to cease and desist. "Why did you have Rigello under surveillance?"

Callahan transferred her gaze to him. After a moment she answered, "It's part of an ongoing investigation. The shop's a front for a money laundering scheme involving a regional motorcycle gang."

"The Aryan Wolves?" Bolan said.

Callahan nodded. "Now it's your turn. What did you want with Dean Rigello?"

"Last Tuesday Rigello Transport and Tours rented out three helicopters to Bannerside Productions," he said. "It's a phony name. The choppers flew down to Mexico to the well-guarded compound of a drug dealer named Jesús De la Noval."

She raised her eyebrows. "I'm listening."

"Once down there," Bolan continued, "a well-trained team of gunmen conducted a hard assault on the compound. They also brought Chris Avelia back to U.S. soil."

She sat staring at him for several seconds before asking, "And you know this how?"

Now it was Bolan's turn to wait before answering. If he divulged too much information too quickly, it wouldn't be in keeping with his Justice Department persona. Plus, how much information was too much? After waiting a few more beats, he said, "An emergency assault team was sent down there to rescue Avelia, but he'd already been removed from De la Noval's compound."

"Oh?" She canted her head to the side again, and

Bolan figured she already knew this. "How reliable is your information?"

"As reliable as it can get." Bolan gestured toward his partner. "We were both involved in the rescue raid. The other guys beat us down there, and I want to know who, how and why."

Callahan compressed her lips, as if considering giving him more details. He got the impression she knew a bit more than she was telling. "If I didn't know better, I'd say you seem to be taking this kind of personally."

"It's as personal as it gets," Bolan said. "Avelia was a buddy of mine."

Callahan stared at him, and then said, "Sorry to hear that. I'm surprised they allowed you to pursue this investigation."

"I don't know what kind of shape Chris was in when they brought him back," Bolan said. "Or even if he was alive. But I want to find out who set him up. De la Noval was keeping him in a tiger cage at the compound."

Callahan closed her eyes for a long moment. "His body was found just off an exit ramp of I-19. It was an apparent dump. He was killed elsewhere."

"How was he killed?" Bolan asked.

"The cause of death was a gunshot wound to the head." She hesitated, and then added, "His body did show signs of abuse. It looks like he was tortured."

Bolan had figured as much, having seen the blood on the floor of the tiger cage, and the items scattered about the room. Those responsible were going to pay, no ifs, ands or buts.

Valdez reentered the interview room. Bolan wondered how long the man had been standing on the other side, watching and listening. He tossed a fat file onto the table, but kept his fist on top of it.

"I'd better warn you," he said. "If he was a friend of yours, what you're gonna see isn't pretty."

"It never is," Bolan replied, reaching for the file. He flipped open the top of the folder and saw a spreadsheet of the autopsy photos. An enlargement of each was under the contact sheet. Bolan went through them slowly, examining each for clues of what might have happened. They'd worked him over with a brutal and systematic efficiency.

From the nature of the bruises on Avelia's face and body, as well as the swelling, it was apparent he'd been alive for most of it. Perhaps the only saving grace would be that he most likely had been in shock, and thus oblivious to the pain, when the end came. The entrance wound was in the middle of his forehead—a small, round hole. Starring and powder burns around the entry indicated that the barrel of the weapon had been very close when fired, perhaps even placed against his forehead. The exit wound was more substantial, indicating a high-velocity round, probably from a handgun.

Bolan looked at Valdez.

"Any projectiles recovered?"

He nodded. "The head shot was a through-and-through, but they recovered three other projectiles in his body. Three-fifty-sevens."

"Ballistics find any matches?" Bolan asked.

The sergeant shook his head. "Not yet."

Bolan leafed through the rest of the crime-scene photos. The body was left lying on the embankment, half off the roadway on the dry, brownish earth. A detritus of discarded coffee cups, plastic soft drink bottles, aluminum cans, broken glass liquor bottles, crumpled fast-food bags and used condom wrappers littered the ground next to the body.

"Is this a well-traveled exit?" Bolan asked.

Valdez nodded. "It connects to the main highway going into South Tucson. How'd you figure that?"

Bolan studied the pictures some more before answering. "Obviously, they wanted him to be found. Somebody was trying to send a message."

LASSITER WAS GROWING restless in the small motel room as he waited for a text from Ellen. He had a new burner phone that he wanted to start using, and didn't like to keep the old cell phone turned on for too long. They'd probably be trying to trace that one. But she still hadn't texted him back on the old one, the only number she had for him, so he had no choice. It was now edging into early evening.

The night before, he'd driven into the desert and ditched the van that had been beside the bodies. Then he'd put one of the motorcycles in the trailer for subsequent transportation, and gone over the tractor and cargo with his cell phone app to locate the GSP transmitters. He'd found three, and the wet team's van had a mapping function tuned in to the same frequency. At least he'd assumed it was a wet team. There'd been no traceable IDs or anything in their vehicle or on their persons. That was the way the Company usually did things…the way he usually did things…the way they'd been trained. After removing the devices, he drove off in the tractor trailer with the shipment, wondering where to go next.

He'd decided on the old Wally's Waterworld Park. He'd driven past it so many times when he'd been out here that it had almost faded into the desert scenery. Back in the day it had been a combination amusement park and shopping mall that provided people with an escape from the desert heat and a place to spend money. It had gone out of business after a failed remodeling ran out of financing, and now sat abandoned on a side road in the desert.

Most of the old structures were still standing, including a large section of large department stores that formed the old, cross-shaped mall. A few of the stores on the far end had been partially demolished, providing a couple concrete-walled caverns that proved useful in concealing the tractor. He'd parked the trailer in an old loading bay of one of the stores. Once he had both of them stashed, he took the motorcycle and rode back to town.

By that time it had been early morning, almost seven o'clock, and he needed sleep. He rented a room at their regular rendezvous point under an assumed name, using one of his phony IDs, and paid with some of the cash he'd taken from the Wolves. There was plenty of it, more than he'd be able to spend in a lifetime or two. He texted Ellen that they had to meet, giving her his location. She'd texted him back that she couldn't get away at the moment, and she'd sent another later saying she'd be there and to wait.

Later had stretched into eight and a half hours. He awoke feeling refreshed, but disappointed after he checked his messages. Nothing. But she would call. He knew she would.

Waiting was always the hardest part.

Lassiter looked around the small motel room and decided to do what he always did when he was apprehensive and bored. Dropping to the floor, he began doing sets of push-ups. One hundred in each set. After ten sets, with a minute's rest in between each, he flipped over and hooked his legs under the bed. The positioning was less than ideal, and he quit after knocking out two hundred or so sit-ups. He stood and assessed himself. His muscles felt engorged, strong, yet Ellen had mentioned that he had some kind of medical situation she was concerned about. An aggressive treatment plan, she'd said.

What the hell did that mean?

He didn't feel sick. She had to be wrong. Didn't she?

Lassiter walked over to the bathroom. The ridge of the door frame jutted about an inch or so, and he reached up and managed to secure finger-holds with both hands. He began lifting himself upward, doing pull-ups as easily as if he'd been doing them on a horizontal bar in the gym. It came from having a powerful grip, developed by the rock climbing hobby that he loved. As he began to pull himself up for the twelfth repetition, the burning pain flashed deep inside his gut and he dropped to the floor, landing on his knees. The pain grew steadily worse, causing him to curl up, slightly at first, them all the way, doubling him over into a fetal position.

What the hell was happening?

Damn, it hurt. Ellen had been right. It all made sense now; it all came together. The raid, the snatch of the drug informant, the setup with the drugs and weapons cache, the attempted termination with extreme prejudice by the wet team... He wondered now about the guy they'd removed from Mexico. Was he really some kind of cop? One of the good guys, after all, as he'd said he was? But then again, as he'd told Morris, there were no good guys. No right and wrong, no black and white, only infinite shades of gray.

The pain burned as steadily as a blowtorch, not ceasing at all.

He lay there, desperately trying to focus on something else. Ellen, past missions, his initial tours in Afghanistan and Iraq, being recruited into the GEM program...

The handsome, sunburned face of Colonel Brent Hutchcraft came into view. His helicopter had touched down in the middle of Camp Bravo just outside of Fallujah, the sand whipping and stirring as the blades slowly ceased their rotation. Lassiter and the two other grunts had been told to report to the orderly room immediately. Once inside, the colonel and some guy in a battle dress uniform with no insignias, who Lassiter figured for CIA, greeted them and gave them bottles of soft drinks and snacks. They'd also been given pieces of fruit, which had made Lassiter's mouth water. For months the soldiers had dined on MREs. He couldn't remember the last time he'd eaten a real strawberry.

The CIA guy was thin and had a slinky build that reminded Lassiter of a human snake. It was a no-brainer that he was with the Agency. Not only the way he was dressed, but the situation, with all its special accoutrements, was a little too good to be true. A grunt's dream in a duty station like this.

Mr. CIA stood in the background while Hutchcraft gave them each a good-old-boy slap on the back, as friendly as could be as he explained how Lassiter and the other two guys standing next to him, Rodriguez and Paris, had been "specially selected for a new program." They'd all been through Ranger training, assorted combat ops, and all had some impressive decorations. Each man had applied for Special Forces as well. That's why they thought they'd been called in. But this was something different, the colonel explained, though just as important. Perhaps even more so. All they had to do was volunteer, and they'd be on a plane back to the States and enrolled in a top secret, specialized training program.

Getting out of the sandbox sounded great, and all three of them jumped at it.

The colonel and the CIA guy exchanged nods as they looked at each other. Then they let fly with their haymaker. There were a few catches to the offer. First, they all had to become "casualties" with little or no contact with anybody back home. And if things worked out, possibly worse.

"Worse?" Lassiter asked. "What could be worse than that?"

"You could end up off the radar," the colonel said with a sly smile. "Black ops."

That was fine with Lassiter. He had nobody to speak of waiting for him back in the World. Rodriguez and Paris agreed, as well, and they were flown back to the States that same night. After a thirteen-hour flight, during which their families were falsely notified that they'd been reassigned to Germany for training, the three of them were briefed more comprehensively on the true nature of the situation. They were to undergo "specialized enhancement treatments" to make them better soldiers. Some of the treatments were experimental, but none of it would be harmful.

It still sounded like a great deal. Get out of the sandbox and back to the World just for letting them stick a few needles into you.

"Is this like taking steroids or something?" Lassiter asked.

The CIA guy, whose name Lassiter later found out was Gregory Benedict, showed no change in expression as he glanced at the colonel.

"Or something," the colonel said. "But we assure you, it will all be done under the strictest medical supervision, and all proper safeguards and procedures will be taken into consideration."

Yeah, they talked a good game.

What I fool I was, he thought, to believe them.

That had been seven years ago. He'd spent the next year in the special desert compound in Arizona, rarely seeing anyone outside the walls, except Dr. Lawrence and his staff and a guy they all called "Mr. Godfrey." He looked like a freak in a fat-suit, standing there watching, occasionally stopping in the medical room to chat, but always keeping a cool detachment from everyone else, especially Lassiter and the other two guinea pigs.

After each medical procedure, which consisted of injection on top of injection, blood draws and all kinds of other tests, the exhausting exercise regimes started. They were put through the most rigorous programs he'd ever been exposed to, each one incrementally more difficult that the last. Rodriguez and Paris lasted only a few weeks and mysteriously washed out. They were there one day, complaining along with him, then gone the next. Vanished in the night, like dust in the wind. Word was that they got sent back to Iraq or Afghanistan. Further word came that both of them had died in a firefight. Lassiter never saw either of them again.

Not that he had time to look, or even think about them. In the meantime, his body developed into something he'd only dreamed of being in his youth as he'd looked at the muscle magazines and lifted the weights: He was now a virtual superman. The reflection in the mirror showed a Herculean physique so ripped that he periodically had to ask himself, *Is that really me?* Doing one-arm push-ups and pull-ups, running the 100 yard dash at lightning speed, or trotting along through the twenty-six miles of a marathon and barely breaking a sweat, he felt, and looked, like a real-life Captain America.

Mr. Godfrey was there, occasionally coming in to touch Lassiter's biceps after a workout or watch while he took on four or five guys in rough-and-tumble mixed martial arts training matches. Lassiter began to wonder what the old guy's angle was. One day Lassiter asked Dr. Lawrence, the snake in charge of the medical stuff, why Godfrey was always lurking around.

"He's the money," Dr. Lawrence answered. "The guy who pays for all this. In one manner or another, we all work for him."

Owned by him, was more like it.

Then the missions started, covert operations—no insignias, no name tags, sometimes no uniforms. His life became a blur of black ops.

Lassiter was paired with other teams, hitting places all over the world—Iraq, Afghanistan, Europe, South America—and pretty soon he was leading them. He was the fastest, he was the strongest, he was the best at everything. And everything was good. Everything was a dream come true.

He'd never had any closeness of "family," so when he became a "ghost" after Benedict told him that he'd officially been listed as KIA, he hardly blinked. It didn't matter. There were more missions to complete, more worlds to conquer. Little by little, the missions became less exciting and more tedious. Many times he was ordered to do things that he wondered about, or didn't like, but he put it off to being a small part of the big picture. "We don't pay you to think," Benedict had told him once. "Only to be the best."

The best small cog in a big wheel.

Then he'd met Ellen and all that changed. He remembered the feeling when she'd touched his arm that first time in the examination room in the GDF complex. It had felt electric, as if someone had flipped a switch somewhere, shocking both of them. That had been a while ago, too.

Now, the burning in his gut intensified and he clenched his fists and gritted his teeth.

What the hell was going on? Where was Ellen?

The answers to his questions slowly edged forward in his mind's eye like a march of somber mourners at a funeral.

All proper medical procedures and safeguards will be taken into consideration.

We don't pay you to think. Only to be the best.

An aggressive treatment plan.

He remembered his teacher in high school talking about the guy who wrote *The Great Gatsby*, F. Scott Fitzgerald. One of the quotes they had to memorize was "There are no second acts in American life." No second acts…and his first act seemed to be coming to an end. The pain continued to burn, even as his cell phone finally chirped with an incoming text. She was on the way, and he knew he could absolutely count on her.

One other thing's absolute, he told himself as he lay there, writhing in pain. Justice…my justice, will be served. Things will be set right.

He had always known he was expendable, but just how expendable never dawned on him until now. He should have read between the lines of the bullshit Benedict and Godfrey and the rest of them had fed him.

Harmless injections, my ass, he thought. He remembered Ellen's face as she'd told him about the side effects. She'd made it sound as if it was still medically treatable. As the pain continued, he wondered. Maybe she wasn't telling him everything. Maybe she was holding back as to how bad it really was. Maybe he should have read between those lines, too.

It was bad now. Really bad. Otherwise, why would they have sent the wet team to kill him? They wanted to shut him up, make him disappear, put him in an unmarked grave somewhere in the desert and forget he ever existed. But he wasn't going down without a fight. Or without setting things straight. Now it was all about getting revenge on those who'd betrayed him. He hoped he had enough left for one more mission.

His mission: a quest for vengeance.

CHAPTER SIX

"A motorcycle gang being sophisticated enough to pull off a helicopter raid on a drug cartel south of the border?" Bolan shook his head. "Sounds a bit far-fetched to me."

They'd moved from the small interrogation room to one of the larger briefing rooms. Valdez had spread a big map of the area on the table next to the array of crime-scene photos of Avelia's murder.

"Nevertheless," Callahan said, "that seems to be the case. At least until we can come up with a better theory."

"Avelia's body was recovered here," Valdez added, tapping the eraser end of a pencil on a section of the map. "The Wolves have their clubhouse here." He moved the eraser a few inches north along that stretch of road. "It makes sense they're the ones that dumped the body, given their previous association with the De la Noval Cartel."

"What exactly is that connection?" Bolan asked.

Callahan shrugged. "Hard to say. We know for sure they're a conduit for drugs and weapons to-and-fro across the border."

"If you know about it," Grimaldi said, "why the hell don't you jump in and stop it?"

"That's not as easy as you might think," Callahan said. "We have to build a case."

"We been working on it," Valdez added. "Surveillance, wire taps, but so far we've no substantial proof. You got any idea how much manpower is involved trying to surveil a bunch of knuckleheads like the Wolves?"

"We've got an FBI team down here as well, sharing the burden," Callahan said. "But even so, we seem to come up short at all the wrong times."

"So what you're saying," Grimaldi stated, "is that these motorcycle dudes are either really smart or really lucky."

"Or have somebody on the inside," Bolan said.

"Hey, Cooper," Valdez said, straightening, "I don't appreciate anybody bad-mouthing my people. We don't have anyone on the take, if that's what you're saying."

"What I'm saying is run some internal checks to see if you have any leaks," Bolan said. "I told you that when we went down to rescue Avelia, somebody had already snatched him. And they left De la Noval's compound looking like it'd been hit by the Eighth Army. Somebody knew we were on our way down there to get Chris, and they sent their own assault team in first. Whoever that is had a pretty strong reason to send in that preemptive strike, and the information that it had to be done fast. They also apparently knew we were on the way. That seems to suggest a connection with someone in this phase of the investigation."

Valdez narrowed his gaze but said nothing. Finally, after a good five seconds of staring at Bolan, he nodded. "Okay, I'll run some checks."

Bolan looked at Callahan, who raised her eyebrows.

"Certainly you're not suggesting that someone in the Bureau leaked this information," she said.

"Heaven forbid," Grimaldi told her. "But maybe somebody whispered something inadvertently to someone else."

Bolan decided to let it lie. Aaron Kurtzman was checking along those lines, anyway. Instead, he changed the subject. "Does the name Artie mean anything? He supposedly was the one who paid for the rental of those helicopters from Rigello."

Valdez shook his head and looked at Callahan.

"Doesn't ring any bells," she said.

Bolan considered that, then asked, "What else can you tell me about the Wolves?"

Valdez took a deep breath and started talking. "Regional motorcycle gang. They're definitely one-percenters…drugs, guns, the usual stuff like that, along with bringing illegals across the border. They're affiliated with the major gangs, but pretty much stay in the South Tucson area. The club has maybe thirty-five to forty members and is led by a musclehead by the name of Clay Stafford, aka Animal."

"If they're into all that, how come you haven't arrested them?" Grimaldi asked.

"They're very selective about who they let into the club, and who they work with," Valdez said. "If they even suspect someone talked to us, they'll make an example out of him. It isn't unusual to find some 'snitch' alongside the road with his tongue cut out." He stopped and glanced down at the crime-scene photos.

"Is that what happened to Chris?" Bolan asked.

Valdez nodded slowly, and then added, "Among other things."

"You mentioned a headquarters," Bolan said.

"'Headquarters' sounds too sophisticated." The officer leaned over the table and placed the pencil eraser on the map. "They call it their clubhouse. It's an old farmhouse in the middle of nowhere, off Devil's Fork Road." He tapped a line indicating a road that branched off from the main highway and twisted into a barren area until it split into two distinct prongs. "It's in an unincorporated section and is pretty much deserted, except for the clubhouse."

Bolan studied the map. "Do you have any police helicopters?"

"Of course," Valdez said. "But I don't have any pilots working right now."

"That's okay," Grimaldi said. "If it's got wings or rotors, I can fly it."

Valdez looked at Bolan, who nodded.

"What have you got in mind?" the sergeant asked.

"A little recon," Bolan said. "We've still got some daylight left."

"Recon?" Valdez asked. "For what? You planning on going in there?"

"Sometimes," Bolan said, "the quickest way to get information is to get up close and personal."

"I hope I don't have to remind you that I'm with the Bureau," Callahan said. "We're the lead agency on this investigation, and we do things strictly by the book. So if you're considering anything illegal that violates proper procedures and protocol—"

"Illegal? Us?" Grimaldi said, feigning shock and surprise, as he shot Bolan a quick wink. "Why, we wouldn't dream of it, would we, partner? If there's one thing we're all about, it's proper procedures and protocol."

Bolan looked at him, a slight smile ghosting across his lips.

Washington, D.C.

THE ASSEMBLED GROUP of supporters, well-wishers and contributors in Senator Brent Hutchcraft's newly opened campaign headquarters in downtown D.C. cheered as the huge, flat screen TV played back his recorded conference. It showed him standing against the backdrop of a huge American flag, flanked by his family as he spoke into the microphone mounted on the lectern.

"And so, after much deliberation and careful consideration," Hutchcraft's larger-than-life on-screen image said, "I have decided to announce my candidacy for my party's nomination for president of the United States."

Scattered questions emerged from the gaggle of reporters hovering around the campaign office now. One asked, "Senator, will this announcement affect your planned participation in the upcoming D.C. Iron Man competition?"

Hutchcraft leaned back and laughed, recovering with a flash of his perfect teeth. "Only if one of you tries to interview me when I'm swimming or cycling."

Another smattering of cheers erupted throughout the crowded room.

When the ad hoc interview was over, Anthony Godfrey crept up behind the beaming Hutchcraft, who was talking to two female aides, and placed his hand on the senator's shoulder.

"A word in private, Brent?" Godfrey asked.

Hutchcraft glanced over his shoulder, saw who it was and smiled his politician's smile. "Of course." He then uttered one of his standard witticisms that left everyone laughing.

The two men walked to an office off to the side of the room. Godfrey closed the door and adjusted the privacy blinds. Hutchcraft tilted his head and pointed to the desk. "I think they keep a bottle in there." He went behind the desk and started rifling though the drawers, coming up with a half-full bottle of Scotch whiskey and two paper cups. "Hope you don't mind the lack of elegance, but I need this one."

He set the cups on the desktop and poured a healthy shot in each one.

"You looked good today," Godfrey said. "A cross between a young Ronald Reagan and a dark-haired Bill Clinton."

Hutchcraft smirked as he handed Godfrey one of the cups. "That's covering all the bases." He picked up his own cup, drained it and poured himself another shot. "What's up?"

Godfrey took a sip of his own drink, savoring the taste before letting it burn its way down his throat. "I assume Greg briefed you on the latest developments out West?"

Hutchcraft's smile faded slightly and he nodded. "Yes. Disturbing development, to say the least. Is there anything new to add?"

"Just that I've got Artie running checks on all our personnel. He's also mending fences with the motorcycle miscreants and attempting to locate the shipment."

Hutchcraft's mouth twisted into a scowl. "That damn shipment. How the hell did you let that one get away?"

"In a word," Godfrey said, "Lassiter."

Hutchcraft's scowl deepened. "This could derail everything if it comes out.... If those missiles are traced back to GFD Industries—"

"They won't be."

"How can you be sure?" Hutchcraft's brow furrowed and he massaged the bridge of his nose. "And rumor has it, they're forming another damn committee to look into this latest mess with that agent."

"Smoke and mirrors," Godfrey said, but secretly he was worried, too. "Window dressing."

"All those damn contracts I steered your way when I was on the Defense Appropriations Committee. All the low bid estimates I secretly sneaked in."

"Relax," Godfrey said, trying to sound more upbeat than he actually felt. "Like I told you, I've got Artie Fellows working on straightening everything out. There's no better fixer than him."

"I hope you're right."

Godfrey felt a tightening in his gut, but knew he had to feign confidence lest Hutchcraft fold up under the pressure. He'd been like that since Godfrey had found him as a young Army officer years ago and groomed him for public office. "Besides, if all goes as planned, those Stingers will be on their way to the Middle East via our pal Chakhkiev in a couple of days."

"I hope so, but…" Hutchcraft frowned again. "I don't like dealing with that guy Chakhkiev. I don't trust him."

"Trust has nothing to do with it," Godfrey said. "It's all about keeping your cards close to your vest."

"What do you think I've been doing?"

Godfrey held up the paper cup containing the remnants of his drink. "Here's to Brent M. Hutchcraft, the next president of the United States."

Pima County, Arizona

CLOAKED IN DARKNESS, Bolan moved across the bumpy field toward the lights. The Aryan Wolves clubhouse, as they called it, was actually an old farmhouse that looked like an oasis in an isolated expanse of dusty ground. An asphalt road, aptly named Devil's Fork, branched off from the highway and traveled perhaps a quarter mile to a distinctive fork. The left section ran to a wooded area with a grove of forty-foot-tall Argentine mesquite trees and a smattering of smaller acacias, where Grimaldi now waited in the blacked-out Escalade. The other fork in the road led to the old farmhouse and barn. Each roadway was perhaps half a mile long.

The clubhouse itself was a dilapidated wooden, two-story structure. A barn sat about 150 feet from the house, and Bolan knew from their late afternoon fly-over that the roofs of both buildings were in need of repair. He didn't think any of the gang members were aware of his nighttime approach, but he flattened out and used his night-vision goggles to survey the scene.

The house was definitely occupied, and numerous figures milled about inside wearing typical biker apparel. A dark Chevy Tahoe was parked outside the front doors. The angle made it impossible for Bolan to see the license plate, but he made a mental note of the make and model. The big doors of the barn stood open and looked large enough to allow a couple semi trucks with trailers to enter. The structure appeared empty at the moment, except for some motorcycles parked just inside the doors. Seven more bikes were parked next to the Tahoe. A white guy in a solid-colored polo shirt and dark slacks came into view through one of the windows. He appeared to be engaged in a conversation.

Bolan keyed his radio, activating the throat mike. "Looks like some kind of meeting going on. I'm going in for a closer look."

"Roger that," Grimaldi's voice said in Bolan's earbud. "Watch yourself."

They'd made their way, totally blacked-out, up the

left branch of Devil's Fork, and parked in the seclusion of the trees. Bolan had then begun his trek across the open expanse of field toward the clubhouse. He was wearing his customary blacksuit, with his Beretta 93R holstered under his left armpit and his folding Espada knife in a slit pocket. He'd also taken the time to smear combat cosmetics on his face and hands. Their earlier air reconnaissance had given him a good idea of the basic layout of the place. Moving across the open field entailed a certain amount of risk, including navigating under a three-strand barbed wire fence that ran along the edge of the road, but the trip was only about a quarter of a mile.

The night air was still, and the oppressive heat of the day lingered. Bolan idly wondered what kind of crop the farmer had tried to grow in this arid climate. Beans, most likely. Now it was overgrown with stunted weeds, mesquite and a few wildflowers

He stowed his night-vision goggles and resumed his trot. After a few minutes he reached the fence line. Despite a few dips and bumps, the area between the two roadway branches was basically flat. The fence had obviously been erected to prevent someone with an all-terrain or four-wheel drive vehicle from traversing the field to get to the clubhouse. It was basic perimeter security, in no way sophisticated. Bolan wondered how many more measures of this sort he'd come across on his nocturnal visit.

He dropped again and rolled onto his back, going under the wire fence with the aplomb of a professional soldier. Once past the fence he rolled onto his stomach again and took a quick look around. Only fifty feet remained before he'd reach the clubhouse, but the yard was well-lit by floodlights on poles scattered throughout the area. However, the circles of illumination didn't totally overlap. There were a few darkened gaps.

Nothing moved in the immediate area. Bolan sniffed the air and listened. Some telltale odors of burning tobacco and marijuana floated from the open windows of the house, but not much else. He saw no signs of lookouts or guard dogs, so he rose to a crouch and sprinted across the road, zigzagging into a triangular patch of shadows near the back of the building.

No alarms sounded. He took care to duck out of sight under each open window as he passed, moving toward the front, where he'd seen the guy in the polo shirt. Bolan stopped just short of the last window, about ten feet from the front of the house. The angle still made it impossible for him to see the plate on the Tahoe, but he could hear voices coming from inside the house.

"I don't care," someone said in a loud voice that had a Southern twang. "Nobody messes with the Aryan Wolves, Artie. Nobody."

"Hey, we lost some of our men, too."

"That's your problem. We ain't forgetting that your rogue boys took out three of our biker brothers. Stole one of their hogs, too."

"Singular," the guy in the polo shirt said.

"Huh?"

"It was one man who did that."

Bolan adjusted his position so he could see into the room. It was a den of some sort, with a few dilapidated chairs and a rickety-looking wooden table. The guy in the polo shirt was slim and waspish, with a shaved head. He looked to be between forty and fifty. The bulge on the right side of his belt told Bolan he was armed. The other man was at least half a foot taller and clad in blue jeans and a biker vest. His brown hair hung down to his shoulders, and the cutoff sleeves of his T-shirt displayed massively developed deltoids and hugely muscled arms. Bolan recognized him as "Animal," the leader of the gang, from the picture Valdez had shown him and Grimaldi earlier.

The big biker shook his head. "One guy? Ain't no way."

The other man smiled. "His name's Lassiter, and believe me, he's more than a match for any three of you. That's why I need you to back off any thoughts of retaliation, and concentrate on helping us find that missing shipment."

Bolan made a mental note of all this.

Animal ran his tongue over his teeth, his expression thoughtful. "What about the drugs you still owe us?"

The waspish man shrugged. "Find out where he hid the semi and trailer, and you'll find your drugs."

"That ain't the way it was supposed to work. You said if we set you up with Rigello to use them choppers, and took care of that snitch, we'd get our stuff right away, like always."

"That was our agreement," the man in the polo shirt said. "But we didn't figure on these complications."

"Complications, my ass," Animal scoffed.

Bolan heard the whine of approaching motorcycles and glanced toward the road. The headlights of five bikers were rapidly approaching.

"Well," Animal said, as he withdrew a large chrome revolver with a six-inch barrel from his belt, "we kept up our end of the bargain. Losing everything's your problem. We want our stuff and then some." He held up the gun and began to point it around the room.

"Put that damn thing away," the other man said. "You think you're intimidating me?"

Animal grinned and looked down at the gun. "This here's my snake. Colt Python .357. It's the one I done your snitch with. After I cut out his tongue."

So Animal was the one who'd pulled the trigger. An image of Chris Avelia's smiling face flashed in Bolan's memory and he fixed Animal's features in his mind. He wanted to remember it for the reckoning.

The sound of the approaching motorcycles grew louder. They were almost to the house.

No sudden moves, Bolan thought, as he hurried forward and flattened himself against the side of the structure, melting into the darkness.

The motorcycles came around the front and abruptly angled to their right. Bolan found himself suddenly engulfed in a glare of headlights.

"What the—" one of the newly arrived bikers yelled. "Who the hell's that?"

Bolan raced toward them, knowing surprise was his only advantage at this point. Standing still meant certain discovery and death. One of the bikers was already raising a snub-nosed revolver as he reached him. The Executioner grabbed the man's outstretched arm with his left hand and jerked it to the right. The snub-nosed gun exploded with a bright flash. Bolan used the momentum of his run to force the biker over, sending him crashing into his buddy next to him. That caused the other four to topple over, taking their motorcycles with them, like a row of dominoes.

As the first biker got to his feet, Bolan kicked him in the stomach. The man doubled over, and Bolan drove a quick right uppercut into his face. He grunted and fell face-first on the ground. A second biker rushed at Bolan. The soldier pivoted and caught him with a left hook. That man fell, too.

A sudden roar from behind Bolan, along with an accompanying whine, rushed by his right ear.

Gunshot!

He crouched and unleathered his Beretta 93R and flipped the selector switch to 3-round burst as he pivoted toward the house, pulling the trigger. Animal was leaning out the window, the big chrome Python in his hand trailing a wisp of smoke from the barrel. The rounds pock-marked the wooden boards around the window as the big biker ducked back.

Bolan felt a crashing blow hit the back of his head, and swung around. Another of the bikers was on top of him, swinging a short chain. As Bolan brought the Beretta around, the chain encircled his forearm and pulled him forward. The Beretta slipped from his grasp. He bent, trying to retrieve it, but a second assailant plowed into him, knocking him backward. Bolan used the momentum of this new assailant as they both fell, shifting his weight and forcing his knees into the biker's gut as they dropped together. The thug went flying.

As Bolan rolled to his feet, a fist caught the side of his head. He managed to slip the blow, and drove a hard left into the substantial belly that loomed in front of him. His assailant grunted and fell forward.

Bolan heard a commotion coming from the front of the house, and saw a group of bikers clambering down the steps. He didn't have time to look for his Beretta in the darkness.

Time to go, he thought, and grabbed the closest fallen motorcycle. He pulled the heavy bike to an upright position and straddled it. The keys were still in the ignition; a quick twist and it roared to life. Bolan depressed the clutch, slammed the machine into first gear and peeled out. Several bullets whizzed by him as he flew straight down the driveway toward the asphalt road. He skidded around the turn and shifted into second. Glancing over his left shoulder, he saw several gun flashes, but felt nothing, figuring he was now a more difficult target for their handguns. He didn't know if they had any rifles, and didn't want to wait around to find out.

"What's going on?" Grimaldi's voice asked in the earbud. "Sounded like gunfire."

"It was," Bolan said, keying his own radio. He shot another quick glance over his shoulder and saw a swarm of pursing headlights leaving the clubhouse. "I'm coming your way and I've got some bogies on my six."

"Jeez, Sarge. Sounds like you're riding a Harley or something."

"Ha, ha," Bolan said. "A little help would be nice."

"That's you leading the pack, I assume?" Grimaldi asked.

"Roger that. For the moment, anyway."

"Bring 'em on up to me," Grimaldi said. "I'll be waiting. Just stay far enough ahead of them."

Easier said than done, Bolan thought. Some of the bikers seemed to be gaining on him. Obviously, the hog he'd picked wasn't the fastest of the lot.

Bolan hit third gear and glanced back one more time. His pursuers were about a hundred yards behind him now. He was approaching the fork in the road. Gearing down, he made a skidding right and turned up the connecting road of Devil's Fork. He wound it out in second, then shifted smoothly to third. Behind him the pursuers were approaching the fork. A couple tried to take a shortcut, leaving the road, but bumped over the uneven terrain and flipped on their sides. The others stayed on the asphalt and executed the hairpin turn with the ease of professionals.

They had to know this road led nowhere, Bolan thought, as the group of motorcycle headlights assembled in a wedge about fifty yards behind him.

"Coming to you, Jack," Bolan said into his throat mike.

"You still in the lead?" Grimaldi asked.

"Roger that, with at least twenty on my six."

"Just stay a hundred feet in front of them," Grimaldi said. He sounded out of breath.

"Roger that," Bolan said, wondering what little surprise his pal had planned.

Seconds later he shot by a small grove of the tall Argentine mesquites. In his peripheral vision he saw the idling Escalade, its dark framework next to the base of one of the large trees.

"Pull over and come join the party," Grimaldi said. "The clothesline party."

Bolan immediately knew what Grimaldi had planned, and braked to a quick halt and spun. Behind him he saw the approaching gaggle of headlights. In the shadows, the Escalade jumped forward, and the first of the motorcycles lurched off to the right in an out-of-control spin. Several of the subsequent bikes followed suit, spinning and falling, causing the inevitable crashing of the group. Crafty Jack had obviously found some kind of line to string across the road at chest level.

The last motorcycle swerved to avoid the carnage, lurching off to the left and zooming through the trees. Its driver had evidently spotted the ambush and managed to avoid it. He could obviously ride. Bolan watched the big Harley bounce over the uneven ground and then turn toward his position. As it got closer, he saw who the rider was: Animal.

The big biker steered his hog right into Bolan's without slowing, and both men and machines crashed to the ground in a tangled heap. Bolan found himself on his back, looking up as Animal was raising the big chrome .357 toward Bolan's face. The Executioner reacted in an instant, slamming his left palm against Animal's right forearm. The Colt Python was knocked from the biker's grasp, but Bolan still found himself in the bottom position, with the muscular man on top.

Animal started raining blows on Bolan, who brought his arms in front of his face to absorb most of them. He began rolling with each punch, to further lessen the impact. The big biker wiggled his way higher on Bolan's supine torso, still continuing the flurry of punches. Bolan sensed a hesitancy and figured Animal had temporarily punched himself out.

The Executioner used the opportunity to drive his fist into the other man's crotch several times. As his adversary grunted in pain, Bolan pushed him off. Both men scrambled to their feet.

Animal lumbered forward, and the soldier smashed a one-two punch combination into the man's hairy face. Blood spurted from the biker's nose, but he still kept coming. Pushing Animal's outstretched arm away, Bolan smashed an overhand right to the bigger man's left temple, then followed with a left uppercut to the side, under the other man's arm. The biker grunted and shook his head. Bolan delivered another combination, this one a left-right-left, to Animal's face, the last blow, a left hook, catching him on the point of the chin.

The big biker froze for an instant, his arms still outstretched. Bolan knew this was the crucial moment, and drove home another overhand right to the big man's exposed jaw. He sagged to his knees and fell forward, catching himself with his arms. He rested that way for a few seconds.

"You can surrender now," Bolan said, "and I promise you I'll take you in to stand trial for the murder of Chris Avelia."

Animal spit out some bloody mucous as his body shook with a spasmodic laugh. Like a released whip-cord, he suddenly lurched to his feet, pulling a large Bowie knife from a sheath inside his dirty leather vest. He held up the knife in his right hand and smiled. His teeth were smeared with blood. "I'm gonna cut you up good, boy."

The wide blade gleamed in the moonlight.

Bolan took two steps backward and reached into a pocket, taking out his Espada and flicking it open. Animal saw the blade pop outward to a locked position, and grinned.

"You think that thing's gonna save you?" he asked.

Bolan said nothing, but stepped back, away from the wrecked motorcycles.

Animal ran forward, slashing with his big blade, which had a serrated edge along the top. Bolan stepped back again, letting the biker's blade go sailing by, and then dealt a quick, hooking slash to Animal's big deltoid muscle. He followed that up with a second, backhand slash that sliced across the biker's right forearm, then zipped the blade over the man's right thigh. Each slice was punctuated by a burst of crimson.

The biker whirled back with a sweeping slash that he easily avoided, then, stepping inside, Bolan grabbed Animal's outstretched right hand and plunged the Espada upward, just under the sternum. As quickly as he'd delivered the death blow, he danced back out of range of the biker's futile and desperate thrashings.

The Executioner watched as his assailant stumbled forward on increasingly unsteady legs, his right arm still managing some weak slashing with the oversize knife, his left hand clasped to the wound in his gut. Blood seeped through his thick fingers like water from a broken pipe.

"Who ordered the hit on Chris Avelia?" Bolan asked. He figured the biker knew he was finished, and might answer in an attempt to put things right, but the only thing that came out of Animal's mouth was more blood and a few bits of profanity. The man stumbled and fell to his knees, the Bowie slipping from his fingers. He clutched at the wound with his right hand, too, as if trying to hold the precious crimson fluid in. He looked up at Bolan and opened his mouth once more. This time all that escaped was a last, hacking breath as the biker fell forward.

Grimaldi joined Bolan and held his SIG Sauer on the prone biker.

"He dead?" Bolan nodded.

"Let's be sure," Grimaldi said, kicking Animal in the head so that his profile was extended. The pilot bent down and touched the barrel of his SIG to Animal's open eye. No reaction.

Grimaldi straightened. "Why didn't you just shoot the son of a bitch?"

"I lost my Beretta back at the house," Bolan said.

"You lost your baby?" Grimaldi said with incredulity. "That explains why you put such a beat-down on that asshole." He gestured toward Animal. "I'd have come over sooner, but it looked personal, so I didn't want to interfere."

"It was." Bolan moved over and picked up Animal's chrome Python. "He's the one who shot Chris."

Bolan's body was beginning to ache now from the aftereffect of the crash, the fight and the adrenaline leaving his system.

"So it's over then?" Grimaldi asked.

Bolan shook his head. "He's just the one who pulled the trigger. I still want the ones responsible for setting Chris up and sending that team to grab him in Mexico."

"Works for me," Grimaldi said, as he and Bolan walked toward their SUV.

"Nice clothesline, by the way," Bolan said. "What did you use?"

Grimaldi grinned. "Remember that nice coil of nylon rope we saw in the Pima County helicopter?"

Bolan blew out a slow breath. "You didn't."

"I did," Grimaldi said. "Can I borrow your knife?"

Bolan gave him the Espada and Grimaldi sliced the still-taut rope that had been tied around the SUV's door-post with a clove hitch. The rope fell to the ground like a limp snake. "I figured it must have been lost or stolen property, seeing as how it was in a police helicopter and all. So I kept it for safekeeping."

"Yeah," Bolan said. "Right."

"And now I'm going to report its whereabouts to the authorities like any responsible and trustworthy citizen should." He took out his cell phone and dialed 911. "Sheriff's Department? There's been a terrible accident on this side road called Devil's Fork off Route 86." He paused and listened. "Yeah, looks like it." Another pause. "Hard to say." Pause. "That's the place. A bunch of motorcycles crashed. I can't really see them too well from the road, but they're up a ways." He paused again. "Sorry...I don't want to get involved. Just list me as an anonymous Good Samaritan."

Bolan quirked an eyebrow as Grimaldi terminated the call. "An 'anonymous Good Samaritan'?"

"Damn straight," Grimaldi said as he hit the starter and then shifted into gear. "I wouldn't want anybody else driving along this road and maybe getting into a wreck."

CHAPTER SEVEN

Fairfax County, Virginia

Godfrey rubbed the sleep out of his eyes and glanced at his bedside clock as he picked up the cell phone.

Five-fifteen. What the hell was Artie Fellows doing calling him at this hour? It had to be, what…2:15 a.m. in Arizona.

"What?" he said into the phone.

"Lassiter," Fellows said.

"You got him?"

"Uh-uh, he got us. He took out a bunch of your motorcycle morons in the process. And I think he saw me, too."

Godfrey breathed in and out a few times to digest the information. "You're sure it was Lassiter?"

"Who else do you know who could take out twenty-five bad-ass bikers in one fell swoop?" Fellows asked. "Plus he left behind a little bonus prize. A Beretta 93R."

That stunned Godfrey. "A 93R? They don't even make those damn things anymore."

"Exactly. So who besides Lassiter would have one?" Godfrey heard him sigh. "Recovering it was the only bright spot in an exceptionally bleak evening experience."

Godfrey massaged the bridge of his nose. He had to shake off the lethargy of sleep and assess the situation. Figure things out. Look at it logically. "Did he say what he wants?"

Fellows laughed. "What he wants? You think I stuck around to ask him? I was trying to smooth things over with that jerk, Animal, like you told me. He's dead now, by the way."

"Back up. Start from the beginning."

After listening to the account, Godfrey had little doubt it was Lassiter, as well. "I'll try texting him again."

"Like that's going to do any good," Fellows said. "He obviously put two and two together and knows Benedict sent the wet team to get him. He's probably gotten rid of that cell phone, or at least has it turned off, with the battery out of it."

"Perhaps," Godfrey said, "but that doesn't mean he won't still want to establish communication with us at some point, which makes it all the more important to keep monitoring that number."

Fellows said nothing.

"We have to see what he wants," Godfrey said, "especially with him having the shipment. And while we're on that subject, any progress on locating it?"

"None. He must have disabled the GPS trackers."

"Well, don't stop looking. Find the damn thing. And what about finding that leak?'

"I'm working on it," Fellows said.

That irritated Godfrey even more. Being woken up in the middle of the night just to tell him nothing…"What the hell am I paying you for again?"

"To be your chief of security," Fellows said. "It's a long process. I'm backtracking through everyone's personnel files and their recent financials, but so far, no significant irregularities."

"Well, get that nailed down, too, damn it. And don't call me back unless you have something substantial."

Godfrey terminated the call. He sat in the darkness, thinking. It probably wouldn't do any good, as Fellows said, but Godfrey pulled up the number for Lassiter's cell phone and texted, Are you there? What do you want? Still waiting to hear from you.

Perhaps if he could establish contact with Lassiter and somehow regain his trust, they could establish a new dialogue. Once that was accomplished, it was only a matter of keeping it going until they could triangulate his position. And that would lead them to the shipment.

After what seemed like an interminable time he stopped waiting for a reply and got up to go to the bathroom. Godfrey splashed some warm water onto his face, then stumbled back to his bedroom.

He was awake now, wide-awake, thanks to that idiot Fellows. Heaving another sigh, he glanced at his cell phone and was surprised to see he'd got a new message. He quickly pressed the button. The reply was there staring back at him:

Soon, GOD, soon.

Godfrey immediately tried texting back, but no further response came. He tossed away the cell phone in frustration.

Soon.

What the hell did that mean?

Pima County, Arizona

ELLEN CAMPBELL NOTICED Arthur Fellows, chief of security for GDF Industries, wiping the sweat off his bald head as he walked down the hallway. She smiled and nodded as pleasantly as she could when they passed. Fellows had always acted a bit aloof toward her.

Of course, that's what someone in his position was supposed to do, she thought.

But it still bothered her. She managed to sneak a quick glance backward as she adjusted her backpack and caught sight of Fellows again. This time he'd stopped and was standing off to the side of the hallway, watching her.

A shiver went down her spine. Did he suspect something?

Campbell shifted the backpack off her shoulders and paused to get a better grip, managing to take another furtive look. Fellows was gazing the opposite way now. Perhaps he'd been surveying the entire hallway instead of watching her. Or maybe he'd just been casting a surreptitious glance at her butt. He was a man, after all, and she was wearing rather tight-fitting slacks that morning. Fellows turned his head in her direction again and their eyes meet. She smiled, shifted the backpack once more, as casually as she could manage, and headed toward her office.

When she unlocked and opened the door, she was surprised to find Mickey Potter sitting behind her desk, going through a sheaf of papers.

"Mickey?" she asked. "What are you doing here?"

Potter stood, flushing, and flicking his tongue over his chapped lips. "I was looking for the test results on Trang's acclimation to the serum yesterday. Dr. Lawrence wants them."

"You couldn't call me?" she asked. "And how did you get in here?"

"I had Artie let me in," Potter said. "He's Security.

He's got a master key." The tip of his tongue flicked again and he started for the door, still holding the papers. "I'll tell Dr. Lawrence you're here. He can call you directly."

She stepped in front of him, blocking his exit. "My papers?"

He stopped, pursed his lips and tossed the sheaf onto the desktop. Some sheets scattered and fell to the floor. Campbell shot him a look of shock over his abrupt action. "What is wrong with you?"

"Sorry," he said, and sidestepped around her.

Campbell watched the door swing closed behind him. Now she knew why Fellows had stopped to watch her as she passed. He was probably wondering if she was going to catch Potter in the act, going through her papers. But why was Potter snooping? He was a little worm, and nobody liked him. "Mickey the rat," everyone called him behind his back. He would do anything to court favor with Dr. Lawrence, including trying to steal results from other people's research.

But Campbell had a more pressing concern. She squatted and picked up the scattered papers. They were the test results she'd run on Trang's blood work. She'd been careful to hide the results she'd gotten on John's blood tests. No hard copy, only a flash drive. She stood and integrated the recovered pages with the rest of the ones on her desk. Potter could have been telling the truth. He could have been merely looking for Trang's numbers. But he also could have been looking for something else.

The phone on her desk buzzed and she picked it up.

"Good morning, my dear." It was Dr. Lawrence.

"Yes, Doctor, I just got in."

"I'm glad you're here. Could you bring me those test results on Trang from yesterday? I'm in the main lab."

She decided to ask him outright. "Did you send Mickey to go through my notes? He was in my office when I arrived."

"Oh?" Her boss sounded distracted, off guard. "Yes, I told Artie to let him in. We came in early this morning to run some more tests. I needed the results from the samples you ran yesterday. Did he get them?"

"No." She purposely left off her customary "sir" to indicate her displeasure at him allowing Potter to go through her desk. "I have them here."

If Lawrence noticed, he didn't let on. "Well, get down here, then. I tried calling you last night to let you know I wanted to get an early start, but evidently you didn't check your voice messages." His tone had gone back to the preemptory, aloof one that she was used to.

"I'm sorry, sir," she said, reverting to the obedient assistant. "Just let me change and I'll be right there."

He mumbled something and hung up, the good doctor totally immersed in his scientific endeavors.

He did seem to be looking for the results, just as Potter had claimed. Or could Potter have called him after he'd left and persuaded Lawrence to phone her? No, she decided. The little worm didn't have the balls to do that. She was probably reading too much into Potter's snooping.

Campbell leaned back and took a breath. Was John's paranoia starting to rub off on her? Of course, he certainly had reason to be distrustful of Dr. Lawrence and GDF, didn't he?

And now they both did.

CHAPTER EIGHT

The midmorning sun shone through the high windows of the sheriff department's substation. Bolan and Grimaldi sat on one side of the large table in the briefing room, while Valdez and Callahan were on the other. "I don't suppose you have anything to say about what happened to the Aryan Wolves last night, do you?" the detective asked.

Bolan remained silent.

Grimaldi grinned. "The Wolves? The motorcycle gang? Something happened?"

Valdez glared at him, then took out a recorder and pressed the play button. A voice that sounded just like Grimaldi's said, "Sheriff's department? There's been a terrible accident on this side road called Devil's Fork off Route 86."

"Is anyone injured, sir?" a female dispatcher's voice asked.

"Yeah, looks like it."

"How many vehicles are involved, sir?"

"Hard to say."

"This is on Devil's Fork Road at Route 86?"

"That's the place. A bunch of motorcycles crashed. I can't really see them too well from the road, but they're up a ways."

"Can you stay on the line with me until the units arrive, sir?"

"Sorry."

"Well," the dispatcher said, "could you give me your name and call-back number?"

"I don't want to get involved. Just list me as an anonymous Good Samaritan."

"Sir—" The call disconnected.

Valdez waited a beat and then shut off the recorder as he stared at Grimaldi.

"Is that it?" the pilot asked. "I wanted to hear what happened next."

"I'm certain you can figure that out," Callahan said.

"Well, one thing I'm sure of is whoever that anonymous Good Samaritan was, he sounds like a real straight-up guy," Grimaldi stated. "Great voice, too."

"What really frosts my ass," Valdez said, "is that it appears as though someone clotheslined just about the whole group of them. Using a length of nylon cord." He paused and stared first at Bolan and then at Grimaldi. "Coincidentally, the SWAT team's missing a five-hundred-yard coil of nylon rappelling rope from that chopper I let you guys borrow yesterday."

Grimaldi's jaw dropped in an exaggerated fashion. "You don't say? Did they file a police report?"

Valdez pursed his lips. "I don't like smart-asses."

"You don't seem to have much to say about this, Agent Cooper," Callahan noted. Bolan shrugged. "My interest in the Wolves only goes as far as to how it relates to Chris Avelia's murder."

"Speaking of murders," Valdez said, "Clay Stafford, aka Animal, was found dead at the scene."

Grimaldi made a tsking sound. "Those motorcycles are dangerous. My mother would never let me ride one."

Valdez's nostrils flared. "He was stabbed to death after somebody beat the holy hell out of him."

"He probably had it coming," Grimaldi said. "A guy like that must've had lots of enemies."

"Yeah. And maybe two of them are sitting in this room."

Grimaldi raised his eyebrows. "You two had a beef against him?"

Valdez snorted and shook his head.

"I don't need to remind you, gentlemen," Callahan added, "the Bureau takes a dim view of vigilantism."

Grimaldi started to say something, but Bolan held up his hand. "Let's stop dancing around. We're here to look into Avelia's murder, just like you are. You said the Wolves were tied to the Rigello brothers, who rented that trio of helicopters to someone who did a preemptive raid down in Mexico. I've come across the name Artie in my investigation. Does that sound familiar?"

"Let me run it through NCIC right away," Valdez said sarcastically.

Bolan glanced at him. He couldn't blame Valdez for feeling out of the loop, but the clock was ticking on this one.

"Actually," Callahan said, "we did find something pertaining to the Avelia murder out of last night's fiasco."

Both Bolan and Grimaldi turned toward her.

"As you know, Agent Avelia was tortured and beaten antemortem." Callahan took a deep breath, exhaled and then continued. "The official C.O.D. was a gunshot wound to the head, but he was shot three more times. We were able to recover the projectiles from his body, and our preliminary ballistics tests have given us a strong indication that a .357 Colt Python that was recovered from last's night's scene may be the murder weapon."

"That's a pretty quick ballistics test," Bolan said.

"When the death of a federal agent is involved," Callahan said, "we pull out all the stops."

"I'm assuming you found prints on the gun, as well?" Bolan asked.

Callahan nodded. "Clay Stafford's. We're also doing DNA tests of some blood splatter present on the weapon."

Bolan nodded. While he'd left the weapon at the scene in the hopes that it would be recovered and traced back to the murder, he still had to track down those responsible for setting up Avelia.

"How long will that take?" Grimaldi asked.

"The standard rush time is a minimum of twelve hours for confirmation," Callahan said. She took a deep breath and looked at Bolan. "If these splatter samples turn out to be Avelia's, I've been directed to exceptionally close the investigation."

"What?" Bolan said. "That doesn't make sense. Animal might have pulled the trigger, but he didn't have the brains to set the whole thing up. That group wasn't sophisticated enough to organize a raid down in Mexico."

Callahan's lips tugged into a thin line. "My orders are coming from Washington."

"Well," Grimaldi said, "someone in Washington needs to get his head out of his ass."

Bolan tapped his partner's arm, signaling for him to cease and desist. The "exceptionally close" tag meant that the investigation could be reopened if new and exceptional circumstances could be uncovered. "What was Avelia working on?"

"We're trying to find that out," she said. "Last report was that it involved the De la Noval cartel and an illegal arms shipment."

"We know the Wolves were involved in trafficking back and forth over the border with that group," Valdez interjected.

"De la Noval was building a small army down there," Callahan said. "That's why we were delighted when Avelia was able to infiltrate the cartel, even though he wasn't officially with the Bureau. It took years for us to place a man inside their organization."

"He was this close—" Valdez held his thumb and forefinger about a millimeter apart "—to finding out who was supplying the arms to De la Noval."

That's what I have to find out, Bolan thought.

Fairfax County, Virginia

"THOSE DAMN HEARINGS are set to start next week," Hutchcraft said. He dropped into a chair in Godfrey's den and grabbed the whiskey and soda that he'd made for himself at the nearby wet bar. "Did you see the news? And Greg's definitely on the list to be called on Tuesday."

Godfrey watched this man who would be king, assessing how difficult it was going be to mold him into an effective, yet malleable chief executive. He had the looks, the charisma and the brains. If they could just get past this latest bit of unexpected unpleasantness, they'd be over the hump.

"But I think I've got that problem covered. For the moment, anyway." Hutchcraft took a long sip, then tilted his head back and swished the alcohol around in his mouth. "What else do you need me to do?"

Eminently malleable, Godfrey decided. "You're certain he's going to be called?"

Hutchcraft swallowed and nodded. "Oh, yeah. Word

is already spreading like wildfire in the inner circles about that federal agent's death. And the damn sharks are circling." He took another sip of his drink. "Like they're smelling blood in the water. They're going to put him on the spot by inquiring who sanctioned the mission. And they know about my association with Greg, and his past association with you."

"We worked together in the same governmental agency years ago." Godfrey shrugged, trying to appear more confident than he felt. "So what?"

Hutchcraft took another drink. A larger one this time. "D.C. is a small town. The last plantation, they call it. You can't hang your dirty laundry on the fence without someone sneaking up to give it a sniff."

Godfrey chuckled. "Well, let's talk about things we can control. Like how we're going to work the spin. Did you call your buddy in the Bureau?"

Hutchcraft nodded. "They've recovered the murder weapon, courtesy of your friend Animal. He's dead, if you haven't heard. I've been leaning on my sources inside the Bureau to get them to close the investigation, once it's confirmed that Animal's gun killed Avelia."

"Yeah, I heard about Animal. Good to know we finally have some positive news." Godfrey smiled. "Looks like that motorcycle moron was good for something, after all. Tell me more about Greg getting called before the committee about the operation."

"I've pulled enough markers to get one of the congressmen on the committee to steer the whole matter into 'executive session,'" Hutchcraft said, raising his hands and forming imaginary quotation marks with his fingers. "Once things get near any sensitive information, Greg will throw up the usual smoke screen. I'm not sure I should answer that in the name of national se-

curity. Just be glad the damn border remains such a hot
topic nowadays. Once they close the investigation and
put the blame on those bikers, hopefully the whole thing
will just fade away. At least for the moment, anyway."

Hutchcraft almost spilled his drink on the finely
crafted leather divan as he gestured. Godfrey handed
him a coaster so the future president would perhaps
take the hint and set the half-full glass down on the
adjacent coffee table.

"What's new out West?" Hutchcraft asked. "You sure
it was Lassiter who took out those motorcycle morons?"

Godfrey nodded. "It had to be him. It was done with
too much precision not to be. But Fellows assures me,
as far as the cops out there know, the Wolves are just
another one percent motorcycle gang. They'll probably
put it off to some typical biker madness."

"As long as they don't connect them to your little
across-the-border dealings." Hutchcraft leaned forward, elbows on his knees, and sighed. "I'm still worried about Lassiter. You said he texted you last night?"

"Yes. I've been periodically trying to establish contact with him by the usual methods, but he hasn't been
answering. He's kept his burner phone out of service,
too."

"What did the text say?"

Godfrey's mind flashed to the response he'd gotten
earlier. "Soon, GOD, soon."

"What? That's it?"

He nodded.

"God? What the hell does that mean?"

"That's my customary text signature." Godfrey
shrugged. "I was hoping the response was a sign he
wanted to open a line of communication, but my subse-

quent messages went unanswered. He evidently turned off the phone and removed the battery once again."

"Any idea why he'd do that?" Hutchcraft gestured with his hands, almost spilling his drink again.

"Will you put that damn thing down?" Godfrey pointed at the glass, then the coffee table. "That divan is Cordovan leather from the south of Spain."

"Well, ex*cu-u-use* me." Hutchcraft grinned. He took a small sip and set the glass on the coffee table. Godfrey sighed, picked it up and placed a coaster underneath it.

The liquor must be getting to him, Godfrey thought.

"And that coffee table was crafted in 1928 for the McCormick family."

"You know, for a billionaire industrial arms dealer and international death merchant," Hutchcraft said, "you're something of a fuddy-duddy."

"Speaking of international matters, Dimitri is due into JFK later today. His buddy Chagaev's meeting him there."

That seemed to sour Hutchcraft's good spirits. "Another mess. Where do we stand on that? Have you found our missing shipment yet?"

"Fellows assures me he's on track to find it."

Hutchcraft snorted in disgust and grabbed his drink again. His clumsy fingers tilted the glass and more liquor sloshed over the side. "Sometimes I don't think that idiot could find his ass with both hands. And putting him up against Lassiter is like sending a poodle after a tiger."

"Artie knows his limitations," Godfrey said. "But when he locates Lassiter, he locates the shipment. We'll send in Trang to take him out this time."

Hutchcraft drained his glass and glanced toward the wet bar. "How's he looking?"

"Ready, willing and champing at the bit," Godfrey said. "According to Dr. Lawrence."

"Lawrence." Hutchcraft frowned. "Dr. Franken-stein himself. How do we stand on finding that leak out there?"

"Fellows assures me he's working on that, too."

Hutchcraft grunted an approval and started to get up. "And what about our other buddy, Jesús?"

"No word on him yet." Godfrey shook his head. "But as long as he stays secluded in Mexico we can keep him on the back burner for now."

"And what if he doesn't?" Hutchcraft leaned forward. "What if he decides to come to *el norte*?"

"Then we'll deal with him," Godfrey said. He held out his hand for Hutchcraft's glass, figuring it would be better to mix him a weak drink than to have the senator make it himself. "But let's keep our eye on the ball, shall we? Minimizing the fuss here in Washington, finding Lassiter and the shipment, and keeping Dimitri happy."

Hutchcraft handed him the empty glass. "I don't need to tell you that I can't have that ex-commie and his *Mafiya* pals, or any of this other stuff with that dead DEA guy, derailing my chances of winning the nomi-nation. Not after I just got the campaign ball rolling."

Godfrey stood and went to the wet bar. "Relax, *Mr. President*." He flashed the other man a reassuring smile as he put a splash of bourbon into a glass filled with soda.

"I'm not president yet," Hutchcraft retorted.

"No, not quite yet," Godfrey said, walking back and handing Hutchcraft the half-full glass. "But soon. Trust me, I have everything under control."

"If Chakhkiev makes a stink about those damn Stingers..." Hutchcraft reached toward the drink and grabbed for it, the glass slipping from his fingers. It tumbled to the top of the antique coffee table and the amber liquid spread out over the finely crafted surface. "Oh shit."

Godfrey sighed and went to fetch a few paper towels. Better the coffee table than the Cordovan leather, he thought.

Pima County, Arizona

"I WAS BEGINNING to think you two were having so much fun out there in Arizona that you'd forgotten about us back East," Hal Brognola said over the sat phone.

"It's been a barrel of laughs so far," Bolan replied. "Did you find out anything on that name I sent you?"

"Lassiter? Yeah..." Brognola's voice trailed off. "How much time have you got?"

"As much as you need. Looks like the FBI's getting ready to close the investigation into Chris's murder."

"What?" Brognola sighed. "I'll have to see what I can find out about that."

"You catch a break yet on the arms deal?"

"Apparently the big arms deal in the works involves a major purchase from the cartel's U.S. arms supplier. Any idea who that might be?"

"Plenty of ideas," Brognola said, "but little in the way of proof. It was believed to be someone who could supply a sophisticated array of weaponry, including a shipment of Stinger missiles and M-72 LAWs."

Bolan whistled. "Those could really spell trouble in the wrong hands."

"Yeah. Unfortunately, as you know, somehow Avelia's role got compromised, and that's when they decided to send in the rescue squad."

"Which American arms supplier seems suspicious?" he asked.

"DEA's looking hard at GDF Industries in the South Tucson area," Brognola said. "They do a lot of government business, and have a great reputation here in D.C. You practically have to call the Pope and ask permission to investigate them."

"So call him," Bolan said. "See what you can find out."

"Already in the works," Brognola said. "In fact, Avelia's murder and the investigation of an American firm doing business with one of the Mexican cartels have the Hill all a-buzz. They've convened a special investigation committee to look into the matter, starting this week."

"Marvelous," Bolan said. "At the rate they move, we should know something by Christmas, next year."

Brognola laughed. Bolan could imagine him reaching for a roll of his antacid tablets and washing them down with a cup of Kurtzman's terrible coffee.

"Anyway," Brognola said, "it's set to begin on Tuesday, with them calling in one of the assistant directors of the Agency. Gregory Benedict. Have you heard of him?"

"A few times, and it wasn't flattering." Bolan considered that bit of news. Normally, he ignored the political gamesmanship in Washington, preferring a more hands-on approach, leaving the networking and information gathering to Brognola and Kurtzman. "I guess it wouldn't hurt to check him out, as well."

"Again," Brognola said, "already in process. In the meantime, a couple more interesting things have popped up."

"Oh?"

"Yeah, remember I mentioned that our old buddy Dimitri Chakhkiev was coming to grace us with his presence?" Brognola paused for a few seconds and then continued. "Well, he's in-country. He landed at JFK."

"Somebody tagging him?"

"Of course," Brognola said. "Word is that he's on his way to D.C. I'd bet my last dollar he's involved in this."

"Damn straight."

Maybe you and Jack should head back here if things are drying up out there in Arizona."

Bolan considered this option. With the Wolves pretty well decimated, and the Feds ready to close the death investigation, perhaps they could pick up a fresh trail back in D.C. There wasn't much to follow up on in Arizona.

"I'll tell Jack to fire up the jet," Bolan said. "In the meantime, see what you can find out about everything we discussed."

"I'll do that. See you soon."

CHAPTER NINE

Pima County, Arizona

They sped through the darkness, the hot desert wind whipping over Ellen Campbell's face as the motorcycle propelled them along the thin ribbon of asphalt highway. Dark shapes of cactus and mesquite flew by like disinterested pedestrians, but she couldn't help but speculate whether she and John were truly alone. Had they escaped the prying eyes of Mickey Potter and the ubiquitous tentacles of the GDF compound? She wondered if she was being paranoid or imagining things. Was Fellows really watching her? She and John had always been extra careful to avoid detection, but this night he'd taken things to a new level.

She felt the cycle slow, and John did something with his left foot and hand as they went into a sloping right turn, going past a big metallic sign that advertised WALLY'S WATERWORLD PARK in bright red-and-blue block lettering. The sign looked old, and the paint had been partially worn off the cartoonish face next to the words. A bright orange strip had been plastered diagonally across the front of the sign, stating: Park Closed. Private Property. No Trespassing.

They followed the road for a few hundred feet. It obviously had once been a four-lane drive, leading under an archway with Waterworld emblazoned in the same lettering on a metal strip fitted between two massive stone pillars.

A cyclone fence with a big gate blocked the road. Lassiter came to a stop, and waited until she slid off the rear seat of the motorcycle and removed her backpack of medical supplies before he slammed down the kick-stand and swung his leg over. He went to the gate, which was secured by a thick chain and heavy-duty padlock. Taking a ring of keys out of his pocket, he slid one into the lock and pushed the gate open. Its hinges resisted the motion with a brittle, cracking sound. Once the gate was ajar, Lassiter motioned for her to step through, and went back to the motorcycle.

He jumped back in the saddle and grinned at her. "I'm going to have to teach you how to drive this thing."

She tried her best to smile as he rode the bike through the opening, stopped and went back to secure the lock on the gate.

I'll have to tell him all of it sooner or later, she thought. So far she'd given him only bits and pieces about his worsening condition. It was way too technical for him to understand, anyway. So she'd tried to sound optimistic about what she had told him, masking the grim prognosis in terms of a treatment plan that made the condition sound possibly curable. At least she hoped she had, thinking that telling him the whole, pessimistic outlook would only hasten the oncosis. But his call to her the previous day, telling her about the burning pain and sudden weakness he'd experienced… Should she really hold back the full truth from him at this stage? That it was more serious than she'd let on? Did he have a right to know everything?

These were ethical questions she hadn't had to deal with as a doctor. The vast majority of her work thus far had been genetic research under Dr. Lawrence's tutelage and supervision. He'd always handled the more direct consultations with the patients. At least she'd thought so. She hadn't had to deal with their initial failures, and was led to believe that those men had voluntarily left the program. It wasn't until she'd overheard Dr. Lawrence directing Potter to "look up the old Rodriguez and Paris files and find out about the rate of pyknosis" that she became suspicious of why there were so few men who stayed in the program. This was long after she'd developed feelings for John. He finished locking the gate and motioned for her to get back on the motorcycle. She squeezed between the rear sissy bar and his big body, carefully placing the backpack over her shoulders so she could keep her arms around him. The bike jerked forward, and they swung through the darkness along an old asphalt road toward the dark shapes ahead.

Glancing over his massive shoulder, she could see flat-roofed buildings and the looping structures of water slides. They looked like vague shapes in the night, almost like huge serpents rising between symmetrical rock formations. A few hundred feet beyond them was a large section of buildings. As the bike drew closer, she saw segmented concrete floors rising out of the earth. Parts of the building had broken away, exposing steel netting and twisted portions of rebar.

"This place is creepy," she whispered into Lassiter's ear, hoping he'd be able to hear her above the percussive sputtering of the motor. "Are we allowed to be in here?"

She felt the jerk of his laugh and realized the absurdity of her question.

"It used to be a really fun place," Lassiter said, raising his voice in order to be heard. "They started remodeling the park years ago, but ran out of money. Just closed it down and fenced it off to be a tax write-off."

The two of them whizzed along an asphalt road, dodging several tall weeds that had managed to push through some cracks in the hard surface. Their route curved upward, and Campbell could see the lower section of buildings formed a second story built into a hill. An old metal sign in front advertised the name of a long-since-bankrupt department store chain, still advertising their company slogan in black letters against a white background: Satisfaction Guaranteed or Your Money Back.

They passed a big expanse of level ground that had once been a parking lot, and went past a large archway entrance that was boarded up. Lassiter drove perhaps fifty feet farther and stopped near three doorways, the first of which had a smaller, metal overhead panel about fifteen feet wide. It had once been white, but now showed streaks of rust where the desert sand had blasted off the paint. The two other entrances, a set of double metal doors secured by a chain and padlock, and another regular door, were in equally decrepit states.

The motorcycle came to a skidding stop and Lassiter put his feet down to balance them.

"Are we going to break in?" Campbell whispered, realizing seconds later that the percussive rumbling of the motor had probably obscured her voice.

"We don't have to," Lassiter said loudly. "I have keys, remember?"

At first she was surprised that he'd heard her, then she realized his hearing was still supersensitive, which was one of the by-products of the GEM treatments: perfect vision, exceptional hearing, increased strength—

the bio-enhanced perfect man, the supersoldier...
Except that he was now dying from the inside out.

They got off the motorcycle, and Lassiter moved to
the double doors. The headlight of the idling motorcycle, combined with the moonlight, illuminated his ac-
tions. He took out the ring of keys again and inserted
one into the padlock securing the chain. It popped open,
and he held up a finger for her to wait as he slipped
through the narrow space between the doors. A few
seconds later she heard a rattling metallic sound, and
the overhead door began to rise. As it got higher, she
saw him just inside, hoisting the panel by using a dan-
gling metal chain pulley system. When he'd lifted the
door about seven feet, Lassiter looped the chain around
a metal cleat on the framework and stepped through.
Smiling, he strode to the double doors, relocked the
chain and then wheeled the motorcycle into the building.

Campbell stepped inside with him and he reached
up and undid the looped chain, allowing the overhead
door to begin rolling shut. When it crunched down to
the concrete, they were suddenly engulfed in darkness,
the only light source coming from the headlamp of the
motorcycle. He shut off the engine, leaned the bike over
so that it rested on the extended metal rung, and canted
the front wheel to the left. Reaching into his pocket,
Lassiter took out a flashlight. They walked several feet
along a walled corridor. The place smelled musty and
damp, as if no one had been there in years, but she could
hear a faint thrumming sound.

"What's that noise?" she asked, her voice still a whis-
per.

"I nursed one of the old generators back to life," he
said. "Just took some elbow grease and a bunch of die-
sel. I left it running."

He stopped and reached toward the faint outline of a box mounted on the wall. Campbell heard the groaning protest of the small metal door and heard the popping sound of a switch being thrown. Several lights along the ceiling came on.

They were in a section of offices with glass walls and solid doors.

"How did you find out about this place?" she asked.

"We used it a couple of times as a staging area for one of our raids down south." He put his hand on a larger switch and paused. "Ready for the big surprise?"

She nodded.

Lassiter threw more switches. Successive rows of overhead lights came on, and the entire interior was suffused with brightness.

"This way," he said, taking her hand and leading her through a maze of corridors. The hallway widened, and they passed through some swing doors into a section that had ceramic tiles on the floor. Two doors, one labeled Men and the other Women, were off to their left. Toward the end of the hallway she could see the large glass windows of some storefronts. Suddenly, a burst of noise startled her—abrupt flapping sounds. She cringed and looked up.

Lassiter laughed. "Sorry. Pigeons. They get in through the broken skylight on the roof, among other places."

Campbell took a few breaths to regain her composure, then laughed too.

Pigeons.

She looked around. A film of dust covered the windows of the once bright stores. The glass, however, was still intact, which surprised her. Twelve years of inactivity was a long time. They walked down a wider hallway that connected more vacant stores and ended with an ornate banister between some big pillars. As they got closer, Campbell saw that they were on the second level of what once had been a shopping mall. Below was a center court with a large fountain fashioned from artificial stones. It was totally dry and the area was littered with broken bricks, discarded hunks of lumber, and a detritus of paper cups, plastic bottles and paper bags.

"Down that way," Lassiter said, pointing to a long corridor. They walked past a row of once vibrant boutiques—jewelry and clothing stores, an electronics shop, a phone store, a fast-food restaurant, and finally stopped at a big department store. Campbell looked at her companion, and he motioned for her to keep going. The large Plexiglas sections that had once secured the front of the store had been haphazardly pushed to the side. The interior was dark and dusty. Lassiter used his flashlight to illuminate the way as they walked through the massive, empty space, which was littered with more detritus from sloppy renovators and punctuated with jutting electrical outlets in various places along the bare concrete floor. He led her down another corridor of what had to have once been offices and into another large area.

"What is this place?" she asked.

"Their main stockroom. Come on, it's not much farther."

She was about to ask what wasn't much farther when they stepped into a narrow corridor, and Lassiter pushed open a heavy metal door and shone his light into an expansive area. Under a darkened overhang she saw a rectangular shape that looked like the rear end of a trailer, the kind the big trucks towed down the highway. She blinked and studied it, realizing that's indeed what it was. She could see the license plate hanging below a set of red brake lights.

"What's that?" she asked.

"That's what everybody's looking for," Lassiter said. "Or at least for what's inside. I got the tractor stashed on the other side."

"Tractor?"

"You know, the truck part."

Campbell took a deep breath, deciding not to ask him to explain any more. She wanted to get started giving him the treatment, and they couldn't do it here. It was questionable as to how much good it would do, how much time it would give them, but she knew she had to try.

"Why did you insist on coming here?" she asked.

"I wanted to show it to you." Lassiter's smile looked wistful. "Plus I had to pick something up."

Campbell glanced around. What could he possibly need here?

He led her back through the store and the mall corridors, returning to the office section adjacent to where they'd come in. He turned and went through a door marked Mall Security.

"This is where I've been hanging out while I'm here," he said with a grin.

She smiled at the irony. The place was empty of furnishings, but there were several large cinder blocks piled against the wall. He went over to the heap and started picking up the blocks one by one, setting them to the side, revealing a broken section of concrete that formed an opening in the wall. Lassiter got on all fours and crawled into it, disappearing momentarily, and then came out with a large black duffel bag. The top had been sealed with what looked like several rolls of duct tape.

He stood and struck the sides of the bag several times, knocking off the dust.

"Sorry about the mess," he said with a grin, "but it's the maid's day off."

"What's that?" she asked.

He looked at her. "Your future."

She decided not to inquire any further. All she wanted at the moment was to get the hell out of there. Not only did the place give her the creeps, she wanted to start that IV, and this place was filthy. Stepping forward, she placed her hand on his arm and said, "Can we leave now, please? Get back to the motel?"

"What?" he said, his smile broadening. "You don't want me to show you around some more?"

She was tempted to give his arm a playful slap, but time was of the essence, so she just tugged him toward the door. Time wasn't on their side. Time was their enemy. It brought back the dilemma that had plagued her initially, when he'd picked her up at their secluded meeting place at the restaurant. What was she going to tell him? What *should* she tell him? "John..." she said.

"Yeah?"

"Never mind. Let's just go, please. Now."

BOLAN WATCHED AS Grimaldi went through his final pre-takeoff checklist and radioed the tower for clearance. The lights of the runway stretched into the darkness toward the end of the field. It seemed to mirror Bolan's thoughts as he ruminated over the stalled investigation.

"Why don't you go back and catch some shut-eye?" Grimaldi asked.

"And leave you up here alone to fly this thing?" Bolan grinned. "You'd probably be asleep before my head hit the pillow."

Grimaldi snorted. "Hey, that's what autopilot is for. Besides, I always pack an alarm clock."

The tower radioed back that they were cleared for takeoff and gave Grimaldi his runway.

"All right," he said, easing the throttle forward and revving the turbines that propelled them. He turned to Bolan. "Sit back and enjoy the ride. We catch a good tailwind and I'll have you back in Virginia in no time."

Bolan nodded and closed his eyes as he leaned back. Despite the good-natured banter, his mood was still dark. He was unhappy about the lack of information he'd been able to get from the Wolves, and disappointed that both Callahan and Valdez seemed satisfied enough to close the investigation once the ballistic and DNA tests confirmed Animal's gun as the murder weapon. He'd had no doubt they would, given what he'd heard from his vantage point by the window. The guy with the shaved head in the blue polo shirt was another possibility. He had to track down that guy. He tried to recall the snippets of conversation he'd heard.

"We lost some of our men, too," Baldy had said, adding that he thought it was one man, Lassiter, who'd taken out the three bikers and stolen one of their motorcycles.

Apparently, the Wolves had a bit of trouble holding on to their equipment, Bolan thought. Then he remembered his own missing Beretta 93R and realized the pot was calling the kettle black. It certainly wasn't his first experience with "combat loss," but it still irked him. He'd have to look into getting his favorite weapon back. Not that he couldn't get a replacement at Stony Man Farm, if worse came to worst.

But back to the overheard conversation, he thought, recalling another snippet. "His name's Lassiter," Baldy had said. "And believe me, he's more than a match for any three of you."

Lassiter sounded pretty formidable. Bolan recalled Animal saying that the Wolves had set it up for Baldy to "use the choppers." That most likely meant that Lassiter had been the man in charge of the raid that preceded Bolan's, the one that had hit De la Noval's compound and removed Chris…the "snitch," as Animal had called him.

But a snitch against whom? The arms dealer?

So Baldy was connected to the arms dealer and they had a highly competent operative named Lassiter. But apparently this Lassiter had gone rogue on them. Bolan recalled Baldy's other words: "I need you to back off any thoughts of retaliation, and concentrate on helping us find that missing shipment."

A missing shipment of what? Drugs? Weapons? Both?

"What about the drugs?" Animal had asked, and Baldy had replied, "Find out where he hid the trailer, you'll find your drugs." *Your drugs*, as if they didn't concern Baldy all that much. He was more interested in what was also in that trailer. It had to be weapons.

Bolan reviewed the rest of what he remembered and came up with one more tidbit. Animal had pulled out his big chrome Python, and Baldy hadn't been affected. "Put that damn thing away," he'd said. "You think you're intimidating me?"

Obviously not, Bolan thought. Say what you want about Baldy, but he's one cool customer.

Tucson, Arizona

LASSITER CIRCLED THE block and pulled up in a shady side street. He had an unimpeded view of the restaurant where Ellen had parked her car. He'd dropped her off in a parking lot on the other side of the place so no one would see them. She'd assured him she'd be all right— "It's only a short walk."

She was right, it was, but Lassiter had spent his life backtracking and checking his six. He intended to watch her get into her car, and make sure no one was following her. Once you dropped your guard, once you figured your adversary was nowhere to be found, once you thought you were out of harm's way, that was when you'd get hit. Most of the time these double-back checks proved baseless, but there was always that one that wasn't.

Like this night.

He saw the man in the car almost immediately. A dark blue Chevy Tahoe, the same kind that the security guards at the GDF compound drove. It was idling, too, probably with the air-conditioning keeping the inside cool on this hot, sticky night, and that piqued Lassiter's interest. That meant that the man wasn't concerned about gas, so most likely neither the car nor the gas was his. The position of the Tahoe was another tip-off. The guy had parked down the street in front of a row of darkened houses, left side to curb, so he had an un-impeded view of the restaurant parking lot and Ellen's Toyota Celica. The place was open twenty-four hours, and there were plenty of parking spaces, but he'd parked about a hundred feet away.

Must be one of Artie's boys, Lassiter thought. He shut off the bike and wheeled it over to the curb. It was time to verify, then figure his next move.

It was Saturday night, so Ellen being out and about shouldn't set off any alarms. In retrospect, he was sorry they hadn't chosen the parking lot of a bar or something.

Still, she was far from a barfly type, so the restaurant seemed logical.

Taking this guy out also seemed logical. Lassiter doubted the man had seen them together. They'd been careful enough about that. And if they'd somehow been tagged when they were going to the abandoned amusement park, Fellows would have sent the troops in as soon as they were pinpointed.

Most likely it was a routine surveillance, but why watch Ellen? Had their relationship been discovered? Did the higher-ups suspect something?

Those thoughts ran through his mind as he crept closer to the idling Tahoe. He took out his Beretta 93R and began attaching the sound suppressor. One quick shot through the side window and it would be over with. Lassiter moved to a willow tree in the front yard of the house next to the Tahoe's location. He flattened against the trunk to survey his surroundings, then assumed a shooter's stance, resting the extended barrel on the side of the tree trunk and waiting for a clear sight picture.

Perhaps 150 feet in front of him Ellen unlocked her Toyota, slid in and closed the door.

The man behind the wheel of the Tahoe stirred slightly. Another mistake. His silhouette gave Lassiter the position of his head. He adjusted his aim so that the round would skim over the headrest and into the top of the man's skull.

Lassiter took a deep breath and let it out slowly.

What if Fellows had them following everybody? What if this joker failed to report in after being assigned to follow Ellen, especially in view of her upcoming emergency leave? She'd been insistent that she was accompanying Lassiter to Washington.

"I need to come with you," she'd said. "We've got to continue with the treatments."

And he had to admit he did feel better after the IV. More like his old self. No sudden or periodic flashes of pain or weakness. At least not at the moment.

"John, it's more serious than I led you to believe," Campbell had told him.

"More serious?" he said. "What are you saying? That I'm dying or something?"

Her blue eyes had filled with tears, and she'd looked down instead of answering. That was when he knew for sure. He was a walking dead man. The superman potion they'd given him, which had cultivated him into Captain America, was collecting its due now. Just like Rutgar Hauer in that old sci-fi movie *Blade Runner,* the torch that burned twice as bright lasted only half as long.

Ellen started her car.

Lassiter's index finger caressed the trigger. It would be an easy shot.

"You don't want to go with me for what I have to do," he'd said, seeing an image of Greg Benedict's dead body floating through his mind.

"Yes, I do," she'd replied. "No arguments. But how will you get there?"

"I've already booked my flight. I've got a collection of false IDs and credit cards that they don't know about."

"Give me the flight information," she said. "I'll get on the same one."

"No. They'll never let you go."

"Yes. I'll tell Dr. Lawrence that my mother's ill. She lives in Maryland."

In the end Lassiter realized arguing with her would

do no good. Plus traveling together, a man and a woman, would be less suspicious.

"Then it's settled," she said. "Just one more thing."

"What?"

"You should shave off your mustache," she said playfully. "As much as I like it, it makes you far too noticeable."

They'd managed to laugh about that, and after the conversation they'd just finished, he saw the laughter as a godsend, although it only forestalled the inevitable.

His cell phone started to vibrate in his pocket. He glanced at his target, then at Ellen's car, still parked in the lot. He held the pistol in his right hand and reached for the cell phone with his left. Its screen lit up with the code for a text message. He pressed the button and the letters became visible. It was from her.

Just left a voice mail message for Dr. Lawrence about Mother. Going home to make reservations now.

Her car backed out slowly, stopped, then proceeded forward. The watcher's head bobbled a bit, and Lassiter saw the brake lights illuminate, accompanied by the flicker of white backup lights. The guy had shifted into gear. Lassiter adjusted his aim, traced his finger around the trigger again, but hesitated.

The same thought burned through his brain once more: What if this joker doesn't report in?

The guy had obviously been assigned to watch Ellen, but it seemed no more at this point than a routine surveillance. Perhaps Fellows and company suspected her, perhaps they were following everyone. Shooting the guy would be akin to killing the messenger, and it would tip off Fellows that Lassiter had been with her, or at least watching over her. Let the guy report back what he saw: nothing more than her going into a restaurant for an hour or two. Unless the guy had gone in himself, or had a partner who went in… But then why would he have stayed in the car?

Ellen pulled out of the lot and turned right. The Tahoe followed, and Lassiter saw an immense puddle of water staining the street where the Tahoe had been idling. The guy hadn't shut off the engine for quite a while. It was probably safe to assume he'd stayed in the car the whole time.

Lassiter flipped the safety on his Beretta and shoved it into his waistband as he ran back to the motorcycle. After starting it up, he pulled away from the curb and zipped over to the freeway. He knew Ellen would be taking I-19 north to her condo. Sure enough, up ahead, he saw both of them on the entrance ramp. Staying a good distance behind, he followed until Ellen dutifully signaled and made her exit. The driver of the Tahoe exited the freeway as well, and continued following her at a discreet distance.

Lassiter stayed close enough to keep the distinctive taillights in sight, but far enough away that he would be hard to notice. He sped up a little when Ellen made the right turn on the block where she lived. The Tahoe did likewise. The street was deserted, except for the usual empty cars parked along the curb. Lassiter shut off the motorcycle's headlight and coasted around the corner, bumping up over the curb next to a tree in the parkway.

Down the block the gate for Ellen's town house loft opened and she pulled inside. Apparently satisfied that she was going to her house, the driver of the Tahoe kept going. Lassiter sprinted across the street and pulled into dark shadows a few buildings away. He kept watching in silence until a few lights flickered on inside Ellen's loft. The street remained devoid of traffic. A few minutes later his cell phone vibrated once more with another text.

I'm home. See you tomorrow. Take care. E

He waited ten minutes more, continuing to watch the street and parking lots for any more surveillance vehicles. Nothing stirred. The Tahoe didn't come back, even for a drive-by. Lassiter got the feeling that it had been more of a routine, random surveillance rather than a specific action. He started the motorcycle, taking time to recheck the belts securing the black duffel bag to the sissy bar before he took off. He'd have to make those bank stops soon. Getting back on the freeway and heading toward his motel, Lassiter felt he'd made the right decision letting the surveillance man live this time, to report back on his lack of findings. The guy really hadn't done anything to him, anyway. No harm, no foul.

But he knew that duplicitous bastard Benedict wouldn't be so lucky.

CHAPTER TEN

Stony Man Farm, Virginia

Early Sunday morning Bolan and Grimaldi touched down on the Farm's airstrip, secured the plane, then headed to the farmhouse. Bolan had taken a brief combat nap and awakened refreshed and ready to meet the day's challenges. He decided it was best to let Grimaldi sleep, since he'd been flying most of the night.

Two of the Sensitive Operations Group's action teams were still in the field, so Hal Brognola had flown by helicopter to the Farm the previous night to get a firsthand report. Bolan found the big Fed in his office, hunched over his desk, wrestling with a stack of paperwork. He looked up as Bolan entered and pushed his reading glasses up on his forehead.

"I didn't figure you for an early riser this morning, considering the time change and all," he said.

"One time zone's as good as another," Bolan replied as he went to the coffeemaker sitting on the adjacent table and poured himself a cup.

"Well, I did some checking like you asked," Brognola began. "Where do you want to start?"

"How about Chris's investigation. Who knew about his assignment?"

"Just a select few in the joint federal agencies. Not even the Mexican *federales* were privy to that knowledge." Brognola stopped and heaved a sigh. "Avelia reported that De la Noval was supplying the other cartels with a lot of weapons. Sophisticated, heavy-duty stuff that rivaled the Mexican National Police's arsenal. Rumor had it that they were getting ready for an all-out war to put their own people in power in the government."

"Sounds a little like what Pablo Escobar tried in Colombia back in the nineties."

Brognola nodded. "The question on everybody's mind is who was supplying that kind of firepower? We know that most of the exchanges of drugs and weapons were being done through the Wolves, or it was rumored."

Brognola pressed a few buttons on a small metal plate off to the right side of his desk. The lights in his office dimmed and a screen descended from the ceiling. Bolan watched as the overhead projector's light changed from red to green.

"This guy look familiar?" Brognola asked as a mug shot of Animal appeared on the screen.

"He's deceased," Bolan said. "As of a few days ago."

Brognola grunted. "Glad to hear it. He was a real scumbag, from the looks of it. He was also the leader, for lack of a better term, of the Wolves. Long rap sheet of arrests ranging from grand theft to assault and battery to attempted murder."

"He was the trigger man who killed Chris," Bolan said.

Brognola raised his eyebrows, then continued. "He served time in Alabama, his home state, before migrating out West, and served time in Nevada and Arizona, too. He hooked up with the Aryan Brotherhood during his frequent stays in the big house, and assumed a leadership role in the motorcycle gang when he got out three years ago."

"That much I already know," Bolan said. "I don't think he had the brains to be in charge of much more than strong-arming the other members to keep them in line."

"Probably not," Brognola said. "And it's even more doubtful that he could set up an operation as sophisticated as the one they had with the cartel. De la Noval may have been a lowlife, but he was no dummy. So the question still remains, who was really running things?"

Brognola paused and rubbed the bridge of his nose with his index finger and thumb.

Bolan recognized that as a sign that something unpleasant was about to follow. "I get the feeling I'm not going to like what you're about to tell me," he said.

The big Fed sat up. "Remember that scandal back a ways when the Agency was involved in peddling arms shipments to foreign governments in exchange for various things like American hostages, drugs and money?"

Bolan felt a tightening in his gut. "You're telling me our own government's involved?"

Brognola held up his palm. "Hold on. We're not talking fast, hard proof here, nor are we talking about officially sanctioned operations. The framework was in place since the days of Iran-Contra, for Christ's sake. Since the Agency pretty much flies under the radar, it leaves a lot of options for people with certain connections to set up independent arrangements and get rich."

"So somebody inside the Agency found out about Chris," Bolan said. "And about the rescue mission, and that's how they were able to mount a react team to beat us down there and extract him."

Brognola nodded.

"Do we know who yet?" Bolan asked.

He shook his head. "I'm on it. They have a congressional hearing scheduled to begin tomorrow morning, looking into the whole mess. Naturally, Aaron and I are pushing our sources, too. We'll get to the bottom of it."

"Sooner rather than later, I hope." Bolan regretted letting the irritation and skepticism creep into his voice.

"You know we'll do our best."

He nodded. "There was a guy with the Wolves the night of my little dance with them. White guy, maybe forty-five to fifty, shaved head. Animal called him Arnie or maybe Artie."

Brognola smiled and turned back to his keyboard. A face appeared on the screen. "Is this him?"

Bolan studied it for a few seconds. "Looks like it. I didn't get a real good look at him."

"This is Artie Fellows," Brognola said. "Former Army major, served in both Afghanistan and Iraq in Military Intelligence. Reserve duty. His regular job is working for GDF Industries as head of security."

"GDF Industries? Interesting."

"Their compound is in Arizona, close to South Tucson. That's where they do research and development."

"Research and development of what?" Bolan asked.

Brognola's smile was grim. "Weapons systems, for one thing. They're also a major arms supplier to the U.S. government. Everything from M-4s to the more sophisticated stuff like Stinger missiles."

"Stingers? Even more interesting. Who runs the show at GDF?"

"Brognola clicked the mouse and another picture appeared, showing a middle-aged man with a pear-shaped face, a balding head and sagging jowls. "May I pres-

ent Anthony Garfield Godfrey." He had a sinister looking smile.

"Looks like a bundle of joy," Bolan said.

"Yeah. He comes from a very wealthy family. He
cut his teeth working in government service until the
death of his father, at which time he resigned to take
over leadership of the company." Brognola paused and
glanced at Bolan. "Bet you can't guess which branch
of the government he worked for."

"Surprise me."

Brognola smiled. "The Agency."

That explained a lot. How GDF got involved in the
arms business, why Baldy, aka Artie Fellows, was as-
sociated with the Wolves, and why he'd rented those
helicopters that beat Bolan's rescue mission of Chris
Avelia to the punch.

"What about that Lassiter guy?" he asked. "Did you
find any connection?"

Brognola shook his head. "Not yet, but Aaron's been
working round the clock to crack through a couple of
supersecret firewalls to find out."

Bolan nodded.

"In the meantime," Brognola said, "since you and
Jack are back in town…"

The big Fed clicked the mouse again. The picture of
two men, one short, with slicked-back dark hair, and the
other fair-skinned, athletic looking and tall, appeared.
Bolan recognized the short one.

"Our buddy Dimitri Chakhkiev," he said.

"Right. With one Oleg Chagaev, Brighton Beach res-
ident and Russian *Mafiya.* After Chakhkiev landed at
JFK, he met with Chagaev. Reports initially said that
Chakhkiev was headed to D.C. solo, but they're both
en route to the area now."

"To do what?"

"That's the sixty-four thousand dollar question," Brognola said, placing his elbows on the desktop and leaning forward. "I've got somebody following them, but I thought maybe you and Jack could look into that."

Bolan set the coffee cup on the edge of Brognola's desk and stood. "Will do. I'm going for a run. Keep me advised."

"You bet I will."

"And have Aaron keep digging on that Lassiter name," Bolan said. "Whoever he is, I got a feeling he's a big part of this."

Pima County, Arizona

ALTHOUGH THE GATE guard thought it was unusual for Ellen Campbell to be coming in early on a Sunday morning, he greeted her with his usual courteous smile.

"Dr. Campbell," he said. "I didn't expect to see you here today."

"I forgot something in my office," she said as she handed him her ID card.

"And early, too."

It was seven-thirty. "On my way to church," she said.

He eyed the van she was driving. "New ride?"

She flashed him a quick smile as he scanned her ID. "Actually, it's a rental. My other car's in the shop."

The guard grunted something about being partial to vans himself as he handed her back her ID and pressed the button to open the gates. Campbell waved as she drove through, trying to make her visit look as nonchalant as she could. The GDF compound, which housed the laboratory and research facility, was surrounded by a twelve-foot-high cyclone fence with three strands of barbed wire along the top. The road leading to the main buildings had to be a tenth of a mile, at least. And even on this quiet Sunday morning she caught sight of one of the security patrols that roamed the grounds twenty-four-seven. It was more like a military base than a research facility. They even had a fleet of helicopters. And knowing what she now knew about the facility's true purpose, none of it surprised her.

Campbell drove slowly, taking her time, yet not wasting any of it. She had no doubt the roving patrol had confirmed her sighting with the gate guard. She wondered how far they'd take it. Would they give good old Artie Fellows a call to let him know? Maybe they'd wait, considering the relatively early hour.

In and out, that's what John had told her. He hadn't liked the idea of her driving the rented van, but agreed, since they were going straight to the airport after this one stop. She'd told him she needed to keep giving him the doses of the powerful meds. So far the bouts of weakness had been occasional, but she knew they were bound to increase in frequency eventually. Anything she could do to forestall the inevitable was preferable, especially in view of what he had planned: his mission.

She thought about that, too. Revenge. Did he have the moral right to embark on such a quest? There was no persuading him otherwise. She knew that. She'd tried, to no avail.

"I'm a walking dead man, thanks to them," he'd said the previous night. "And that's not good enough for them. They've already tried to kill me once."

He was right, she knew, but did she really want to be a part of it?

But that wasn't a choice anymore. She was with him now, and would stay regardless.

For better, for worse, she thought. And this was the worse.

As Campbell pulled into a parking space adjacent to the lab entrance, she noticed two other vehicles. One was the black Tahoe that Fellows usually drove. Could he be here, too? God, she hoped not. Luckily, she'd brought her oversize purse. It was big enough to hide whatever supply of meds she needed. John had told her not to worry about the accessories. He'd said he had enough cash to buy the rest at a medical supply store in D.C., and anything else they might need, as well.

Still trying to look nonchalant, in case someone was watching her with the ubiquitous cameras that were spread all around the facility, she put the van in Park and turned off the ignition. She tossed a scarf into the almost-empty purse and got out of the vehicle. As she walked toward the building , she took out her cell phone and thumbed a quick text to John.

I'm in.

After erasing it as she walked, Campbell swiped her ID card in the slot by the door, which popped open. The hallways were deserted, as she briskly walked toward the lab section. She kept the cell phone in her hand, calling up the special app that John had installed the previous night.

"It'll jam any signal the PTZ camera gets when you're in the lab," he'd said. "We've used it for years. Just press the button."

She did so as she swiped her card in the slot by the door.

Once inside she immediately went to the pharmacy section. She wanted to look up to see if she could tell if the pan-tilt-and-zoom camera behind the plastic half-moon shell on the ceiling was following her movements, but decided not to. It would only make her seem overly suspicious, if someone was watching. She had to trust John's expertise and advice. If he said the app would block the camera, then that's what it would do.

She swiped her card yet again and got into the pharmacy, scanning the shelves for the boxes she needed. It took her less than a minute.

I have to stay on schedule, she thought.

Anything more than that, they'd decided, would make her cover story of having forgotten her reading glasses in the lab seem improbable. She actually had the small metal tube containing the glasses in the zipper pouch of her purse. Pulling the scarf over the boxes of meds, she took a deep breath and knew she had to get out of there.

She walked back through the lab, opened the door and stepped into the hallway. Everything was on schedule until she saw Fellows and Dr. Lawrence standing a few feet away.

"Ellen?" Lawrence said, his thin face twisting into a smile. "What are you doing here?"

Fellows stared at her, saying nothing, the corridor ceiling lights gleaming off his bald head.

"Oh, Doctor," she said, smiling back at him. "I accidentally left my glasses here."

Lawrence's smile stretched into a more sinister looking grin. "Really? I should think it would take more than that to get you here so early on a Sunday."

"Normally, it would," Campbell said, trying not to sound evasive or nervous. "It's just that I'm going out of town. I needed to take them with me."

The doctor raised his eyebrows. "Out of town?"

"Why, yes," she said. "I left you a voice mail. My mother's taken ill. I have to go see her."

"Oh?" Lawrence said. "How long do you anticipate being gone?"

"A few days, perhaps," she said, looking from Lawrence to Fellows, who was standing there like a statue, not moving, his face a frozen mask.

"I'm very sorry to hear that," Lawrence said. "Nothing serious, I hope."

"I—I'm not sure," she managed to say. "I have to catch a plane. You'll have to excuse me."

"A plane?" Lawrence said. "Where are you going?"

"Maryland. She lives near Baltimore."

Lawrence reached out and patted her arm in a fatherly gesture, leaving his hand on her forearm. "Well, we won't keep you. I wouldn't be here myself, but I needed to check on Trang's blood tests. I was experimenting with a new AAV and wanted to see how it affected the dispersal times." He jerked back with an acknowledging smirk. "There I go, talking shop and keeping you from your affairs." She felt him squeeze her arm again.

She smiled and started to walk away.

"Did you find what you needed?" Fellows suddenly asked, his voice sounding so unexpected and intrusive it made her jump.

"Yes," Campbell said, reaching into her purse and pulling back the zipper. She held up the glasses. "They were right where I left them." She was so glad she'd taken the extra time to smooth the scarf over everything else. Then a horrible thought struck her. What if Fellows wanted to go through her purse?

The man stared at her for a few moments, then asked, "That your van outside?"

"Yes." She smiled, deciding to stay with the cover story she'd already used. "My Toyota's in the shop." Her voice sounded a tad hesitant, even to her. She smiled again.

"I guess it's like they say…" Fellows kept staring at her and she felt a shiver run down her spine "…sometimes when it rains, it really pours."

She had to strain to keep her expression neutral and placid as she turned and walked down the hallway toward the exit, maintaining as casual a pace as she could, but all the while wishing she could break into a run.

Fairfax County, Virginia

GODFREY SET DOWN his cell phone and handed Benedict a glass of bourbon when the other man looked up at him with a nervous grin.

"You're smiling," Benedict said. "I take it that was good news?"

"It was Artie Fellows," Godfrey said. "He may have found our leak."

"Oh?" Benedict said, perking up. "Who?"

Godfrey shook his head and went back to his chair. He picked up his own glass and swirled the amber-colored liquid inside it. "One of the female doctors on the GEM project is acting strangely. Nothing definite yet."

"I knew there was a problem out there," Benedict said. "How else would Lassiter have known about the wet team we sent?"

Godfrey smirked and took a sip from the glass. "As I told you, nothing's definite. It may be due to other reasons. She says her mother's ill."

"Horseshit," Benedict said. "Are they watching her?"

"Checking on things at a careful distance." Godfrey

took another sip. "Remember your days in the field. The worst thing you can do in these cases is tip your hand."

"Horseshit," Benedict said again.

Godfrey laughed. "You shouldn't let your nerves get the better of you. I told you Brent has this committee thing covered."

Benedict tipped back his glass, took a drink and held the liquor in his mouth while considering that. He swallowed and said, "Horseshit."

Godfrey laughed out loud this time. "Make your appearance, be your typical, evasive, noncommittal self, and when the questioning gets hot, Brent's crony on the panel will make a motion that they go to executive session to discuss how to proceed." He paused and looked at Benedict. "I need you to meet with Dimitri afterward. Tell him to make arrangements to meet me in Arizona."

"What? Where?"

"I'm figuring out a good spot. One with easy access and egress. I'll text you the location tomorrow."

"Why the hell do I have to do that?"

"Why, indeed," Godfrey said. "Because I've got a board of directors meeting in the morning. Plus I'm one of Brent's campaign contributors. How would that look if I were to be somehow seen with him?"

"What if *I'm* seen with him?" Benedict asked.

"You're the head spook." Godfrey smiled. "Or you will be. Meeting with a foreign national in a dark alley is considered very James Bondish."

Benedict snorted in disgust. "I just wish this damn testimony thing was over with."

"I told you to quit worrying." Godfrey got up, went to the drinks cart and poured a little more bourbon into his glass. "Once they officially close the murder of that agent, blaming it on De la Noval and our dead motorcycle moron, this whole thing will just fade away." He held up his hand as he spoke, and made a fluttering gesture with his fingers.

Benedict kept licking his lips and glancing back and forth. "Easy for you to say. You're in the private sector now. I still have hopes of getting to head the Agency one day."

"And you will," Godfrey said, "once President Hutchcraft is in office. We just have to bide our time till then."

"They're already plastering my face all over the news," Benedict said, "advertising my testimony tomorrow."

"Much ado about nothing," Godfrey said. "We'll meet at Brent's racquetball club tomorrow afternoon, when it's all over, and you'll see how you were worried about nothing."

Benedict started to say something and then reconsidered. He took another drink of bourbon. "The last thing we need is some damn whistle-blowing do-gooder. Who's this leak at GDF?" he asked. "What's her name?"

"Better you don't know," Godfrey said. "That way the name won't register if someone brings it up."

"And why would they do that?"

"Not now," Godfrey said. "Later on. After things have been taken care of and the dust has settled."

"Plausible deniability?" Benedict said.

Godfrey nodded.

Benedict shook his head and he raised the glass to his lips and drained it. "I'm afraid things have gone way beyond that point."

CHAPTER ELEVEN

Stony Man Farm, Virginia

Bolan had finished his run and workout, showered, and was sharing a cup of coffee and some quiet conversation with Barbara Price at a table in the kitchen when Brognola texted him.

Busy? Got something for you on your boy.

Bolan read it and raised an eyebrow. This might shed some light on a few things.

Price reached over and put her hand on his. "Something important?"

He shrugged. "I don't know yet. Hal's found something on that guy Lassiter."

She nodded. "Well, I need to get back to work, anyway." She stood.

"Maybe we can get together later," he said, rising to his feet.

They walked to Brognola's office together and stopped at the door. No one was around, and she leaned up and gave Bolan a quick kiss.

A promise of things to come, he thought.

He stepped into Brognola's office. "What do you have?"

The big Fed gestured for him to sit in the chair in front of his desk, and pointed to the screen that was descending from its slot on the ceiling. When it was down, he clicked the mouse and a picture of a young recruit in an Army uniform appeared on the screen.

"John Samuel Lassiter," Brognola said, then read off the man's date of birth. "He came from a broken home in Chicago. Father left him and his mother when John was three. His mother did as best as she could raising him, but didn't get much in the way of child support. Daddy dearest was in and out of jail several times, in numerous states, until he was shot to death in a cheap motel just outside Detroit. Apparently it was a lovers' quarrel of some sort. Mama worked various jobs, waitressing and a night shift at the local convenience store until she was killed in a drunk-driving accident, after which young John, age fourteen, went to live with relatives in rural Arkansas. He got into numerous scrapes with the local sheriff's department, the most serious of which was stealing a car at the tender age of fifteen, at which time the judge gave him the option of staying out of trouble by entering an ROTC program in his high school."

Brognola clicked the mouse again, uploading a few more photos, one of which showed a young man in uniform, with a serious look on his face.

"The kid straightened out enough to earn a shot at enlistment when he graduated high school. He went through basic and advanced training at good old Fort Polk, Louisiana."

Bolan smiled. He'd spent many an unpleasant time at that place. "Infantry MOS, I take it?"

Brognola nodded, knowing that MOS stood for military occupational specialist. "Eleven-B, all the way. He went airborne and did well in Ranger training, then shipped off to the sandbox. Did one tour there and one in Afghanistan, back-to-back, got a bunch of decorations and applied for Special Forces."

"What decorations?" Bolan asked.

Brognola read the list, which was pretty standard until he came to the last two. "... and a purple heart and the Silver Star."

"The Silver Star?"

"Right," Brognola said. "He was in a firebase in Afghanistan. They'd gone into a village in Daridank province trying to track some Taliban fighters when his squad got cut off and attacked. The team leader, some green second lieutenant, got hit and Lassiter carried him and led the squad out of there, taking out a bunch of enemy combatants on the way." The screen showed a long shot of a group of soldiers receiving medals in a ceremony. The distance was too great to see their faces.

Bolan nodded. "You said he applied for Special Forces?"

"Yeah, during his second trip to Iraq. Things were winding down there and he got selected for the training." The screen flipped to another picture, this time of three men in BDUs, all standing at attention. One looked Hispanic, one Caucasian and one was a more mature looking Lassiter. The three rigid soldiers were flanked by another man with a black oak leaf on his chest. It appeared that the picture had been taken in some sort of Army barracks against the backdrop of a glass window. Something stirred in Bolan's memory when he saw this photo, but he couldn't quite figure out what.

"Here's where things get interesting," Brognola said.

The image on the screen changed again, this time showing the remains of a crashed helicopter. "The records get kind of murky, but it seems the first two grunts in the previous picture—" Brognola made a few clicks and the three soldiers standing at attention in BDUs returned "—Robert Paris and Juan Rodriguez, were killed in a training accident in Arizona." Brognola clicked the pictures forward again. "And Lassiter was also listed as killed in a training accident a year and a half later." He read off the date as he pulled up another picture of a crashed bird. "Also in the Grand Canyon State."

"Take it back to that picture of all of them," Bolan said.

Brognola backed up the images to the three young stalwarts.

Bolan studied the faces of the men. "That colonel looks familiar."

"He should," Brognola said. "He just announced he's running for President. Senator Brent Hutchcraft."

"He was in the Army?"

"Reservist. Assigned to Military Intelligence."

"How about the guy taking the picture?"

"The guy taking the picture?" Brognola repeated. He stared up at the screen.

"Take a gander at the background," Bolan said, pointing to it. "That looks like a pane of glass. There's a faint reflection on it from the flash. See?"

"Well, I'll be. I'll see if Aaron can wave his magic wand and enhance the pixel resolution to call that up. Think it might be significant?"

"At this point anything might be." Bolan studied Lassiter's face again. "What was the date of that second training accident again?"

Brognola told him, adding, "About seven years ago."

"That's strange," Bolan said, turning to look at Brognola. "The way his name's been popping up lately, he must have been resurrected."

Baltimore, Maryland

CAMPBELL ADJUSTED THE flow of the drip chamber as her companion lay on the bed in the hotel room. The flight had exhausted her, but he seemed to be holding up surprisingly well. The disguises they'd used, him wearing a gray-haired wig, mustache and beard, and walking with a cane, and her in a nurselike medical smock, had worked. No one paid them undue attention. After the couple had checked in their luggage and asked for a wheelchair to get early boarding, the attendants had whisked them through the security lines and onto the plane.

Lassiter seemed unaffected by the rigors of traveling cross-county and the accompanying time change, but she insisted on administering the IV as soon as they'd checked into the hotel under their assumed names.

"An ounce of prevention?" he'd asked, smiling at her.

Campbell smiled back. He seemed to be in a state of temporary remission, but she knew that could change at a moment's notice. It was coming. They both knew it, but exactly when was off in the nebulous future. She only knew that she had to help him as much as she could, help him to fulfill this last mission he was so intent on completing. It wasn't something she really wanted to embrace, but her feelings for him were too strong. Whatever he wanted, she would do. And what he wanted was to finish his vengeance quest.

"Hey, that's interesting," he said, starting to sit up as the television played a segment of news. She placed a gentle hand on his bare chest and kept him from rising, then slipped a pillow behind his head.

"Turn up the volume," he said.

She reached for the remote and hit the appropriate key.

"The hearings, which are scheduled to begin tomorrow morning on Capitol Hill, will deal with an ongoing investigation into the recent death of Drug Enforcement Administration Agent Christopher Avelia."

A picture of a man's face appeared on the screen. He was rather handsome, Campbell thought, with a dark complexion and a looping mustache. She heard John murmur something, and asked him what was wrong.

"A lot," he said. There was a sadness in his eyes.

"Avelia had been working undercover in Mexico and was recently found murdered in Arizona. A congressional committee has been formed to investigate the operation he was involved with, which may have had ties to a U.S. company, as well as the federal government."

The picture changed, and another man was shown walking briskly past a group of news reporters with extended microphones. "Assistant Director Gregory Benedict, of the Central Intelligence Agency, has purportedly been summoned to testify before the committee tomorrow morning regarding the Agency's involvement in operations just over the border in Mexico. As it stands—"

The announcer's voice continued, but Lassiter spoke over it. "Benedict…that's the son of a bitch we came here to see." His face had hardened now.

Campbell looked at the video of the man slinking along. "He looks creepy."

"He's a human snake," Lassiter said. "But at least now I know where he'll be tomorrow morning. It beats spending a couple days staking out Langley, waiting for him."

Campbell closed her eyes and patted his shoulder. He was so intense, so driven. Was all this really happening?

Lassiter jerked with what she assumed was a sudden jolt of pain.

"Are you all right?" she asked.

He nodded. "Yeah, just cold. It always happens that way."

Yes, she thought. It's happening now, and I'm involved up to my neck. But I wouldn't want it any other way.

CHAPTER TWELVE

Washington, D.C.

All roads lead to Rome, Bolan thought. Or in this case, Washington, D.C. He and Grimaldi had started their morning relieving the previous Stony Man team on the surveillance of Dimitri Chakhkiev and Oleg Chagaev. When the Russians went mobile, Bolan switched to the Suzuki motorcycle they'd stowed in the back of their van, while Grimaldi got behind the wheel.

"How come I never get to drive the motorcycles?" he asked with a good-natured grin.

"You're better with larger means of transportation," Bolan said, slipping on the helmet and then testing the radio receiver inside. "How do you read me?"

"A-okay," Grimaldi replied. "Looks like our Russian buddies are heading downtown."

Bolan watched as the big Lincoln swung onto I-395 and proceeded north toward the D.C. area. It was close to 10:00 a.m., and the morning traffic had thinned slightly after the early rush, but he knew that D.C. traffic was always bad no matter what time it was. He sped up, zigzagging through the cluster of vehicles to keep the Lincoln in sight.

"I'm on them," Bolan said, keying his mike. "Drop back and I'll keep you posted."

"That's not a problem," Grimaldi said.

Chakhkiev and Chageav had spent the night at an inn in Fairfax County after driving down from New York. They'd gotten up early and eaten at a nearby restaurant, and then driven to the freeway. Two men accompanied them. Bolan noticed that the Lincoln was going at a steady pace, but not exceeding the speed limit. He radioed that information to Grimaldi.

"Probably wants to avoid one of those damn electronic radar tickets," Grimaldi said. His love for speed always garnered him a few whenever he drove in the Metro D.C. area. "They take a picture of your license plate and mail the ticket to you a month later. Is that fair?"

"He probably learned his lesson the hard way," Bolan said, regretting they weren't close enough for Grimaldi to see him grin when he added, "Unlike some people I know who never seem to learn."

Things slowed to a crawl when they crossed the Potomac and kept heading east. They crept farther, crossing the Francis Case Memorial Bridge and finally exited on Third Street. Bolan kept a few car lengths behind them and radioed their position to Grimaldi.

"Okay," Grimaldi's voice said inside Bolan's helmet receiver. "I'm stuck a ways back. Keep me posted."

Bolan continued to follow the Lincoln as it wound through the city streets of downtown D.C. After the driver made two right turns in a row, Bolan figured the Russians might be nervous about being tailed. He keyed his mike and asked Grimaldi where he was.

"Coming up on your six," Grimaldi said.

"Good. Our target's straight ahead on Fourth Street. They're making right turns to see if they're being tailed, so I'm going straight. Can you pick them up on M?"

"Your wish is my command, Sarge," Grimaldi replied.

Bolan watched as the Lincoln executed a right turn onto M Street. He twisted the accelerator and shot in and out of a line of cars, then turned into an alley and made a U-turn to head back south on Fourth. By the time he got to the intersection, Grimaldi was on the radio again.

"We're heading south now," he said. "Down Fifth."

Bolan adjusted his course, running parallel on Fourth Street. Up ahead he noticed something else that piqued his interest: two black Ford sedans, one with government license plates, one with regular plates, both pulling over to the curb. As Bolan drove by, he saw movement inside the first one. He checked his side mirror and caught a glimpse of a man hurriedly getting out of the car with government plates, trotting back to the second vehicle and climbing inside.

"Turning right on L now," Grimaldi said. "These guys are definitely worried about being tailed."

"Back off a bit," Bolan said. "Don't let them see the van."

"Roger that," Grimaldi said. "Already done."

The cat and mouse game continued for about ten minutes, until Grimaldi reported that the Lincoln was pulling into a multilevel, self-parking garage on Third Street.

"And that isn't all," he said. "I had a black Ford on my six all the way up the block and they're turning into the same parking garage."

Bolan thought about the car switch he'd seen earlier. "Keep going and double back to watch the exit. I'll check things out from the inside."

"Roger that," Grimaldi said. "Watch yourself. That Ford had at least two occupants."

Bolan made a right turn and went down Third Street.

He could see Grimaldi's van making a quick right at the next corner. In between he saw a silver BMW X-5 slow and stop. A man got out of the vehicle and jogged across the street toward the self-parking garage. Bolan was too far away to see what he looked like, but the guy was tall and well-built, and he moved like a running back. The BMW continued down Third.

"Jack," Bolan said. "We've got another drop-off at the parking garage. White male wearing black jeans and a black sweatshirt with the hood over a baseball cap."

"You're getting a little bit outnumbered. Want me to come back you up?"

"Negative," Bolan said. "But keep your eyes out for a silver X-5, unknown driver, last seen southbound on Third."

Bolan swung into the driveway for the parking garage and pressed the button for a ticket. The card popped out of the slot and the wooden, segmented arm of the gate retracted. Bolan noted that he could have probably squeezed around it with the motorcycle. A conspicuous camera was affixed to the upper right corner of the entranceway. He drove by an empty office area with darkened windows and a sign that read, In Case of Trouble Call: A phone number was posted underneath.

The structure itself had seven levels, and without knowing which the Lincoln had headed for, Bolan decided to go to the top and work his way down. He roared up the first ramp, glancing from side to side. Each consecutive level was visible through a triangular space that narrowed as the ramp ascended to the next level. He made it all the way up to the fifth before catching a glimpse of some movement through the narrow confines of the shrinking triangular space showing level four. Bolan continued up to six and spun, shutting off the motorcycle and jamming it into a space between the elevator and stairwell. He still had the helmet on to maintain radio communication with Grimaldi, and gave him a fast sitrep.

"No sign of the Beamer," Grimaldi whispered after Bolan's report. "Standing by in front."

The thought flashed through Bolan's mind that the BMW might not be involved in this, after all. Perhaps it was someone dropping off a colleague to pick up his car. But the guy had moved with the catlike grace of a big predator. The movement sparked a familiar tingle in Bolan's memory, but he couldn't put his finger on it. Plus he had other things on his mind at the moment.

He disconnected his radio mike from the helmet and set it on the floor next to the motorcycle. After giving a quick glance around the area he crept over to the ramp he'd just exited and knelt so he could look through the acute angle of the opening to the level below. All he could see was row after row of cars. The lot extended a good distance on either side of the ramp. The soldier moved downward in a crouch, and when he was at the midway point, slipped under the rungs of steel cables that ran along the side.

Time for a closer look, he thought.

LASSITER SLIPPED OFF the cap and hoodie.

They were too restrictive, he thought, even for a clandestine op.

Quickly he took stock of how he felt. Ellen had warned him that the sudden weakness might come back at any time, but at the moment he felt strong. The trek up the stairs to the fourth level hadn't even winded him. He was certain he'd seen the black Ford, the one Benedict had gotten into back on the street, slow on that level and turn into one of the parking aisles. After taking out the Glock 19 that he'd bought on the street the previous night, he pulled back the slide a fraction of an inch to make sure there was a round in the chamber. Unnecessary, he knew, but old habits died hard. It was a good, reliable weapon and gave him nineteen 9 mm rounds. He wished he'd been able to get a few spare magazines, but in a clandestine street deal beggars couldn't be choosers.

He realized the irony of that and smirked.

A beggar, he thought. A walking dead man.

But not quite yet. It was time to give that title to someone else.

After a quick peek through the crack of the stairwell door, Lassiter pulled it open a bit more and moved through, darting to the closest parked car and assuming a crouch. Then he listened.

No signs or sounds of the motorcyclist who'd turned in after him. He wondered if that guy was part of this or not. Benedict was obviously meeting someone in this garage. That guy on the bike maybe? He'd heard the motorcycle going up to the next level. He scanned the area as he held the Glock, looking for any telltale movements and listening for any noises.

The calm silence was broken by the sound of car doors closing. Three of them.

He crept toward the sounds, going from car to car, pausing to scan the area ahead. Through the smudged windows of a white Lexus, he could see three men walking toward each other. One of them was Greg Benedict.

BOLAN WATCHED AS the three men approached each other with a wariness obviously borne out of previous experiences. These guys were pros, all right. He was crouched in front of a pickup truck and edged around to the side of the vehicle to get a better vantage point. Two men, one in a gray suit and tie, the other in a black jacket and pants, moved toward the third. This guy was short, but broad shouldered, and kept his sunglasses on. Bolan knew he was one of the Russians he'd seen with Chakhkiev earlier that morning.

Russian *Mafiya*, most likely.

It's time to take proper precautions, he thought and withdrew his .44 Magnum Desert Eagle from his belt holster. In this place it was like bringing a cannon to a gunfight. The weapon didn't hold as many rounds as his beloved Beretta 93R, but the Eagle's penetration power would give him an edge if things got nasty. "Where's Dimitri?" the guy in the suit asked. His tone was gruff, demanding. He obviously didn't like dealing with underlings. Bolan recognized him as Greg Benedict. What was a guy high up in the Agency doing meeting with Chakhkiev?

"He is in the car," the Russian said. He gestured toward the guy in the black jacket. "Who is this?"

"My bodyguard," Benedict said. "Get your boss out here. I've got a message to deliver, and then I'm out of here."

"You can deliver it to me," the Russian said.

Chakhkiev was obviously staying in the Lincoln, which was parked in the middle of the aisle about thirty feet in front of the black Ford. Bolan ran across the aisle so he could move a bit closer to get a better look, and that's when the first round was fired.

LASSITER COULDN'T CARE less about a clandestine meeting between Benedict and some Russian goons. The tough looking Russian was probably an underling, anyway.

The important thing was that it brought Benedict out in the open with only one bodyguard to contend with. Lassiter knew he wouldn't get another chance like this.

He straightened to give himself a better sight picture, and shot the Russian first. The round hit the man's chest. Lassiter readjusted his aim and acquired a sight picture on his second target, Benedict's bodyguard. He squeezed the trigger once more but only let it retract back until he felt the slight click, indicating the weapon was ready to fire again. He put a second round into the bodyguard as the guy was pulling out his own weapon.

Benedict was frozen in space, his face showing utter panic.

Time for a reckoning, Lassiter thought. Then something moved in his peripheral vision and he instinctively ducked. The glass of a window in the Lexus shattered, accompanied milliseconds later by a hard, thumping sound of a large-caliber bullet piercing the metallic frame of the vehicle behind him.

Another shooter, Lassiter thought, as he rolled on the ground and scurried to the rear of the adjacent parked car.

WITH ALL THE obstructions between them, Bolan wasn't sure if he'd hit or missed. The guy had seemed to drop a split second before Bolan had squeezed off the round.

He might've seen my movement, Bolan thought, as he rose quickly from his position by the pick-up. He trotted across an expanse of aisle and ducked just as several rounds plunked into the vehicle next to him. Whoever this guy was, he wasn't shy about returning fire.

Russian *Mafiya* maybe?

Bolan crouched and ran about twenty feet, which took him to a better vantage point and new cover position. He did a quick peek through the windshield of the Jeep Wrangler he'd stopped in front of, keeping the engine block and front wheels between him and the last known position of the shooter.

He heard the screech of tires and glanced over to see the Lincoln peeling down the aisle, heading toward the exit ramp. A flurry of shots came from the guy in the suit, who was now armed. He was firing wildly as he glanced around.

"I know you're out there, you bastard," Benedict yelled. "It wasn't me. It was all Godfrey."

He turned and locked eyes with Bolan. They exchanged a millisecond's stare-down, then Benedict raised his pistol and fired. The bullet cracked through the windshield of the Jeep. Bolan brought his own weapon around to return fire, but Benedict's head jerked spasmodically to the right and made a semicircular motion as an accompanying burst of red mist filled the air. Bolan switched his sight picture back to the other man and saw him once again ducking.

Bolan lowered himself to floor and scanned the aisles between him and the shooter. No telltale feet to fire at. He estimated the guy's position based on the last sighting, and fired a round from the Desert Eagle. It struck the concrete floor and skipped onward. Seconds later, Bolan felt several rounds zip by him as they skimmed off the concrete and under the Jeep.

Time to change positions, he thought, and ran to his next cover point, by a solid, three-foot-thick pillar. He did a quick peek around the corner and saw no movement. Backing up so as not to hug cover, he extended the Desert Eagle while in a firing stance and surveyed the rows of parked cars.

No movement.

Somewhere in the sea of vehicles a starter groaned and a car engine came to life. A maroon Chevy Suburban lurched from a parking space and tore down the aisle, heading straight for the black Ford, which was still parked in the center of the aisle. Bolan zeroed in on the shadow behind the tinted window of the driver's side, but he held his fire. He couldn't rule out the chance that an innocent civilian had been inadvertently caught in the firefight.

Seconds later he doubted this supposition as he saw the shattered rear window on the driver's side. The Suburban rolled over one of the supine bodies in the aisle without hesitation and smashed into the left rear quarter panel of the idling Ford. The vehicle lurched forward from the impact and crashed into a parked Mercedes. A car alarm sounded with loud, intermittent blasts.

The Suburban forged ahead, the right front tire whining from scraping against its crumpled fender. The vehicle wheeled around toward the exit ramp and continued downward, but the abrasion of the tire seemed to be slowing it.

Bolan thought about running after it, but decided that even in its battered condition the Suburban would be too fast for him to catch on foot. Holstering his Desert Eagle, he ran back toward the ramp to level five and jumped up on a parked car, moving over the top of the vehicle as if scaling an obstacle course. From the roof, he leaped forward, grabbing the steel cables that separated this parking level from the ascending ramp, and swung himself through the opening. His subsequent landing was uncomfortable, and he felt the scraping pain on both his left elbow and knee as he skidding to a stop. Rolling to his feet, he raced on up, heading for the motorcycle, and keying his mike as he ran.

"Jack, shots fired. Three men down inside," he said. "Call for an ambulance and watch for a maroon Chevy Suburban coming your way."

"Looks like something—" Grimaldi started to say, then stopped. "Damn. The Lincoln just busted its way out of there. Want me to stop it?"

Bolan was on the motorcycle. He twisted the key in the ignition and hit the kick start. "Negative. It's Chakhkiev. The guy in the Suburban is our shooter. Armed and very dangerous. Watch yourself."

The motorcycle's engine roared to life under him. Bolan jammed the gearshift downward and popped the clutch. The bike's front tire reared up and he pressed down on the handlebars to get it back on the floor. He peeled down the entrance ramp, leaving a spoor of burned rubber, leaning to the side as he went into the first turn, then straightening to take the descending exit ramp to the subsequent level.

He passed the carnage of the fourth level, the smell of gunpowder and scorched rubber hanging in the air, and proceeded down to the third.

No sign of the Suburban yet.

He rounded the next corner and suddenly the maroon SUV was in front of him, crashed into the left side wall. He couldn't tell if it was empty. Bolan slowed the bike to a stop and began reaching for his Desert Eagle. Suddenly a blur appeared out of nowhere on his right and an expertly thrown flying karate kick slammed into him. His assailant's boot caught Bolan's ribs, and the Executioner flew off the motorcycle and tumbled onto the hard pavement. He rolled to lessen the impact, and landed on all fours, looking up just in time to catch a split-second image of a heavy boot coming at his face.

Bolan twisted his head down and to the side to try to

slip the blow, but it caught the bulky helmet and he fell
backward onto the garage floor. He rolled to his side,
still trying to extract the Desert Eagle from its holster
when the third kick landed in his right side. Seconds
after the impact he felt the pain and knew the blow had
hit his liver. He fought to overcome the agony and temporary paralysis. Bolan forced himself to make a grab
for the Desert Eagle, but felt the whipping impact of
another blow to his head. The helmet lessened its effect, but he collapsed again to his knees and tried to
marshal his strength.

The sound of the motorcycle's high whine as it sped
off came seconds later, and he glanced up in time to
see it peeling away down the exit ramp.

Bolan keyed his mike and said, "Jack, he's on my
bike."

No response.

"Jack, he's coming your way on the bike," Bolan
repeated.

No answer.

Still in pain, he forced himself to stand, and began
trotting down the exit ramp, feeling as if a knife was
rotating in his guts with each step. As he ran, he drew
the Desert Eagle with his right hand and traced over the
wire connecting his microphone to his radio with his
left. When his fingers got to the junction, he realized
it was broken. He tore the radio from his belt, stripped
off the helmet and keyed the mike using the side button.

"Jack, are you there?"

"Yeah, where the hell are you?"

"Still inside," Bolan said, managing to escalate into
a run. "Tango's coming your way on my bike."

"Aww, shit," Grimaldi said, the disgust obvious. "He
just shot out of here, popped a U-ey, and doubled back

down the sidewalk toward the next block. I thought it
was you tearing out of here."

"Damn," Bolan said as he slowed his pace slightly,
but continued his trot. In the distance he could hear
the wailing of a siren and knew it was time for them
to disappear.

"He took your bike?" Grimaldi asked.

Bolan nodded and slammed the Desert Eagle into its
holster. "Let's get out of here."

CHAPTER THIRTEEN

Stony Man Farm, Virginia

A few hours later, Bolan stood shirtless, hunched over the sink in his quarters as Barbara Price was getting ready to wipe the road rash on his left arm with more disinfectant. The biting sting reminded him of the cost of dropping one's guard in the midst of a firefight. But all things considered, it could have been worse. Instead of kicking him off his bike, his assailant could have shot him. Bolan wondered why he hadn't. Perhaps he was out of ammunition.

"This is going to sting a bit again," Price warned as she applied more disinfectant to the gauze pad and held it over the wound site.

"It can't hurt as much as my pride," he said.

She dabbed with the gauze and he felt the burning sensation once more. It was a good reminder to keep his eye on the ball and his head in the game. But what exactly was the "ball" in this instance? They'd been tailing Dimitri Chakhkiev to see who he met up with, and had walked into the middle of a firefight.

But it wasn't as much a firefight as it was an ambush.

"I know you're out there, you bastard," the guy in the suit had yelled. "It wasn't me. It was all Godfrey."

Godfrey. Bolan had asked Brognola to do more checking on GDF industries as well as try to find out the names of the shooting victims. He doubted any of the three had survived, especially Benedict, who was both shot and run over, but stranger things had happened. Grimaldi and he had left the area before the arrival of the police and the emergency services. Bolan was certain that Chakhkiev had escaped, too, in the Lincoln. The Russian was well versed in assassination attempts from his days in the KBG and his subsequent ties with the *Mafiya*. It was anybody's guess where he would be heading now.

"You want me to bandage it?" Price asked.

He shook his head. "Just smear on some antibacterial cream. It'll heal faster if it's uncovered."

"It'll also hurt more."

"Yeah, but I deserve it."

He felt her fingers probing his right side, where he'd sustained the impact of the flying kick. It was a bit tender, but he didn't think any of his ribs were cracked.

"You're going to have a pretty nasty bruise there," she commented.

"On you it would be pretty," Bolan said. "On me, it'll just look like a dark spot on a punching bag."

His cell phone vibrated. He reached over, feeling a twinge of pain, and grabbed it off the countertop.

Come by when you're ready, Brognola had texted. Got some news for you.

Maybe this was like the ten-second warning for the seconds to vacate the ring. He was ready for the next round to begin.

Washington, D.C.

WISPS OF STEAM rose in the air. Hutchcraft got up and went to the shower nozzle to douse himself with cool water. He turned back toward Godfrey, the room's other occupant. The man's face still looked as if it had been dipped in hot vinegar.

"I thought you said Lassiter was out in Arizona someplace?" Hutchcraft said. "Are you sure it was him?"

"No, I'm not *sure*," Godfrey said. "But looking at it logically, who else could it have been? Who else had the motive?"

"Motive." Hutchcraft frowned. "Why should that freak want to take out Greg? And how could he get here without anybody noticing? Isn't his name on the TSA—Transportation Security—watch list?"

Godfrey used his towel to wipe his forehead. The steam was becoming more uncomfortable for him, but he had to get Hutchcraft settled down. He also had to figure out the next prudent move. "Remember, Lassiter doesn't officially exist. He hasn't since his *death* several years ago. And he's got a plethora of false IDs, passports and credit cards at his disposal from his years with the Agency."

"In other words, instead of a supersoldier, we created a monster."

Godfrey laughed. "That's one way of putting it. Greg sent that damn wet squad to take Lassiter out, and they blew it. It stands to reason that he's a bit peeved, doesn't it?"

Hutchcraft's face assumed a more alarmed expression. "You don't think he's after me, do you?" He swallowed and glanced around. "I mean, what could he possibly have against me?"

"Nothing," Godfrey said, "other than the fact that you and Greg recruited him into the GEM program."

Hutchcraft appeared to shudder, which struck Godfrey as ironic in a steam room. He wondered whether his

hand-picked hero actually had the chutzpah to be commander-in-chief. Perhaps it was time to give him all of it.

"Time is on our side, though," he said.

Hutchcraft stared at him.

Godfrey continued. "Dr. Lawrence used a special
method for the gene modification treatments. It's called
a vector."

"So what?" Hutchcraft said. "How does that help us?"

"They used an AAV—adeno-associated virus—to
administer the dystrophin for the gene enhancements.
It attached directly to his cells that way. They thought
it was harmless. Nonpathogenic." Godfrey paused and
smiled. "Lawrence recently discovered he was wrong.
The virus apparently mutated. Lassiter's dying."

"What?"

"He's a walking dead man. That's when Greg and
I decided it was best to take him out. Before he found
out."

Hutchcraft smiled. "Well, that is good news, relatively speaking. How much longer has he got?"

"That we don't know. It could be days, it could be
weeks…." He paused. "It could be even longer."

Hutchcraft's frown returned. "You should have been
a politician. You're so good at double talk."

"We think he's being given special treatments by
one of the doctors on Lawrence's team."

"One of the doctors?"

"Yes. Ellen Campbell. Artie was doing a routine security screening and check of all the employees, and
she's been acting strangely." Godfrey used the towel
to wipe his forehead again. He'd had about all of this
incessant heat that he could stand for one afternoon.
"Plus she said she was coming here, to the East Coast,

this week. Ostensibly to visit her sick mother, which proved totally false."

"Great," Hutchcraft said. "Grab her. Make her tell us where that son of a bitch is and then send another wet team."

"That might be a lot harder than it sounds," Godfrey said. "Tipping our hand and letting both her and Lassiter know we know would only send him deeper underground. Better to let them return to Arizona, where we can track them. It's a simple matter of putting a GPS on her car, and eventually she'll lead us right to him and the shipment."

"And then what?"

"And then we send in a squad of Artie's best men, led by Trang, to finish the job."

"Trang's ready?"

Godfrey nodded.

"Is he dying, too?"

Godfrey shrugged. "I suppose. Lawrence is optimistic that, given enough time, he can find a nonhazardous method that works just as well. For the next supersoldier."

"Given enough time," Hutchcraft said, his tone laced with sarcasm. "How much time will we have before Trang finds out what we've done to him and goes rogue, too?"

"Enough," Godfrey said. "This time we know in advance it's coming. We didn't find out about Lassiter's condition until about six months ago."

"Why didn't you terminate him then? When you first found out."

"Several reasons, not the least of which is it provided Lawrence with an ideal test subject to trace the pathology of the deterioration. I'm sure you remember the quick degeneration of those first two."

Hutchcraft blew out a long breath. "Yeah, what were their names again?"

"Rodriguez and Paris." Godfrey sighed. "Lawrence thought he had things licked with Lassiter, but he miscalculated. But now we have a good idea of the rate at which the virus manifests itself. The only problem is that woman, Campbell, discovering it as well. Which is why we need to use her to ferret him out."

Hutchcraft sat there, sweating profusely. His chiseled features had regained a bit of their elegance now. He almost looked handsome again. "Okay, what makes you think he'll go back to Arizona?"

"Because that's where the bait's going to be," Godfrey said.

"The bait?"

Godfrey smiled as he stood. It was time to get the hell out of there. "Yes, Brent, the bait. You and me."

Stony Man Farm, Virginia

WHEN BOLAN WALKED into Brognola's office, Grimaldi was already sitting in one of the chairs in front of the desk with a mug of coffee. He held it up. "Care for some witch's brew?"

"I've got enough problems," Bolan said. He turned to Brognola. "You mentioned some news?"

The big Fed took a long drink from his own mug, set it down and tossed an antacid tablet into his mouth. He began to chew, then drank some more coffee.

"You want the good news first, or the bad news?"

"Save the best for last," Bolan said.

Brognola nodded and glanced downward.

The soldier knew from experience that he wasn't going to like what was coming next.

"My sources tell me the authorities have officially closed the Avelia death investigation case," Brognola said. "The ballistic and DNA tests confirm that the Colt Python that was recovered from one Clay Stafford, aka Animal, in Pima County, Arizona, was the murder weapon. Stafford is presumed to be the killer, and since he's now deceased, along with a good portion of the rest of the gang, they've closed the book on it."

Bolan had seen that one coming. He nodded. "What else?"

Brognola pointed to the screen, which was descending from the ceiling. He took a quick sip of coffee and flipped the switch to activate the overhead projector and dim the lights. "The three fatalities from the parking garage shootout have been identified." The first picture, a passport photo depicting a heavyset man with a scowl on his face, appeared. "This is, or was, Oleg Chagaev. Apparently he and Chakhkiev go way back in the mother country."

"He looks like a hard case, all right," Grimaldi said.

"Well," Brognola replied, "he's now officially deceased. One 9 mm round to the chest. It was a good center mass shot, which took out his heart."

Bolan replayed the shootout in his head as Brognola talked.

"Second victim." The photograph on the screen changed, to one in color showing a white male in his late thirties with an Ivy League haircut. "George Norman. He worked out of Langley as a special bodyguard and driver to this man."

The picture on the screen shifted again, showing another white male, this one slender looking with a waspish face and hawklike nose. "And here we have Greg Benedict, who is a known entity."

"Yeah, you mentioned Benedict. What's his background?" Bolan said. "Besides him being deceased, you mean?"

"Well, he's been with the Agency for about twenty-three years. I guess I should be using the past tense. He was in the field in Europe, South America and the Middle East for a number of years before being assigned to Langley in charge of some special ops program. It was pretty hush-hush, but Aaron's been able to break through a couple firewalls and find out some details. Apparently, Benedict and Anthony Godfrey are buddies."

"So Anthony Godfrey, the late Greg Benedict and Artie Fellows are all connected to what's going down," Bolan said. "Benedict was screaming something about Godfrey right before he got shot."

"Well, they did know each other," Brognola said.

"Benedict said something about it not being him," Bolan said. "About it being 'all Godfrey.'"

"Interesting. Well, we found out that much of Godfrey's success as an arms dealer, especially as one of the major suppliers of arms to the U.S. Military, is courtesy of this man." The photograph changed to the smiling face of Senator Brent Hutchcraft.

"This stinks to high heaven," Bolan said.

Brognola nodded. "You got that right." He tilted the chair back and clasped his hands behind his head. "One of GDF Industries subsidiaries, SNTP Laboratories, has received numerous federal grants for a highly classified research project, courtesy of the Defense Appropriations Committee, headed by future presidential candidate Brent Hutchcraft. But all we've been able to find out is the name of the project, which is GEM. Whatever the hell that means. Aaron's working on finding more about that, too."

"So," Bolan said, "let me see if I've got this straight. Russian arms dealer Dimitri Chakhkiev, who was last seen with now-deceased Russian *Mafiya* member Oleg Chagaev, both of whom were meeting with now-deceased Assistant Agency Director Greg Benedict, who used to work with arms industrialist Anthony Godfrey, who's beholden to soon-to-be presidential contender Brent Hutchcraft, are all in bed together."

"That pretty much sums it up," Brognola said. "Except for one more little thing." He leaned forward and grabbed the mouse. "Remember that picture of Hutchcraft, Lassiter and the two other guys?"

Bolan nodded.

"Well, Aaron was able to enhance the pixel quality on that reflection you were curious about." He clicked the mouse and the picture appeared on the screen: the three young soldiers with Colonel Brent Hutchcraft. Brognola centered the mouse on the reflected face and clicked. Another picture replaced that one, this time showing an enlarged image of the reflection. Brognola clicked a few more times, enhancing it each time he did, but the face was still difficult to discern.

"The up-until-now anonymous photographer was none other than—" Brognola clicked the mouse a final time, bringing up the resulting image beside a previously shown photo of a slender looking man with a waspish face "—our deceased buddy, Greg Benedict."

"Well, I'll be damned," Grimaldi said. "Looks like we've come full circle."

"And then some," Bolan added.

Brognola leaned forward. "There's more about Lassiter," he said. "Remember Operation Cat's Cradle? And I've got some other interesting intel…."

CHAPTER FOURTEEN

Lassiter was confident that traveling under the name Michael Jones was safe enough, since it was one he'd never used during his operations. He sat back in the wheelchair, his legs covered by a blanket and with a mustache and beard obscuring the lower half of his face. Ellen pushed him through the special boarding section, bypassing the long TSA security lines. It had worked like a charm on the way to D.C. and appeared to be working just as effectively on their return trip. They'd purchased one-way tickets each time, not wanting to be tied down to any schedule that could be tracked. It had turned out to be a fortuitous move. Going back to Arizona this quickly hadn't been Lassiter's original plan. He'd hoped to stay in D.C. to get a crack at a couple more people, namely that son of a bitch Godfrey and Brent Hutchcraft. But the news announcement that Hutchcraft was using the upcoming congressional three-week break to travel back to his home base in Arizona for campaign appearances had changed things. Especially when it was also announced that one of his major campaign contributors and staunch supporters, Anthony Godfrey, would be hosting a five hundred dol-

lar a plate dinner for the candidate in both Phoenix and
Tucson. That had been a game changer.

He knew Hutchcraft would probably have to be taken
out at a distance if much more time elapsed. At this
point, shortly after the announcement of his candidacy
for the nomination, the inevitable Secret Service detail would follow and make things more difficult. And
Lassiter wanted the final goodbyes to be up close and
personal. He regretted Benedict's hadn't been face-to-
face, but at least good old Greg had known who it was.

The panicked yell floated through Lassiter's memory
as they stopped and he handed his boarding pass and
false ID to the TSA woman. She shone her black light
over the ID, illuminating the official seal, and matched
the picture to his face.

He lifted his upper lip in a weak smile. "That was
taken before I got real sick," he said, which in reality
was true.

The woman nodded and smiled, handing the ID and
boarding pass back to him after scrawling her initials
on it. She then took Ellen's stuff.

Too easy, Lassiter thought, but then again, he had
been trained and equipped to fool the very best.

The best… He thought again about the parking garage confrontation and the unexpected entrance of the
man in the black outfit. He was no ordinary Agency
flunky, but moved like a real pro. Lassiter had thought
about putting a bullet into the guy's brain after kicking
him off the motorcycle, but something had stopped him.
The man had proved to be a formidable adversary, and
had fought well. Plus there was something strangely
familiar about the big guy's moves. And Benedict had
shot at him, too. As if he'd thought he was no ordinary
Agency hack. So Lassiter had just taken off rather than

try to finish him. At that moment, the priority had been
getting away, not staying to go another round with that
tough customer.

Still, there was something sort of familiar about him.

The TSA woman handed Ellen back her boarding
pass and ID and told them to have a nice day.

Yeah, too easy, he thought as he felt the chair move
forward. Way too easy.

"THESE TRIPS BACK and forth to Arizona are getting to be
so routine, I could do one in my sleep," Grimaldi said
as he flipped a switch to verify his preflight checklist.

"I told you we had unfinished business there," Bolan
said. He'd taken the copilot's seat to assist Grimaldi,
but his mind was elsewhere. He was thinking about the
long-ago failed mission Operation Cat's Cradle, and
what Brognola had told him. That had been where Bolan
had seen Lassiter the first time. The guy who'd led the
rescue squad, sweeping in after De la Noval and his
cronies had caught Bolan and the Colombian special
ops team in their ambush. It had been compromised…a
setup. And Lassiter had come to the rescue. There was
no getting around the fact that, all things considered,
Lassiter had saved Bolan's life.

Then there was this last debacle, the mission to rescue Chris Avelia. That one had been compromised as
well, only this time Lassiter, if it had been him, had preceded Bolan's team. He'd hit Jesús De la Noval hard,
killing a bunch of lowlifes and a few prostitutes, and
had taken Chris back, to give to the Wolves for execution. At the behest of whom? The Agency? Greg Benedict? What did he have to gain, or lose, if the arms deal
Chris was working to expose came to light?

How about who was behind it? Maybe the Agency

was trading arms for drugs with the cartel? Certainly, that might not be something the principals would want being broadcast on the evening news. Or in a congressional committee hearing on Capitol Hill. Especially if the arms dealer in question had a connection with a possible presidential candidate.

Weapons meant a connection to GDF Industries, and Anthony Godfrey. His flunky, Artie Fellows, had been explaining to Animal how one man, Lassiter, took out three of the motorcycle gang and some of Fellows's men, as well. Godfrey had double-crossed Lassiter, or at least had tried to do so. And now Lassiter was apparently out to even the score. There was no record of his name on any airline or train passenger lists, but that didn't surprise Bolan. If Lassiter had been with the Agency, he was more than capable of covering his tracks and moving around with the aplomb of a ghost.

What had surprised Bolan was the openness with which both Godfrey and Hutchcraft had made their travel agendas known, filing a flight plan with the FAA and announcing a pair of fund-raisers in Arizona. Not your usual behavior for potential targets, unless they were getting ready for a counterstrike. It was an audacious move.

Fortune favored the bold, Bolan mused. But setting yourself up like a staked goat to catch a rogue tiger was risky. Maybe Godfrey and the would-be president had an ace up their sleeves.

Bolan thought about his own encounter with the tiger in the parking garage. Lassiter had taken out Benedict and the two others without the least bit of compunction, yet he'd passed up a chance to follow up on his advantage over Bolan after executing that flying karate kick.

He could have put a bullet in my brain, the soldier thought. But he didn't. Why?

"Hey, you're not being much help here," Grimaldi said. "I asked you twice to flip that switch, and you're looking like you're a million miles away."

"Sorry," he said. "Just trying to sort a few things out."

"Yeah, something tells me we're headed into a real hornet's nest." Grimaldi flashed a grin. "But then again, when don't we end up with a tiger by the tail?"

"Good point."

Bolan went back to thinking about big cats and stalking tigers.

South Tucson, Arizona

GODFREY FELT A thrill watching Trang go through his paces. He was the best GEM yet. Even better than Lassiter. The Asian supersoldier was facing six highly trained opponents at the same time in the hexagonal cage thirty feet below. Hutchcraft stood next to Godfrey, watching with interest. Godfrey's only regret was that they were in the observation room. He would have preferred to be ringside so he could smell the sweat, and the fear, once the blood started to run.

"You sure he's ready for all six?" Hutchcraft asked. "I mean, the guy's just finished a five-mile run carrying ten-pound dumbbells."

"That was just the warm-up," Dr. Lawrence said, smiling.

"Just think what he could do in your D.C. Iron Man contest," Godfrey said.

The first man rushed Trang, who brushed him away and sidestepped just as the second man stepped forward with a perfectly executed leg kick. Trang pivoted, lifting his own leg up and away, and sent a back kick of his own into that man's midsection. He crumpled to the mat.

Two other opponents jumped Trang, one on his back, the other grabbing Trang's right arm with both hands. The supersoldier merely grasped his right hand with his left and ripped away from the attempted armlock. He then reached over his shoulder and grabbed his other opponent by his hair, stepped back and flipped that man forward. He flew into the other opponent, and they both went down in a profusion of scrambling arms and legs.

"Each of those men is a black belt and experienced martial artist," Godfrey said. "Trang's the best one yet."

The final two fighters advanced a bit more cautiously, circling Trang from opposite directions. He stood calmly waiting, watching, his head facing forward. He wasn't even breathing hard and had barely broken a sweat.

The opponent on the left moved first, feinting a jab. Trang leaned back as the man on the right made a sudden grab for Trang's neck, but was abruptly stopped by a hard elbow to the midsection. Reaching up, Trang grabbed the jabber's extended arm and stepped forward, pulling the man's weight onto his left leg, and then sweeping it out from under him. The jabber fell to the mat, grasping his leg.

"He's good," Hutchcraft said, "but any clown can look good in the martial arts ring. How will he do when the stakes are raised and someone's coming at him with real weapons on the street?"

"We do train for that eventuality as well," Godfrey said. He pressed a button on the console and said into an adjacent, hanging microphone, "Proceed to phase two."

Trang stopped what he was doing and went to the center of the cage. Four men in dark security uniforms entered the hexagonal area and helped the injured martial arts opponents out. Three more men came in, one carrying an axe handle, another a set of nunchakus and a third a samurai sword. Each man also had a holstered sidearm.

"Are those real?" Hutchcraft asked.

"As real as we allow in here," Godfrey said, smiling. "This is practice, after all. The axe handle is made of heavy gauge plastic, not wood, the nunchakus are padded, and the samurai sword is not sharpened."

"How about those guns?"

"The pistols are loaded with rounds similar to paintballs." Godfrey noticed Hutchcraft's smirk. "They still pack a stinging wallop, especially on bare skin, but they're normally not fatal, unless someone is shot in the eye, of course."

"We usually frown on that," Dr. Lawrence said with a sly grin.

"Impressive, but it's still not the same as a real-life combat situation," Hutchcraft said. "How can you be sure this guy's really ready?"

"Watch," Godfrey said, "and then you tell me."

The man with the axe handle moved in first, grabbing it with both hands and swinging it over his shoulder as if he were trying to pound a stake in the ground. Or crush Trang's skull.

Instead of moving away, Trang shot forward, going inside the arc of the man's swing, catching him by the upper arms and thus not allowing him to complete the downward motion. Trang delivered a short, but powerful uppercut punch to his opponent's solar plexus, then pivoted his hip into the man's stomach and executed a perfect judo hip throw. The axe man went over, and struck the mat with tremendous force.

The man with the nunchakus moved forward, spinning the wooden clubs so fast they were only a blur. He swung at Trang's head, but the supersoldier nimbly leaned out of range. As the man retracted the clubs, Trang reached out and grabbed his outstretched wrist, then stepped forward, delivering a pair of snapping kicks, the first to the man's groin, the second to his chin. This opponent collapsed as well.

The last one drew the samurai sword from its sheath and held it in front of him. He, too, was Asian. He moved forward with a catlike grace, spinning the sword up and then forward in a slashing motion toward Trang's upper body. Trang danced away to the swordsman's right side. In a flash he had grabbed his opponent's wrists and stepped behind him, using his leg in a sweeping motion to send the samurai man sprawling backward. When he tumbled, Trang followed him, slamming an elbow into the man's face. He lay still, his feet twitching slightly.

The axe man was on his feet now, bringing his pistol to a firing position. Trang sprang forward, leaping at least ten feet, to land next to him and snatch the weapon from his outstretched hands. He slammed the butt of the gun into the man's left temple, then flipped the weapon in his hand, assumed a firing position and shot each of his opponents in the chest. The paintball-like rounds left red blossoms on each one, accompanied by groans of pain.

"Pretty good," Hutchcraft said. "I'll bet you have a hard time finding training partners for him."

"They're paid well to take a beating." Godfrey

laughed. "He'll be out in the field soon enough, and I think you can see he's more than a match for Lassiter."

Hutchcraft nodded, but then his face took on a serious cast. "What about that cell deterioration thing? He going to be affected by that as well?"

Godfrey shrugged and then looked toward the doctor.

"We've changed our procedure a little," Dr. Lawrence said. "Used a different vector and modified the AAV-IGF-X5. It should make a difference, but we initially thought that with John, too." He sighed. "I should know more in time. When I've had the chance to examine the extent of damage to John's cell structure, once we have a new blood sample." He smiled. "I'm sure we'll have plenty of samples once Trang gets hold of him, won't we?"

Godfrey chuckled.

Hutchcraft looked contemplative for a few moments and then drew his lips into a tight smile. "You know, gentlemen, perhaps it isn't such a deficiency, after all. Look at the bright side. We create a supersoldier and use his talents for a time, and then a built-in biological trigger gets rid of him for us before he can become too much of a liability. Gives us a modicum of control over a dangerous weapon."

"Planned obsolescence," Dr. Lawrence said, raising his eyebrows. "I've never thought of it quite that way." He smiled and gave Hutchcraft an approving nod. "Interesting observation."

"And spoken like a true commander-in-chief," Godfrey said. He was grinning now, too. "Use the troops wisely, then let them die."

CHAPTER FIFTEEN

The bouts of sudden and unexpected weakness were becoming more frequent now. Lassiter felt a slight bit of relief as Ellen expertly inserted the needle into the distended vein in his arm and started the IV flow. Thoughts of the intimate encounter he'd been looking forward to that afternoon had all but vanished as the weakness began suddenly to tear at him like a riptide. He lay back and closed his eyes, never thinking it would come to this.

"I feel like a junkie," he said. "Waiting for my next fix."

She patted his hand gently.

"Why don't you rest for a bit," she said. "I can drop off the rental and pick up my car."

"No, give me a few minutes and I'll tag along. I want to make sure they're not still following you."

Lassiter could see that prospect disturbed her. She'd been visibly shaken when he'd told her about the tail the other night. Her unexpected Sunday morning meeting with Lawrence and Fellows had shaken her up even more. Lassiter's thoughts turned to Lawrence. That prick had to have known about the side effects. He was on the payback list, too, along with Hutchcraft and Godfrey. They were all in on it. And they'd deceived him into causing the death of that federal agent Avelia. One of the good guys. That was another debt he had to collect on. The question was how to get all of them in one place, especially since the clock seemed to be ticking double-time for him now.

He opened his eyes and glanced down at the needle in his arm, hoping this new batch of meds would make him feel like his old self.

"I'm going to have to go into the lab again," Campbell said matter-of-factly. "We're running low on medication. Plus I want to start you on some interferon."

That doesn't sound good, Lassiter thought. He didn't know much about medicine, but he did know that sounded like some heavy-duty shit. And going back to the lab wasn't a bright prospect, either, especially with both Fellows and Lawrence there. But what choice did they have? He was going from strong to weak as a kitten more frequently now, and without any warning. Just like a junkie, as he'd said.

There was only one way for him to go, and that was down, but where did she go from here? All he'd been thinking about was the completion of his personal mission, his vendetta. That would be closure for him, and most likely the end of the road, but Ellen… She still had her whole life ahead of her.

Campbell reached into her purse and took out two long plastic objects with protective wrapping over one end. "I'm going to leave you these auto-injectors. If the weakness should come on suddenly, and I'm not here, you can use them to inject yourself. Do you know what I mean?"

"Yeah, like an atropine syrette?"

"Exactly." She compressed her lips and looked down at him again, massaging his temple. "Hopefully, you won't need them."

"Speaking of need…" He reached over with his left

hand and grabbed his ditty pouch from the nightstand. "We need to make plans for you get away from here."

"Don't move so much," she said.

He ignored her and set the bag on the bed, unzipping the back pocket and taking out three small, red envelopes.

"What are those?" she asked.

"Safety deposit box keys," he said. "Each from a different bank. You're listed as a co-signer for authorized access."

She compressed her lips and looked away. "Should I ask what's in them?"

"That bag I had at Wally's World," he said. "There was a lot of money in it. Over four million dollars. I want you to take it all and get out here. Get a new start. Far, far away."

She didn't move. He thrust the three little envelopes at her. "Take the keys."

No response.

"Take them."

She turned back toward him and patted his head as she closed her eyes. He could tell she was fighting tears.

"There's plenty of time for that," she said. "We don't have to talk about it now."

"Can you think of a better time?" he asked.

She kept her eyes shut, but a tear managed to escape between her lids.

He took a deep breath. Perhaps now wasn't such a good time. Perhaps he should come up with a plan that would end this damn thing sooner rather than later. That way they could maybe leave with the money, share together whatever time he had left, and then he could fade away and make sure she was off to a new start.

He needed a new plan, one with a quicker resolution.

Lassiter reviewed the current setup, the proximity of all the principals, and slowly an idea came to him. Everybody was in this same geographic area at the moment.

Maybe, just maybe, he could get all of them in the same place at the same time.

BOLAN AND GRIMALDI waited in the lobby of the Pima County Sheriff's Substation as the desk clerk talked on the phone. The clerk hung up and said, "He'll be right up."

About thirty seconds later a door to the left cracked open and Sergeant Sergio Valdez poked his head through. "Well, what do you know," he said, "Batman and Robin are back."

"Yeah," Grimaldi said, holding up his left arm and pointing to his watch. "We wanted to catch you before quitting time."

Valdez frowned and held the door open wider, motioning for them to enter. He was dressed in a short-sleeved shirt and khaki pants, with his badge and pistol clipped to his belt. Valdez led them down a hall and into an office where two other people, a man and woman, sat in front of a large gray desk covered with stacks of papers.

Bolan noticed that the woman was Special Agent Callahan. She was dressed in typical federal agent attire, a blue pantsuit.

Callahan looked up at them and smiled. "Just when we were discussing how quiet it's been around here the past few days, since you two left. So how was Washington, gentlemen?"

"The usual," Grimaldi said. "You should've come with us. I could have taken you around to see the sights"

"I've already seen them."

"I'm sure you have," Bolan said. "But how did you know we were in D.C.?"

Callahan smiled. "Let's just say that word gets around."

"Keeping tabs on us?" Bolan asked.

"Just like that old commercial," Valdez said, straddling the chair at the head of the table and resting his forearms on its back. "Interested parties want to know. We kind of like to anticipate where the bodies will be falling next."

"There might be quite a few falling around here," Bolan said. "You've got some storm clouds heading your way."

The wry grin faded from Valdez's face and he sat up. "Okay, I'm listening."

Bolan's eyes moved toward the other man sitting at the desk. Valdez noticed this and told the guy to go grab a cup of coffee.

After he'd left, Bolan asked, "Did you hear about the shooting in a D.C. parking garage a few days ago?"

"An assistant director of the CIA was killed," Callahan said. "You have knowledge of that?"

Bolan nodded. "One of the other men killed was a Russian national. His name was Oleg Chagaev, and he was a close associate of Dimitri Chakhkiev."

"The international arms dealer?" Callahan asked.

Bolan nodded in acknowledgment. This woman's done her homework, he thought.

"I know who Chagaev is, too," Callahan said. "Or was. He had suspected ties to organized crime."

"There's no 'suspected' about it," Grimaldi stated. "He was Russian *Mafiya*, as is Chakhkiev."

"I know that also," Callahan said.

"Did you know Chakhkiev's on his way here?" Bolan

asked. "And that he's bringing along a bunch of *Mafiya* muscle?"

"How many?" Valdez asked.

"The flight plan he filed listed fourteen passengers," Grimaldi told him.

"We've also heard rumblings that Jesús De la Noval has been assembling a strike force just south of the border," Bolan said. "He got hit pretty hard in that raid a week or so ago, and he could be looking for revenge."

"Not to mention the arms shipment he was supposedly buying," Grimaldi said.

"We have information on that, too," Callahan said. "That's what we were discussing before you got here. So far, however, it's unsubstantiated."

"You can take it to the bank," Grimaldi said. "It's connected to the Avelia murder, a case you guys closed."

Callahan's face flushed. "I can assure you that wasn't my decision."

"Let's take a look at whose decision it was," Bolan said. "I have a hunch there was a lot of pressure from high places to close that one. Am I right?"

Callahan compressed her lips, then nodded.

"Some high muckity-mucks want this whole thing swept under the rug," Grimaldi said. "What does that tell you?"

"It could be a lot of things." Callahan raised an eyebrow, "but I get the feeling you've got a theory."

"We were sent down there to rescue Avelia," Grimaldi said, "Because his undercover op had allegedly been compromised. Somebody tipped off De la Noval because Avelia was about to blow the lid off a clandestine arms deal that'd been going on."

"We know he was working on one," Callahan said. "But unfortunately, we don't have all the particulars."

Grimaldi snorted. "I thought all you Feds were supposed to be sharing information since 9/11? Seems like the left hand still doesn't know what the right hand is doing."

Callahan blushed.

"Aside from Avelia's murder," Bolan said, "and that incident involving the Aryan Wolves last week, have you had any other unusual homicides recently?"

"Unusual?" Valdez asked, leaning back. "Like what?"

"Like three motorcycle gang members and some other unidentified male victims," Bolan said.

Valdez narrowed his eyes. "How the hell did you…" He paused. "What if we did? How's this all fit together?"

"I'm glad you asked," Bolan said. He gave them a brief rundown of the arms deal Avelia had been working on, the tie-in to GDF Industries and the apparent role of the Agency in the process.

"You're stretching things a lot to ask me to believe that a government agency is involved in these kinds of dealings," Callahan said. "It's against their charter to operate within the borders of the United States."

Grimaldi barked a laugh. "Since when has that stopped them?"

"Look," Bolan said, "for all we know this could be a rogue element within the Agency itself. They could be totally unsanctioned operations. But it all comes back to this guy Godfrey and GDF Industries. That's where we have to focus. Can you get us a federal warrant to search his compound out here?"

"I can look into it," Callahan said. "But we're going to need a bit more than supposition."

"That figures," Grimaldi stated. "We practically

hand you the case you're looking for, and you're looking for ways *not* to act on it."

Callahan frowned. "A warrant requires probable cause. The Bureau operates on a little thing called proof."

"We know that there's a large arms shipment missing that was supposed to go to Jesús De la Noval in Mexico," Bolan said. "We also have reason to believe it's been hidden somewhere around here. If we could find out where it is, that might lead us to the principals involved in this. And to the person who ordered Avelia killed."

He turned to Valdez. "Sergeant, you know this area better than any of us. A shipment of that size wouldn't fit in a motel room. Where could they hide something like that?"

Valdez raised his eyebrows and blew out a long breath. "The desert's a mighty big place. I guess there are a few areas where we might look...."

"Keep in mind we've had satellites souring the area, along with surveillance drones," Grimaldi said. "We've come up with nothing. It's got to be well hidden somewhere."

Bolan gave him a sharp look.

"I mean 'we' in the collective sense of 'we, the government,'" Grimaldi added with a grin.

"That seems to be a role you two slip in and out of as easily as changing your clothes," Callahan said.

"Let's just say we have resources," Bolan said. "Now let's use them."

Wally's Waterworld

AFTER LEAVING THE message for Jesús De la Noval at the number he'd retrieved from a cell phone he'd taken from the compound during the raid, Lassiter busied himself with setting the charges and Claymore mines along the perimeter and inside the structure. The last transfusion was still working like a charm, and he felt like his old self: strong, competent and tireless. Even working in the midmorning heat wasn't bothering him. He did miss Ellen, though, and worried about her going back into the lion's den to retrieve more medicine. But what choice did they have?

He set the plastic case, with This Side Toward Enemy facing outward, on the two-by-four brace next to the main entrance, and connected the wires to the circuit he'd set up. The area was completely wired, both levels of the old mall as well as the water park. It had been transformed into a kill zone. Now all he had to do was lure his targets to it.

The cell phone vibrated in his pocket. Lassiter glanced at the number and saw it was listed as Unknown.

Most likely, it's a call from Jesús, he thought.

He answered it and heard an unfamiliar voice ask in rapid Spanish, "*Quién es?*"

"Speak in English," Lassiter said. "And I know you know how."

After a pause, the voice said, "How you know that?"

"Because we've done business before," Lassiter said.

More silence, then, "And how do I know this is true?"

The guy's English was getting better all the time. "Is this Jesús?"

No response.

"Look," Lassiter said, "I want to talk to Jesús De la Noval. I made it clear in the message I left earlier that I have something that belongs to him. If he wants it, I'll be glad to do business. If not, there are plenty of other buyers I can deal with."

The voice on the phone was silent for a few moments more, and then asked in almost perfect English, "And what might this be?"

"The items that were taken from your *casa*. Do I need to go on?"

After a few more seconds of silence, the voice said, "How do I know you are who you say you are? How do I know this isn't some kind of *truco*? A trick? How do I know you have what you say you have?"

"I'll arrange a little demonstration," Lassiter said. "Proof."

"Proof?"

"Yeah. You have eyes and ears up here in *el norte*, right?"

"Yes."

"Keep them watching your motorcycle buddies, the Aryan Wolves, later tonight."

"It is already night. What time?"

"*Medianoche*." Lassiter paused. "Their *casa es mi casa*."

"You talk in riddles, my friend."

"I'm not your friend," Lassiter said. "Now give me a number where I can reach you after midnight so we can talk about the money you're going to pay me."

GDF Compound

CAMPBELL HAD GONE to work at her regular time and busied herself in the lab, examining blood and tissue samples and catching up on her paperwork. Dr. Lawrence stopped in, welcoming her back and asking how her mother was doing.

"She's fine," Campbell said, hoping she wouldn't have to explain more and perhaps sound vague. But she and John had discussed her sticking to the cover story and making her appearance seem as normal as possible.

"Glad to hear it," Lawrence said, stepping around her desk and resting his hand on her shoulder as he gazed at her computer. He'd moved closer than normal, invading her personal zone. This was uncharacteristic of him, and she slid her chair back slightly.

Lawrence stepped back as well, a somewhat embarrassed expression on his face.

"I'm sorry, my dear," he said. "I was merely curious to see what you'd been working on this morning."

She'd been going over the effects of the latest meds combating John's necrosis, but she could hardly say that. But if he had seen it on her computer screen… Being evasive about it or trying to come up with some sort of subterfuge would most certainly be more problematic. Getting caught in a lie wasn't an option. She decided on the truth, or at least part of it.

"I was comparing the blood cells from one of our earlier subjects with Trang's latest samples," she said. "Remember I asked you about the possible long-term effects of degeneration and possible necrosis a few months ago?"

Put it back on him, she thought. He'd blown her off back then. Perhaps he'd do the same now, hoping she hadn't caught on to what the genetic enhancement was actually doing to these poor men.

Lawrence looked thoughtful for a moment, canted his head to the left slightly and glanced upward. "I do seem to recall you mentioning that. I believe I did look into it. Why? What have you found?"

Oh, great, she thought. The last thing she wanted was

to get involved in a discussion of the syndrome. She remembered John's advice of forging ahead with your plan, and his soldier's creed of fortune favoring the bold.

"I've just been reviewing my old research," she said. "I needed to get updated samples for both Trang and Lassiter, but I haven't seen John recently. Will he be available soon, do you know?"

Before Lawrence could answer, the cell phone on his belt jangled. He smiled and answered it.

Campbell could hear an indistinct, but panicked voice on the other end. The skin between Lawrence's eyebrows creased and he said, "I'll be right there." He ended the call and looked down at her. "Meet me in the gym ASAP. There's a problem with Trang."

She nodded as she closed the computer file and then started to get up. But Lawrence was already hustling out the door, a look of grave concern plastered across his thin face. So she sat back down and transferred the file to a flash drive, which she then put in her purse, along with the new supply of medications that she'd gotten on an earlier trip to the pharmacy.

Saved by the bell, she thought.

GODFREY WATCHED AS Trang continued to beat the three men unmercifully. The training session had begun the same as they always did, but this time one of the opponents had managed to strike Trang in the head with a nightstick. The blow had glanced off Trang's cropped black hair and suddenly sent him into a frenzy. Ripping the nightstick from the man's grasp, Trang began systematically beating him. His two other opponents jumped in to stop him, but they, too, quickly became semiconscious punching bags for the Asian whirlwind.

"Christ, he's killing them," Hutchcraft said. "Aren't you going to stop it?"

Godfrey watched a few seconds more in fascination, before standing and saying, "Trang, that's enough."

That did little good, and Godfrey's mouth tightened into a thin line. There were several security men standing there, as well as Fellows, who made no effort to step forward when Godfrey said, "Get in there and stop it, but don't injure him."

Three of the security men glanced nervously at Fellows, who nodded curtly. They moved in, removing their stun guns from their holsters. Trang was so intent on beating the third man that he didn't whirl to meet the new threat until it was almost too late. The first security guard fired his stun gun, but Trang nimbly leaped to the side, letting the extending wires sail past him. The second man fired. Trang pivoted, and those prongs missed, as well.

"Give him a drive-stun," Fellows yelled.

The first guard stripped off the expended cartridge from his stun gun and stepped forward to use it. Trang had landed lightly on his feet after his spinning step, and as soon as his toes hit the floor he jumped and whirled again. This time his right foot shot upward in a hooking motion, and collided with the security guard's right temple. The other guard pushed his stun gun toward Trang, who pivoted once more and struck his forearm with a chopping, knife-hand blow. The guard cringed in pain, dropped his weapon and grabbed his arm. Trang bashed his fist repeatedly into the stunned man's face, causing a profusion of blood to cascade from his mouth and nose.

"Hold it," Fellows said, stepping back out of range of the whirling kicks as he pulled a large pistol from a holster. He snapped down a front grip and flipped the selector switch.

Trang started forward as Godfrey yelled, "Don't you dare shoot him."

Trang's mouth curved into a smile as he continued moving toward Fellows.

The security chief shot a burst into the mat area in front of Trang's feet. That stopped him.

Suddenly, a voice from the other side of the room called out, "Stop." It was Lawrence, jogging forward in his white lab coat. Godfrey noticed that Ellen Campbell was about twenty feet behind him, her eyes wide as if she was in shock. Coming up at the rear was that little worm Mickey Potter.

"Trang, no," Lawrence said. "Please. Stop."

The big Asian's head bobbled back and forth as he looked first at Fellows, who still had the big pistol extended, and then back toward Lawrence. Godfrey could see Trang was in a bit of a quandary.

Potter handed Lawrence something, and the doctor managed to step over the fallen bodies and place his hand gently on Trang's shoulder. The big supersoldier jerked away from him. Potter then grabbed Trang's right arm and held it with both hands. Trang smashed his left palm into Potter's face, crushing his nose and sending him sprawling on his back, his face a bloody mess. Then he leaped upward, drawing his feet under him, and pounced on Potter. One foot landed on the lab assistant's gut, the other struck the front of his neck. Trang ground his feet, his face contorting into a prolonged grimace. Potter lay there jerking spasmodically.

Lawrence, almost out of breath, said, "This will make you feel better." He stuck a hypodermic syringe into the supersoldier's massive deltoid muscle.

Trang jerked back and for a second looked as if he was going to strike Lawrence. Then he took a couple stumbling steps and smiled. "Feels real good."

Lawrence wiped his forehead with the back of his hand and said, "That's quite enough for today. We've got to run more diagnostics."

The word seemed to puzzle Trang, but at least he stopped advancing. Godfrey threw a sharp look toward Fellows, who was still pointing the gun, and said, "I told you to put that thing away, damn it. And pick up that brass."

Lawrence had his arm around Trang's shoulders now, and they were walking toward Potter and Campbell. Lawrence was muttering something about them all needing to go back to the lab, and Godfrey heard him tell the woman and a few security guards to take Trang there and he'd follow shortly. Then he knelt and began administering aid to the unconscious Potter. Trang looked suddenly calm, almost placid.

Godfrey regretted that Campbell had seen this little foray, if, in fact, she was complicit with that traitor Lassiter. Of course, a little forewarning about Trang's fierceness might make him nervous, more prone to indecision and uncertainty. It could prove to be something of a strategic advantage.

Godfrey turned back to Fellows. "Please tell me you weren't serious about shooting a multimillion dollar project."

Fellows was sticking the pistol back into its holster. He said nothing as he stooped and picked up the expended brass shell casings.

"What the hell kind of a gun is that?" Hutchcraft asked, stepping forward.

"It's a 93R," Fellows said.

Hutchcraft raised his eyebrows. "I didn't know they even made those anymore."

"They don't," Fellows said. "It's sort of a trophy piece."

Hutchcraft grinned, nodded and then turned to Godfrey. "What the hell happened to him? He looked like a madman there at the end. He was practically foaming at the mouth." The senator looked at the array of still-unconscious bodies on the big mat.

Godfrey surveyed the scattered bodies as well. A job well done. Trang had taken them out as if they were papier-mâché mannequins. Even the security guards, who weren't even scheduled to be part of it.

"What better preparation training could you ask for?" Godfrey said.

"Mickey needs an ambulance," Lawrence stated, walking over. He was still a bit ruffled. "It must be a synergistic effect of those new steroids," he was saying. "We can adjust the dosage and—"

"And nothing," Godfrey said. "I like him this way. Lean and mean, no mercy, no quarter."

"You've got a point, Tony," Hutchcraft said. "Hell, give me a battalion of men like him and we'll roll over anybody, anywhere, in no time at all."

"We're working on it, Mr. President." Godfrey smiled as he looked at him. "Still worried about Lassiter?"

Hutchcraft shook his head and smiled back. "Not anymore."

CHAPTER SIXTEEN

"What exactly are we looking for again?" Valdez asked Bolan as they scanned the desert terrain through the open door of the helicopter. His voice sounded distorted and mechanical due to the radios in their helmets.

"Anything out of the ordinary," Bolan said. "Someplace they could hide a shipment of arms where it wouldn't be conspicuous."

Valdez shook his head. "I guess that would depend on how big, huh?"

Bolan considered how much to tell him. The sergeant knew just about everything, except for a few details about the exact nature of the confrontation with the Wolves and the shootout in Washington. Cooperation was a two-way street, and Bolan had a gut feeling that Valdez was trustworthy.

Callahan, who had opted out of the helicopter surveillance in favor of trying to find an angle on getting a warrant to search GDF Industries, was another matter. Bolan didn't doubt she consulted her FBI manual before getting dressed every morning to make sure she was within Bureau parameters. But having her look into the recent business dealings between GDF and the DOD might yield something interesting, especially since Kurtzman had hacked into several secure governmental data banks and found out that a large supply of weapons originally ordered by the DOD from GDF for combat operations in Afghanistan had conveniently slipped into the ether as the timetable for the war wound down. If Anthony Godfrey, the prime mover of GDF, had made arrangements to sell the shipment to De la Noval and Chakhkiev, it would explain why it was so hard to trace. The government would frown on Stinger missiles and M-72 LAWs ending up in the hands of a Mexican drug cartel or Chakhkeiv's buddies in Libya and Syria. But the shipment had been small enough to disappear without too much notice, and could probably be stashed inside a trailer somewhere. Even an arroyo with a camouflaged tarp could provide adequate concealment.

"You see anything?" Bolan asked Grimaldi.

"Nothing but a lot of sand and cactuses," the pilot replied. "Hey, what's that over there?" He pointed to a large, cross-shaped building surrounded by a perimeter road.

"An old water park and shopping center," Valdez said, "that closed down about twelve years ago. It used to employ a bunch of people in the area."

"Let's take a look," Bolan said.

Grimaldi nodded and canted the helicopter downward.

As they flew over, the chopper dropped to about three hundred feet. They could see clearly how the roadway opened into a kidney-shaped park of empty pools, boarded-up concession booths and waterslides. Beyond that lay the large cross-shaped structure. Bolan saw that the southern portion had been partially destroyed, leaving a two-story wall of broken concrete sprouting rebar supports. Huge piles of smashed concrete blocks dotted the adjacent sea of weeds and overgrowth. The doors and windows in this part of the damaged brick building had plywood boards nailed over them. The other sections had exposed and rusted metal I-beams. Some areas had sheets of dirty house wrap covering the walls. Others showed no visible signs of damage.

The perimeter of the whole complex was lined by a cyclone fence. Many of the parking lots and connecting roads had been covered with blowing sand, and persistent weeds had broken through the asphalt in scattered places, lining the cracks with green, like a random mosaic.

"Looks in pretty bad shape," Grimaldi commented. "Want me to set her down?"

"Might as well," Bolan said. "It's worth taking a quick look."

Grimaldi zoomed low over the large expanse of flat roof and circled the place before setting down on the parking lot near the damaged section.

"I've been meaning to ask you," he said to Valdez. "You guys ever think of putting sand filters over the Jesus nuts on these things?"

"Jesus nuts?" Valdez said. "I don't even know what the hell that is."

"If you fly in a chopper, that's something you need to find out about," Grimaldi said. "Suffice it to say it secures your main rotor. If your Jesus nut goes bad, you can be assured of everything else going to hell in a handbasket. With a bird this old, you should make certain the gears aren't picking up a whole lot of sand in the rotors."

"I don't fly in them," Valdez said. "In fact, I don't like to get any higher than two stories, usually."

"In that case," Bolan stated, "I'll check out the roof if we have time. You guys hit that section over there, and the perimeter fence."

"The fence? Way over there?" Grimaldi raised his

hands to his eyes, mimicking a pair of binoculars. "Looks fine from here."

"Check it out, anyway," Bolan instructed. "The gate appeared to be chained, but see if it shows any signs of being opened recently."

"Why do I always get the plum assignments?" Grimaldi groaned. "It's got to be at least a hundred degrees out, and that damn gate's probably a quarter mile away. Plus it's uphill."

"I'll take a look," Valdez offered. "I'm used to walking in the desert."

Bolan glanced at his watch. It was closing in on 5:00 p.m. He also wanted to do a fly-over of the GDF compound. "Let's just give it quick check," Bolan said, as the men exited the helicopter, "unless we find something suspicious or out of the ordinary."

He turned to Grimaldi. "Do we have enough fuel for that other fly-over?"

"Just barely," the pilot said.

"We can check the roof that way." Bolan started jogging toward the incline leading toward the gate. "I'll take the gate. You two nose around the mall perimeter. Meet me back here in fifteen."

FROM HIS VANTAGE point on the roof near the broken sky-light, Lassiter watched the three men who'd gotten out of the helicopter go in different directions. From their mannerisms and gaits, they didn't look especially purposeful or determined, except for the big guy who was jogging toward the front gate. Lassiter was glad he'd continued to lock it after he entered, even though it was a pain in the ass. The other two were moving toward the broken-out section, which led to the corridor into the main mall, where he'd secreted the truck. Luckily, he'd taken the time to obscure the tire tracks, and it was dark in there, but there was a slight chance they'd see it if they could find their way inside.

Lassiter considered his options as he looked through the reticule of the Barrett sniper rifle. The helicopter had Pima County Sheriff Department markings on the side. A police chopper. That meant it was probably outfitted with radar and infrared imaging, but no weapons. He'd been inside when he'd heard their initial fly-over, so he was probably safe if they'd done any thermal scanning.

But why the hell were they here?

He checked the big guy's progress. Something was familiar about him. The way he moved…easy and smooth. No wasted motion. And he was jogging, even in the late afternoon Arizona desert heat…not the usual moves of a run-of-the-mill copper. No, this guy was something more.

From the Agency, maybe?

But they wouldn't be mixed up with the sheriff's department. No way. They weren't even authorized to operate within the borders of the United States. Officially, that was. But the helicopter made this look official.

The big guy was heading toward the front gate. He wouldn't find squat there. Lassiter checked on the other two. One of them, a Hispanic, was heading straight for the partially demolished corridor opening. He was bound to find that the plywood barrier had been recently pried off the door and put back in place, and behind it was the Peterbilt tractor. Once they found that, they'd keep looking until they found the trailer to go with it.

Lassiter weighed the option, as unpleasant as it was, of taking all three of them. He didn't like the thought of killing cops, but he couldn't risk being found out. Not as close as he was to ending this thing and getting Ellen her new start. But killing three good guys wasn't really an option, either. He still felt bad about having had a part in the death of that guy Avelia. Plus, if they disappeared, failed to report back after maybe radioing that they were checking out the old amusement park, someone would notice. The place would be crawling with police in no time, and his plan was already in motion.

Better all around to practice a bit of cover and concealment, he thought.

Lassiter picked up the Barrett and ran over to the other side of the roof. There was a four-foot wall around the edge, and he crouched as he drew close. He got within six inches or so of the broken edge of the roof and peeked down. The Hispanic guy was still pushing his way through the weeds toward the far plywood barrier. Lassiter figured the height of the structure would provide him with enough obscurity, so long as the guy below didn't look up.

He heard a scraping noise below him. The Hispanic guy was pulling on the plywood, feeling to see if it gave a little. It didn't. He stopped and put his hand on a pistol in the holster on his belt, and stood there, arms akimbo. Lassiter saw that the weapon was a Glock. A huge, pie-plate-shaped badge was affixed next to the holster, indicating that the man was law enforcement. Otherwise, he was in plain clothes: khaki cargo pants and a light gray polo shirt. Pima County was emblazoned on the shirt pocket.

He moved cautiously to the next boarded up section—the one Lassiter had taken apart to drive the tractor through. If the guy saw signs of recent tampering, it could spell trouble. He reached out to grab the edge of the board, and almost lost his balance and slipped. Then he swore and looked down at his shoe.

"I hope you didn't step in anything you can't wipe off," the second man said. He was standing at the top of the slight incline, looking down at the cop. This guy didn't wear a badge.

"Very funny," the cop said. He gave the edge of the board a little wiggle. It held.

His cell phone rang and he answered it.

Lassiter strained to hear the conversation, but couldn't make much out.

"Okay, we're on our way now, the cop said, then told the other guy, "Call Cooper and tell him that Callahan needs us back at HQ ASAP. That warrant she was working on came through."

The other guy took his cell phone and punched in a number. Lassiter curled back out of sight, but managed to hear, "Meet you at the copter."

Warrant? Were they getting a warrant for this place? But why would they come nosing around here then? Plus, if they had a warrant, why would they leave? They'd just keep searching with more vigor. No, it had to be someplace else. But they were getting ready to fly out, and if they saw him lying on the roof they'd certainly stop and investigate, even if they were bound for their base. Time to go back inside.

Over the rim of uneven concrete he could see the cops strolling with careless abandon now, exchanging insipid conversation.

Almost home free, Lassiter thought.

Then he felt it: a trickle of weakness working its way, slowly radiating from his gut. He did his best to control it, but the wave of pain continued, dancing through each section of his abdomen and down into his legs. He felt like curling up and holding his gut until the pain subsided.

If it subsided.

He took a couple shallow breaths and assessed the distance: about five hundred feet.

More pain. Sharper this time. His legs wouldn't work.

Five hundred feet... The way he felt he'd be lucky to crawl a couple yards.

Deep breaths, he thought. Respiration. He dug in his pants pocket for one of the syrettes that Ellen had given him. His fingers found it, and he tore off the plastic cover on the front end, placed the syrette against his thigh and pressed the button. The long needle pierced his skin and went deep into his leg muscle.

It felt like ice going into his veins.

Below, he heard the swishing sound of the rotors warming up. He glanced back at the five hundred feet to the door.

Let's hope this works, he thought. Sooner rather than later.

BOLAN SURVEYED THE AREA as the helicopter lifted off, the decrepit mall and water park fading from sight. There was something about this place that bothered him, but he couldn't figure out just what it was. He reached between the seats and grabbed a tan rag and wiped some oil off his fingers.

"You need a moist towelette or something?" Valdez asked with a grin. "Has our less than pristine landscape offended your sensibilities?"

"There were some spots of fresh oil up by the front gate," Bolan said.

Valdez shrugged. "Maybe somebody broke down."

"It was on both sides of the gate," Bolan told him. He pointed out the door. "See anything interesting down there?"

"Not much," the sergeant said. "Some trampled-down weeds, but that could be from periodic security checks. Same with the oil spots. I doubt anybody's been in there for years."

"What's that place called again?"

"Wally's Waterworld," Valdez said.

Bolan nodded and leaned back, thinking about the news that Callahan was successful on getting a search warrant. He took one more fleeting glance at the now desiccated and abandoned water world, and tried to figure out what was bothering him. Maybe it was just the incongruity of the situation: leaving a once-popular attraction in the desert abandoned, in a state of slow-motion decay. Maybe it was the traces of engine oil. But it all added up to something else. Unfinished business. Like his own unfinished business: finding the guys who had set up and ordered the execution of Chris Avelia. They were still out there and unpunished.

But that's going to change really soon, Bolan thought.

CHAPTER SEVENTEEN

Campbell watched as the liquid flowed from the IV bag into the plastic tube. John lay on the tiled floor with a rolled up blanket under his head. His color was looking better than when she'd arrived. He smiled at her.

"Good thing you made me get you those extra keys," he said.

She smiled back, her mind still racing as she considered all the available treatment options. The bouts of sudden weakness were coming with more frequency now, with a shorter time lapse between each one. She had copious notes on the times and dosages she'd administered, but she had yet to put them all together. The past several days had been a whirlwind, and she needed time to assess things, compile her research. What she really needed to do was sit down and analyze all the data she had, along with anything from Dr. Lawrence's special files, and get John to somewhere safe, like the Mayo Clinic.

Somewhere sterile and safe, she thought as she looked around the dusty office. Anything would be better than this. Perhaps it would be a good time to broach the subject.

"How are you feeling now?" she asked.

"Almost back to normal," he said, glancing down at the needle in his vein. "As I said before, just like a junkie."

"You're no junkie," she said. "But we do need to

get you someplace to begin a more aggressive treatment regimen."

"Aggression is my middle name."

She forced another smile. "John, I'm serious. We need to get out of here."

"Here, meaning the mall? I thought you liked the place."

Campbell compressed her lips to keep from snapping at his attempt at humor. She wondered if this was how general practitioners felt dealing with ill patients who wouldn't listen.

"You know what I'm talking about," she said. "If we could go check into somewhere good, like maybe the Mayo Clinic up in Minnesota, we might be able to—"

"To what?" His face still had the same amused expression. "Give me a few more months of wasting away on clean bedsheets?"

She closed her eyes. It wasn't that he hadn't been listening. He'd listened too well. He already had come to terms with his grave situation. The best she could do now was ride it out with him, and hope for the best.

But was the best yet to come? Like in the song?

She adjusted the IV flow and looked at her watch. It was almost six-thirty. She'd left the lab in a rush after receiving his text earlier, saying that he was in trouble. Hopefully, Dr. Lawrence had bought her story about having to get to her dry cleaning before the shop closed at seven. It was the only excuse she could come up with after he saw her leaving in such a huff. But she'd forgotten to take the medications she'd gotten from the pharmacy. She'd hidden them in her desk. If they searched her office they'd find them for sure, and that might be a little hard to explain. Would they go through her desk drawers? She couldn't imagine Dr. Lawrence doing that, although he had seemed a little strange lately. More brooding, less communicative. Of course, it could be due to the trouble with Trang. Especially with those VIPs present to see it.

"What are you thinking about?" John asked.

"Nothing." She saw this wasn't going to satisfy him, and added, "I have to go back to the lab to get more meds."

"Do you have to? I don't think that's such a good idea." He sighed. "You probably shouldn't even have come here."

"That wasn't an option," she said. "And if you're that worried about it, I'll wait, okay? I just wish we could take off and leave all this behind us."

Share what good time we still have, she added mentally.

It was almost as if he heard her. A faint smile brushed over his lips. She felt the tears begin to well up in her eyes, and she turned away.

Don't let him see you like this, she thought. Change the subject. Fast.

She walked to the door and looked through the film of dust covering the glass portion.

"Do you want me to go back and lock the gate and the doors?" she asked.

"You left them open?"

"I wanted to get here as fast as I could." She wiped her eyes as surreptitiously as she could, and turned back toward him. He was still smiling.

"It'll keep," he said.

She couldn't help but smile, too. He was such a special person...with such a special place in her heart. "I left the new supply of meds in my desk. That's why I need to go back there."

"Won't it look suspicious if you return during non-working hours?"

She went over and stood next to him, feeling almost back in control of herself now. "I doubt they'll notice. Dr. Lawrence will be busy. They had some trouble with Trang this afternoon. Dr. Lawrence will probably be working late himself, going over test results. I can say I wanted to check back in on him."

"What kind of trouble with Trang?"

She debated how much to tell, but then again, there wasn't much John didn't already know. He'd been through it all himself.

"He began beating up some of his trainers."

"So? Isn't that what he's supposed to do?"

"Not like that," she said. "He almost killed a couple of people. One of Dr. Lawrence's assistants is in the hospital. He may not survive. Trang was so completely out of control. Dr. Lawrence said he thought it was a synergistic effect of—" She stopped. This was definitely something John didn't need to hear. "The whole thing turned into a complete embarrassment. It was scary. Mr. Godfrey was showing that guy who's running for president around, and they saw it."

"President? What guy?"

She thought for a moment. "What's his name? Hutch-something?"

"Hutchcraft?"

"That's it."

John was silent for a few moments and looked very contemplative. She wondered what he was thinking.

"You got those safety deposit box keys in a safe place?" he asked.

"They're in my purse. Why?"

"Let's plan on leaving this town tomorrow night." He smiled up at her. "How does that sound?"

"Wonderful," she said.

If it's really true, she thought.

GDF Industries Compound

GODFREY WAS GROWING impatient listening to the Russian bastard's rant on the phone. It was bad enough when the prick was in New York or D.C., but having him here in Tucson was almost unbearable.

"Dimitri, my friend," Godfrey said, after the other man had stopped his current bout of threats. It was like handling a primed and loaded antique flintlock—the slightest slip and the damn thing would go off. "I told you we're in the process of tracking down your shipment as we speak." He tried to keep his voice even, his tone cordial, even though the whole series of screwups was starting to really annoy him. To add to his stress, Hutchcraft sat across from him in one of the padded easy chairs, sipping bourbon and looking as worried as a turkey the day before Thanksgiving.

"I have heard this before," the Russian said. "Especially, it doesn't not ring true now that I have already made the payment to your offshore accounts. Need I remind you, my ship is en route from Cuba to the port in Mexico?"

"Everything will be there on time." Godfrey took a deep breath. "I assume you have arranged your own escort?"

"I have," Chakhkiev said. "After my recent experience, I have called in a squad of men, all ex-Spetsnaz."

Spetsnaz was the name of Russian special forces. And these guys were, no doubt, also under the current employ of the Russian *Mafiya,* which meant they could present a tough adversary if push came to shove. But hopefully, it wouldn't.

Artie Fellows walked into the office and held up his hand.

Godfrey acknowledged him with a nod and said into the phone, "Listen, everything is under control. I've just got some new information I have to go over. I'll call you back."

"New information," Chakhkiev said. "It had better be good."

He terminated the call.

Godfrey set the cell phone on the desk and closed his eyes. "Tell me you have something worthwhile to say."

"I think we might have figured out where he's hiding the stuff," Fellows said.

That perked Godfrey up. "Oh? Where?"

The security chief stopped in front of the desk. Hutchcraft set his drink on a small, circular table next to his chair and leaned forward.

"Needless to say, she didn't go to her dry cleaning place," Fellows said. "The GPS tracker we placed on her car traced her way out of town to this old, abandoned water park. It used to be called Wally's Waterworld."

"I went there years ago," Hutchcraft said. "It's been closed up for at least a decade."

Godfrey silenced him with an angry look. "A water park? That sounds too much out in the open."

"It was combined with a shopping center," Fellows said. "There are lots of old, partially demolished buildings to hide in."

"Big enough to hide a truck and trailer?" Godfrey asked.

"Plenty big enough."

Godfrey considered that for several seconds, and then said, "Are we sure Lassiter's there now?"

"I think it's a fairly safe assumption," Fellows replied.

"I don't want 'fairly safe,'" Godfrey said, his voice rising a few decibels. "Is she still there?"

The security chief shook his head. "She's on the freeway, heading in this direction now."

"There's a chance he could be with her then," Godfrey said. "Track and intercept her. If Lassiter's with her, I want them both placed under strict observation until we can get a team in place to deal with him."

"I thought you said he was sick?" Hutchcraft said.

Without telling him that what he'd just said was classified, above Fellows's pay grade, Godfrey hoped his stare was enough to communicate to the senator that he'd made a faux pas.

"Sick or well," Godfrey said, "he's still a force to be reckoned with. Get a team together to hit that water park."

"Knowing Lassiter," Fellows stated, "he's probably got the place rigged. It won't be easy. And if he's ensconced in there…"

"Would a squad of ex-Spetsnaz soldiers be a good augmentation?" Godfrey asked.

Fellows raised his eyebrows. "Yeah, sure."

"All right," Godfrey said. "First things first. Find out if he's with the woman. If he is, observe and contain them until you have backup. If he's not, grab her and bring her here. And in the meantime, assemble a squad of our best men, along with Dimitri's, to hit that water park tonight. Do it fast and quick, and as surreptitiously as possible."

"I assume then you mean with the helicopters?" Fellow said. "Our own this time, and not those pieces of crap from Rigello's."

"Of course," Godfrey replied. "It'll be just like a nighttime version of *Apocalypse Now*. Only a lot quieter and without all the music and the explosions." He smiled at the thought.

Things were finally coming to a head.

"A RAID ON the Wolves' clubhouse?" Bolan said. "I was hoping for one on the GDF Industries compound."

"One step at a time," Callahan said. "We got the Avelia case reopened on the basis of the DNA evidence on Clay Stafford's weapon. Now we have the authority to search their clubhouse for more possible evidence. And if, during the course of this search, we happen to find something to connect them with GDF…" She paused and smiled. "I told you the Bureau operates within certain parameters."

"I remember you saying that."

"Parameters, shrameters," Grimaldi said. "We'll find something to make it work. When are we hitting them?"

"What do you mean, 'we'?" Valdez said. "This is a joint federal and municipal operation."

Grimaldi gave him a sideways glance. "Meaning what?"

"Meaning the Pima County SWAT team is going to serve the warrant." He paused and looked toward Callahan. "Under the auspices of the FBI, of course."

"You two are more than welcome to observe," Callahan added.

"Observe?" Grimaldi repeated.

"Yeah. Those Wolves can be pretty tough customers," Valdez added.

Grimaldi's face reddened. "Who do you think—"

Bolan placed a hand on his friend's shoulder, afraid he'd say more than he should in his moment of hubris.

"That sounds fine. We'll be glad to assist in any way possible."

Valdez was still staring at Grimaldi with a sly smile. "You got something more you want to tell me? Like if you'd had any previous mix-ups with the Wolves?"

Grimaldi returned the sly smile with one of his own. "I could tell you a lot of things, but I won't."

"What time is the raid?" Bolan asked.

Valdez glanced at his watch. "We're planning on moving in at midnight. The team's going through some dry run rehearsals now. We like to go in prepared."

"The best laid plans of mice and men," Grimaldi said. "We'll be close by in case you need any professional help."

Valdez glared at him.

"We've got all the professionals we need," Callahan stated reproachfully. "And we know all about your methods."

"You know," Grimaldi said, turning to Bolan, "I think she likes me. She *really* likes me."

IT WAS CLOSE to eight by the time Campbell finished her packing and lugged the suitcase to her car. She'd been overjoyed when John suggested that they leave the following day. The thought of getting him away from this big mess, the stress and danger of his quest for vengeance, relieved her. If she could convince him to go up to the Mayo Clinic, then maybe she could work on finding a cure, or at least figure out a way to bring the necrosis under control. Even a period of remission would give them a little more time together. It would be a chance, perhaps, for him to get well. A long shot, sure, but a chance. If they could really leave…

She had only one more stop to make.

After leaving her place, she noticed a pair of head-lights from some kind of pickup truck or big SUV in her rearview mirror. They'd been behind her now for a while. She sped up a bit and changed lanes. The head-lights receded into the distance.

It had to have been nothing, she told herself. Just some of John's paranoid thinking affecting her. Not that it was all baseless. They were in a mess, that was for sure, with some really dangerous people. John's plan to exact vengeance had been a terrible idea, but she understood. It was his way. The way he operated. She was so glad he seemed to be abandoning the plan now. Getting away, finding a treatment to beat the necro-sis—that would be the ultimate revenge.

Living well is the best revenge, she thought. Or should that be just living?

Campbell glanced in her rearview mirror again. The headlights were still way in the distance. Checking her speedometer, she saw she was doing eighty, and eased up on the pedal. No wonder the other car didn't keep up. Campbell decided to violate another traffic law as she swooped over toward the exit without signaling. The GDF facility was only a few minutes away. If she could get in and out, grab the supply of meds and equip-ment she needed for their getaway, enough drugs to last until they could get to Minnesota, they'd be home free.

Almost there, she thought. Almost there.

GODFREY WAITED AS Fellows took the report on the cell phone from his operative following Ellen Campbell. He flipped the phone off and smiled.

"Looks like she's on the way here," the security chief said.

"Excellent," Godfrey replied. "It saves us the trou-

ble of grabbing her where somebody might see it. Call
the gate guard and make sure he lets her in without
spooking her."

Fellows nodded and made the call. Godfrey turned
back to the small table where Hutchcraft and Chakhkiev sat. The two men held their drinks, bourbon and
water for Hutchcraft, vodka on the rocks for the Russian. Chakhkiev had kept one of his ex-Spetsnaz goons
with him as a "personal assistant." His other twelve men
were with Fellows's team of security guards, preparing
for their midnight excursion to the water park. Hopefully, the group would be able to take out Lassiter and
recover the shipment. Then everybody would be happy.
Godfrey had thought about sending Trang along, just
in case, but decided that was one ace he'd keep up his
sleeve. If, for some reason, Fellows failed to get Lassiter, they'd still have the girl.

Godfrey's own whiskey and soda was untouched.
He'd mixed it only to be sociable and appear relaxed to
the other two men, but he never drank during an ongoing operation. There'd be time enough for booze later,
when this last little problem was rectified. He smiled
at his guests and reached for the remote for the large,
flat-screen television mounted on the wall.

"Our pigeon has arrived," he said, flipping on the
TV and scrolling through a series of boxes showing different camera views. He stopped on one that held the
picture of a slice of road and some high, white curbs.
"We can watch it all on closed circuit."

After a few seconds Fellows, who was still on his
cell phone, looked over and said, "She should be pulling up anytime."

As if on cue, a silver-colored car swung into the
picture and stopped. The camera lens gave a close-up

view of the driver's window, and Godfrey watched as Campbell lowered the window and extended her hand with her ID card. He activated the audio feed and heard her saying, "Yes, I forgot something in my office." She flashed a smile at the gate guard.

"She is a very beautiful woman," Chakhkiev said. "Are you going to terminate her?"

"When she's outlived her usefulness," Godfrey said. "Why?"

The Russian shrugged. "A woman with her looks could bring good money in certain circles. Of course, this would depend on how amenable she is in certain situations." He grinned, showing a set of perfectly capped teeth.

"Okay, Dr. Campbell," the gate guard said as he handed her back her ID. "Have a good night."

"Thank you," she said.

Godfrey switched the camera view to a long shot that showed the car moving through the front gate and toward the laboratory building. "We're about to find out about her amenity," he said, turning to Fellows. "Go get her. Bring her here."

The chief of security nodded and headed for the door.

CHAPTER EIGHTEEN

Lassiter flattened out in the field adjacent to the Aryan Wolves clubhouse and waited in the darkness. About a hundred yards away the house was lit up and full of screaming morons. About fifteen Harleys were parked haphazardly along the side of the house in three rows. Lassiter had a pair of M953 night-vision binoculars on his tactical helmet and flipped them down so he could get a closer view of the drunken movements of the motorcycle gang members prancing around inside their house. A couple strippers, looking more like well-used biker old ladies, danced to the loud beat of rock music.

The party's about to get a little hotter, guys, he thought as he removed the binoculars and replaced them with a set of night-vision goggles, which he flipped up onto his helmet. He'd need them for phase two of his plan. Lassiter checked the time: 2352. He slipped the cotter pin out of the first M-72 LAW. The maximum effective range was approximately 200 meters, and he was a lot closer than that. He had only a short hundred-yard run to his own parked Harley, so getting out of here, after creating the appropriate confusion, would present no problems. The metal covering on the front part of the launch tube fell away and the rear cover dropped down on its hinge. He pulled the rear section back, extending the tube to its ready length. The front and rear sights popped up, and he pulled out the arming handle.

Might as well hit them where it'll hurt the most, he thought as he looked at the three rows of Harleys. Taking out their choppers would not only break their hearts, but it would effectively eliminate any means of pursuit, should he be somehow discovered. He looked again at the ongoing festivities and didn't think hot pursuit would be too much of a factor.

Lassiter got the other two LAWs ready to fire, then picked up his cell phone. He had to make sure the rest of his plan would unfold as he wanted. He had to make two calls. Lassiter selected the first number, the one Jesús De la Noval had given him, and pressed the button. It rang three times before a masculine voice said, "*Bueno.*"

"You got my million dollars U.S.?" Lassiter asked.

The other man gave a harsh-sounding laugh. "*Sí, amigo, sí.* You got my weapons?"

"I do. Where are you?"

"Close, my friend. Very close."

"Close enough to see the Aryan Wolves clubhouse?"

Another laugh. "Let's just say I have somebody watching now."

"Good," Lassiter said. "He's going to have quite a show in a few minutes. Afterward, I'll call you and tell you where to meet me."

"*Sí,* but why you not tell me now?"

Lassiter considered that. He knew that De la Noval planned a double-cross, that he no doubt had already crossed the border and had his small army with him, so why not give them a heads-up as to where to go, besides straight to hell, that was? Lassiter thought for a moment more, and then said, "You ever heard of a place called Wally's Waterworld?"

Silence. Obviously De la Noval was conferring with someone. He finally said, "I think I can find it."

"Meet me there in thirty minutes," Lassiter said, doing the mental calculations. He figured it would take him no more than fifteen to get from here to there. And if it looked as if De la Noval beat him there, he could always come in the back way.

"Okay," the drug lord replied. "I will be waiting."

"*Hasta luego*," Lassiter said, and clicked off. He then scrolled to the message section of the phone and clicked on the Messages Waiting to Be Sent section. There was only one in the folder. He clicked on it.

Hey, GOD, want your stuff back? Willing to deal. Bring one million dollars to Wally's Waterworld at 0030. Lassiter

Hopefully, with a little luck, he could sit back and watch as De la Noval's group took on Godfrey's goon squad, then he'd set off the charges to take care of any survivors. He'd then head over to the GDF compound to make his final call on Hutchcraft and Godfrey. If they were still there, that was. Hell, where else would the two of them be but hiding in what they thought was the safest place in town?

But would Godfrey see the text right away? The timing didn't have to be exact, but he needed both of them to get there at about the same time. Perhaps confirming that would be best. He clicked back to the last text he'd received from Godfrey, scrolled his options and clicked on Call Back.

"Hello?" It was Godfrey's voice. Lassiter was sure of it.

"Hey, Godfrey. How are you?"

"I'm glad you called me, son. We need to talk. How are you?"

"Cut the shit and listen," Lassiter said. "I've got something you want, and I'm willing to deal. One million cash."

"That's quite a sum. It might take me some time to—"

"I told you to cut the bullshit. You're not the only game in town. Now have one of your bird dogs bring the money to the old Wally's Waterworld Park off Highway 19. Be there at 0030. No tricks. When I know he's there alone, I'll come for the money and give him the location of your shipment."

"And how do I know you'll hold up your end of the bargain?"

"I'll reactivate the GPS signal as soon as he gives me the money. You can verify it on the phone."

Godfrey cleared his throat, obviously wanting to stall and press for more information. Lassiter didn't know if he had the capabilities to trace the cell phone signal, but didn't want to risk it. He said, "That's 0030. Be there." He terminated the call and shut off his phone. He wished he had enough time to call Ellen and tell her to leave without him in the morning if he didn't phone her by six, but then she'd know that he'd planned to finish his quest this night. He hoped she'd believed his earlier acquiescence and his promise of only having to tie up a few loose ends to alert the authorities about the arms shipment.

Lassiter glanced at his watch again. Twenty-four hundred. Time for the party to get hot. Real hot. He raised the first LAW to his shoulder, glanced through the rear sight, lining up the first group of Harleys, and pressed the rubber trigger bar.

BOLAN WATCHED AS the darkened field lit up briefly as a stream of white-and-red fire streaked across the ground toward the Aryan Wolves' clubhouse. A second later the first line of parked Harley-Davidson motorcycles exploded in quick consecutive bursts, going toward the wall of the house. Callahan, who was sandwiched between Bolan and Grimaldi, gasped.

"What the hell was that?" Grimaldi asked. "Valdez's guys using a rocket launcher?"

"Looked more like an M-72," Bolan said, lifting his night-vision binoculars and surveying the field area.

"A LAW?" Grimaldi asked.

Another rocket shot across the field, striking the second group of Harleys. These, too, began exploding, joining the expanding fireball from the first.

Bolan lifted his radio to his mouth. "Valdez, are you okay down there?"

"What the hell's going on?" the sergeant asked. His voice sounded totally confused. "Are you guys responsible for that? Our team's down here, for Christ's sake."

"It's not us," Bolan said as a third rocket blasted its way across the area and slammed into the third line of choppers. He scanned the open field and saw a figure running back toward Devil's Fork Road. "There's our boy." He pointed, still following the runner's progress. The man reached a parked motorcycle and jumped on the seat. Seconds later it roared to life and began traveling down the road, blacked out.

Bolan lowered his glasses. He lifted his radio to his mouth and said, "Valdez, go ahead with the raid. We're on the rocket man now."

"Roger that," Valdez said.

"It looks like Lassiter," Bolan stated, slinging his MP-5 over his shoulder as he ran toward the parked Escalade. "Let's go."

"Oh, my God." Callahan was hustling to keep up with him and Grimaldi. "Do you think we need to call for backup?"

"Valdez can do that if he needs it," Bolan said. "We can't afford to lose Lassiter."

He opened the driver's door, jumped in behind the wheel and twisted the key in the ignition.

Grimaldi pulled open the front passenger door, yelling, "I got shotgun." He tossed his MP-5 on the seat, started to get in and stopped. He turned slightly to pull open the right rear door for Callahan as she reached the SUV.

She jumped in the back, saying, "I've got it, I've got it."

Grimaldi slammed the door after her and hopped in as Bolan jammed the vehicle into gear and took off, making a U-turn.

"I'm perfectly capable of opening a car door by myself," Callahan said.

"Just because we're in an emergency situation," Grimaldi said, glancing over his shoulder, "doesn't mean I stop being a gentleman."

She frowned and made an irritated tsking sound.

"See? I told you she likes me," Grimaldi said, buckling the seat belt and turning his head toward Callahan. "We can talk about our dinner date later. Right now you might want to buckle up real good."

"Worry about your social life later," Bolan said as he twisted the wheel, sending the big SUV skidding back onto the road, and then accelerated hard. "Now be a real gent and see if you can track our buddy on that fleeing Harley. Looks like we're going to have a hard time keeping up."

"*No problemo*," Grimaldi said, bringing up his

USNV-18 night-vision monocular. "The night belongs to us."

"Let's hope so," Bolan said, seeing the red bulb of a brake light flash momentarily way up ahead as the Harley swerved toward the freeway.

As soon as Fellows had pushed Campbell through the door, Godfrey was on his feet. He stared down at her with as much neutrality as he could muster. She had worked for him, for his corporation, and she had betrayed him. It would be slow and painful for her, that much he knew, but now he had to make sure that the major threat, Lassiter, was dealt with properly.

Besides, he thought, I might as well get a little personal enjoyment out of it.

He looked up at Fellows.

"Send Lawrence and Trang in here," Godfrey said. "And then get your contingent and be ready to proceed. He called for a meeting."

"Oh? Where?"

"At that damn water park." Godfrey glanced at the woman to see her reaction. She looked stunned. Good. Let her know that he knew everything, or just about all of it. There were still a few details he had to confirm, and he'd do that shortly. "Put her in that chair first. And get me a pair of pliers."

Fellows shoved Campbell toward an office chair. She struggled as he pushed her onto the seat and then secured her wrists with plastic riot cuffs to the looping wooden armrests. He stood and turned to him. "That good enough?"

Godfrey glanced at her again. She looked rather cowed, as if she'd been beaten already. He nodded and told Fellows, "He thinks you're bringing him a million dollars."

The man smirked. "A million rounds, maybe." He strode toward the doorway.

Godfrey watched him go, then clasped his hands in front of him and rubbed them together. He turned to his captive.

"My dear Dr. Campbell," he said. "May I call you Ellen?"

She stared at him but didn't reply.

He took a deep breath. "Very well. I'm going to give you a few minutes to consider your options, which are quite limited. You can make things a lot easier for both of us, and answer the questions I ask you truthfully, which I will take into consideration." Pausing, he forced himself to smile at her. "Or you can choose not to cooperate, and things will get a bit unpleasant for you." He paused again to let that sink in. "Keep in mind that I used to work in the field for the Agency, once upon a time, and my friend Dimitri here—" he turned and extended his palm toward the grinning Russian "—used to work for the KGB. Between the two of us, we have ways of making you talk."

He smiled again, this time using his most malevolent expression as he stepped closer to Campbell, stopping directly in front of the chair. Godfrey leaned down, placing a palm on each arm-rest, positioning his face a few inches from hers. "We know your boyfriend, Lassiter, has the arms shipment at the water park. Where exactly is it, and does he have anyone else helping him?"

Campbell turned her face away, saying nothing.

Godfrey repeated his question.

She was still silent.

He stared at her, then took his hands from the armrests and tore open the front of her blouse. The buttons popped off and fell to the floor. Godfrey began to grope her, and she screamed. He slapped her face and was just appreciating the red mark on the paleness of her cheek when she brought her foot up and kicked him in the groin.

The sickening wave of nausea washed over him and he stumbled back, out of range of another kick, hunching slightly. It took him a few moments more to become cognizant of someone laughing. Chakhkiev, that son of a bitch.

Laughing. Amused by my pain, Godfrey thought. The Russian prick.

At least his hulking bodyguard was standing there with a stoic expression on his face.

He glanced at Hutchcraft to make sure he wasn't amused, too, but the would-be president just sat there stone-faced. Godfrey recovered enough to step back toward Campbell and give her a hard, backhanded slap across the face. It bloodied her nose.

"Please," Chakhkiev said, the mirth still affecting his tone, "don't destroy such a beautiful face just yet."

Godfrey swung his arm back and gave her another brutal slap, this time on the temple. Her head jerked to one side so hard that for a second he was afraid he'd broken her neck. But she blinked and looked up at him, the blood trailing from her nose and cascading down her chin, dripping onto the bare skin over her collarbone.

"Tony, is this necessary?" Hutchcraft asked.

Godfrey glared at him. What a weakling, he thought as his lips curled back in rage. "Maybe I was wrong backing you. Maybe you don't have what it takes to be the man with his finger on the button."

Hutchcraft appeared flustered. He licked his lips and sputtered, "I—I…"

"Shut up," Godfrey ordered.

Lawrence and Trang entered in the room, with Lawrence looking almost as disturbed as Hutchcraft.

I'm going to have to have a little talk with him, too, Godfrey thought. He glanced at Trang, whose face showed no emotion whatsoever. Fellows came in, looked at the woman's bloody face, raised an eyebrow and handed Godfrey a pair of gas pliers.

"Will these do, sir?" he asked.

"Fine, fine," Godfrey said, snatching them. "Now go get that son of a bitch." He walked in a small circle, still holding his crotch. "In the meantime, I'm going to show the rest of you the finer points of conducting an interrogation."

CHAPTER NINETEEN

Bolan flipped up the night-vision goggles and switched the headlights back on. The red dot that was the fleeing motorcycle's taillight was only a speck now, at least two miles ahead and fading fast.

"He's got to be pushing a hundred and twenty," Grimaldi said. "We'll never catch him in this crate."

"Maybe we won't have to," Bolan said, cracking his window. The rush of the wind sounded like thunder for a few seconds before he raised the glass back up. "I have an idea where he's headed."

"You do?" Grimaldi said. "Where's that?"

"Wally's Waterworld."

Grimaldi's head jerked. "That park we checked out yesterday?"

"The same," Bolan said. He was still going about eighty-five, but luckily, the traffic was nonexistent. Besides, the motorcycle barreling along ahead of them would no doubt catch the attention of any radar unit police out and about.

"How do you figure?" Grimaldi asked.

Bolan sniffed the air. "That motorcycle's burning oil. Smell it?"

Grimaldi worked his nose and then nodded.

"When I was checking out the park I saw spots of oil on the pavement right outside and inside the front gate," Bolan said. "I'd be willing to bet that chopper's got an oil leak."

"Well, damn, Sherlock," Grimaldi said with a grin, "can you tell us what the guy had for breakfast, too?" He glanced back at Callahan. "Isn't he something?"

"He certainly is," she said.

Grimaldi's mouth drew into a fine line as he compressed his lips. He shook his head and looked back at Bolan. "How come all the good-looking girls end up falling for you?"

Bolan grinned. He glanced in the rearview mirror and saw that Callahan was smiling, too. Then something else piqued his interest: a faint pocking sound. He slowed a bit and lowered the window again. The sound persisted, becoming more distinct.

"Hear that?" he asked.

Grimaldi nodded as he lowered his own window and canted his head.

"What is it?" Callahan asked from the backseat.

"Helicopter," Bolan said.

"Sounds like a Bell 412 EP," Grimaldi said.

"Are you sure?" Callahan asked. "You can tell the make from just hearing that?"

"Listen, I know the sound of a composite, four-blade rotor slicing air when I hear it." Grimaldi turned and scanned the dark sky, then peered through the night-vision monocular. "Can't see anything."

"Could it be Pima County SWAT?" Callahan asked.

Bolan shook his head. "Doubtful. I think they're all tied up back at the motorcycle clubhouse. See if you can get Valdez on the horn."

Grimaldi tried several transmissions to Valdez on the police radio. "No dice. He must be tied up on the raid or on the tactical channel."

"I'll try his cell," Callahan said.

Grimaldi shook his head. "But why would Valdez be

coming this way when they're probably still tied up on the raid?"

"Looks like we might get a chance to find out," Bolan said, stretching out his arm and pointing to a distant light visible in the sky through the right side of the windshield. "We seem to be heading in the same direction."

LASSITER GLANCED OVER his left shoulder but saw no one behind him. Whoever was trying to tail him in the SUV was history now. It still bothered him that they'd been on his six when he left Devil's Fork Road. Cops, maybe? Or could it have been De la Noval's boys? Either way, it was a moot question. He swung over to his right and hit the exit ramp, slowing so as not to go too fast around the curve. He managed a quick peek at his watch: 0012. He'd managed the trip back in less than his original estimate. Everything was still on track.

Lassiter slowed to forty as he hit the stretch of highway leading to Wally's Waterworld. It was only a quarter mile. As he approached the turnoff to the water park, he shut off the motorcycle headlight and flipped down the night-vision goggles, leaving the left one off to allow him to keep some of his depth perception. Everything changed to a clear, green view. He eased off the throttle a bit more to slow the percussive throbbing of the engine. His ears were still ringing from it.

Lassiter pulled parallel to the front gate, not bothering to get off his bike as he fished for the keys. He slid one into the padlock and it popped open. Instead of slipping through, he pushed both portions of the gate hard, watching them wheel back.

I might as well leave the front entrance open for them, he thought.

He punched the gear lever down into First, and just

as he started to ease up on the clutch he spotted something off to his right.

Movement.

Pretending not to notice, he angled the motorcycle down the central drive. He saw another flicker off to his left.

De la Noval's boys? But how in the hell could they have beaten him here?

Lassiter started to go straight down the main road, which would have taken him through the sections of smaller, sunken pools and by the waterslides, but at the last minute he gunned it and shot off to his right, feeling the peeling rip of the tires grabbing the asphalt. He felt rather than heard the first shot whiz by him. Then another. He revved it up in First and shifted to Second, doing an in-and-out movement with the clutch. The big Harley shot forward again, and the night-vision goggles allowed Lassiter to zigzag through the far right section of the old water park. He kept going straight, staying as low as he could as he shifted through the gears.

The sound of more rounds crackled behind him.

He tore along the perimeter road and onto the bumpy gravel drive that led into the partially demolished section of the old mall. Something lit up in front of him.

A muzzle-flash!

A split second later he felt the thrill of exaltation, knowing he'd been shot at again and they'd missed. He reached for the Glock 19 he had tucked into the left side of his belt. As he drove, he fired four quick rounds over the handlebars, hoping for a moment's diversion. Angling off the gravel surface, he swerved back onto the asphalt road and headed for the rear portion of the mall—the most dilapidated section. There'd be more cover there, and he'd left a stash of arms, and the detonators for the perimeter and interior explosive devices, under a large metal box that he'd disguised to look like part of an old air-conditioning unit. Plus he had a stack of LAWs and a Stinger missile launcher with three rockets just inside the plywood barrier around the side. If he could get to those, he'd have some real claws and teeth to fight back with. He felt the bump as the Harley jumped over a crumbling curb and onto a stretch of wild grass and weeds.

Almost there, he thought.

Lassiter burst into the tall weeds and drove through, getting back on the paved road that led to where his stash was located. Downshifting, he leaned around a curve and was still going close to forty when he hit the brakes and started his skid. The motorcycle slowed and he angled the handlebars to the right, controlling the motion. A curtain of sparks flashed upward as the metal frame of the Harley scraped the pavement. Lassiter felt a searing, burning pain in his left leg, but he ignored it and rode out the skid, coming to a stop close to the metallic dummy box.

Tossing the heavy bike off him as if it were a toy, he ran straight for the box, scanning the area. Several men rose in front of him. Lassiter put two rounds in each, watching them fall. He dropped to the ground and flattened himself next to the box.

More rounds pinged off the metal surface, some perforating it.

Rifle rounds, he thought, and wriggled deeper into the weeds and dirt. He lifted the Glock over the top of the box and fired off several rounds in the direction of his adversaries. The slide locked back on the pistol and Lassiter dropped it. Kicking over the metallic shell, he grabbed the M-4 he'd stashed there. He had the detonation devices in a black nylon gym bag, and he grabbed that as well before he made a dash for a large concrete block about two feet high. More rounds stippled the ground around him. Lassiter flipped the selector switch to automatic and crawled to the side of the block. Four men advanced toward him. He fired a burst and saw them twist and scream.

More rounds bounced off the concrete block. He fired another burst as he dashed for the corner of the building. This section had enough broken parts and exposed rebar that he might be able to climb to the roof and take the high ground.

Suddenly, he heard the sound of more shooting. A hell of a lot of rounds being expended, but from a distance. Twisting, he glanced back toward the water park area, which was down a gentle slope from his position, and saw a wave of men pouring from a dark van on the front access road. A big limo was behind the van, its front doors swung wide, with men firing pistols around them.

More players in the game, he thought. But who?

Two figures rose about twenty feet away, and Lassiter acquired a sight picture on the first one. The guy held a radio to his mouth and yelled something.

Lassiter didn't fire. Instead, he crept a few feet closer and heard the man speaking in Russian. The man next to him also had a radio, but said something in English.

What the hell? An international strike force?

"Captain Fellows," the guy speaking English said, "we've got a new contingent coming in the front gate, over. A van and a limo."

Captain Fellows… Artie Fellows, Godfrey's chief of security, always used that title and call sign. That meant Godfrey's guys had somehow gotten here first. So the newly arrived contingent in the van and limo was probably De la Noval and his crew. But how did Fellows get here so fast?

Never mind, Lassiter told himself. His plan of pitting the Mexicans against Fellows and his GDF Security force had come to fruition. All he had to do was to help things along a little. He glanced around and felt relatively isolated for the moment. Moving was another matter. He didn't want to rule out the use of night-vision by any of the GDF personnel Fellows might have designated to be snipers, but a new opportunity with De la Noval's arrival had presented itself.

Crawling to the edge of the building, Lassiter was able to look down at the firefight, which was happening about fifty yards away. He unzipped the nylon bag and sorted through his detonators, selecting the ones he'd rigged for the lower perimeter. Twisting the first switch, he watched as seven Claymore mines went off in sequence, each about half a second after the previous one, causing a reddish-yellow blur of explosions throughout the water park area. He turned and selected the detonators for the upper section of the mall parking lot, and twisted the switch again. A half dozen new explosions sounded behind him.

Welcome to the party, he thought as he started to get up.

He began to run, took three steps and then suddenly began to feel weak, the pain starting in his gut again and radiating outward. The heavy ballistic vest he wore under his shirt suddenly felt like a constricting corset.

No, he thought. It can't happen now. Not now.

He had the last auto-injector tucked inside his right boot, but as he started to reach for it something slammed into him and he toppled over, feeling a new, burning pain in his left shoulder. This pain, he knew, had to be from a bullet.

He lay in the weeds, concentrating on his breathing, and trying to reach the rifle or the bag of detonators. But his body wouldn't work. Everything seemed to be just outside his grasp. Several men approached.

The situation was double-timing to hell in a handbasket.

"Looks like a street party in downtown Baghdad," Grimaldi said as they watched the explosions from their vantage point at the rear fence. Bolan had taken a back road up behind the water park and they'd stumbled on the helicopter, which was guarded by a disinterested and lax guy wearing a black GDF Security uniform. Bolan had quickly subdued, gagged and secured the guard with numerous pairs of the heavy-duty riot cuffs they'd brought in anticipation of the search warrant raid. Callahan had insisted on advising their captive of his Miranda rights, "Just in case he subsequently had some forthcoming information."

"Fine, you do that," Bolan said, before he and Grimaldi moved through the hole in the fencing and flattened on the ground overlooking this side of Wally's Waterworld.

"She does everything exactly by the book," Grimaldi said. "I wonder if she ever deviates."

"I do occasionally," Callahan stated, crawling up beside them. "But not where you're concerned."

"Looks like the battle's about over," Bolan said, scanning the area through his night-vision goggles. He then pointed across the expanse of field toward the partially demolished section of buildings. "Check out that corner. They're holding someone prisoner."

Grimaldi peered through his own night-vision monocular. "Sure are, and I'd say it's our boy Lassiter, from the size of him."

"Let me see," Callahan said.

Grimaldi handed her the monocular, slipped a pair of M949 aviator goggles out of his pocket and fitted them over his head.

"If you had those all along," Callahan asked, "why didn't you give me this one earlier?"

"I was saving the batteries in these." Grimaldi grinned at Bolan. "Besides, you didn't ask."

"Stay here and guard the prisoner," Bolan said to Callahan. "We're going down for a closer look."

"Like hell. Bozo-boy here can stay and guard the prisoner. I don't take orders from you."

"Hey," Grimaldi said, "*Bozo-boy* doesn't have a killer figure like you got. If any of those dudes see someone like you walking up on them, they'll think that the playmate of the month's coming to pay them a visit."

Callahan pursed her lips but said nothing.

"Plus we don't want to leave our flank unguarded," Bolan said. He pointed to his radio. "We'll check it out first and get back to you."

LASSITER LAY FACEDOWN and spread-eagled on the ground, with one guy standing in front of him and the other on the side. That one was resting his heavy boot on the small of Lassiter's back. They both had rifles pointed toward his head. All that didn't bother him as much as the pain that was radiating through his body now, robbing him of his strength and ability to move.

If only it hadn't come now, he thought. If only I could've gotten to that damn syrette in my boot.

He knew if the weakness hadn't come he could have

taken all of them out. It appeared that the four who surrounded him now were the only ones left, if the absence of transmissions on the radio were any indication.

"Fellows to unit three, come in," Artie Fellows said into his radio. He was squatting a few feet away. "Fellows to unit three."

Silence.

"Fellows to unit four, come in."

Nothing.

The security chief snorted in disgust and lowered the radio. He straightened and walked over, stopping so his highly shined jump boots were only an inch or so from Lassiter's nose. He unsnapped a low-slung, tactical holster on his right thigh and withdrew a Beretta pistol.

"Well, well, well, Johnny boy," Fellows said. "Looks like you've managed to take out just about everybody else. Not bad."

Lassiter could hear the pop of a few distant rounds going off down below.

"That's the last of my men taking care of the Mexicans," Fellows said. "We've got a take-no-prisoners policy in effect tonight."

"That's good to know," Lassiter managed to say.

Fellows laughed. "Oh, that doesn't apply to you. Don't worry. You've still got to tell me where you stashed the weapons. And you will."

Lassiter took a breath and then managed to say, "Hey, fuck you."

Fellows flicked his boot so that the polished cap slammed into Lassiter's side. He waited a second, then did it again.

"Oh, you'll talk," Fellows said. "Believe me. If not for your own pitiful sake, to save you girlfriend, Ellen Campbell, some lumps."

Lassiter absorbed the pain of the blows and felt a shiver go up his spine. Ellen? Did they have her, or was this prick just bluffing? He knew they had figured out the connection between him and Ellen, but that didn't mean they were holding her. But Fellows seemed to read his mind.

"Yeah, we got her, all right," he said. "She came back to GDF earlier, saying she *forgot* something. I figured it was to get more drugs for you, Johnny boy. We'd tracked her to this location earlier with a GPS. Anyway, I grabbed her and turned her over to the boss." He paused before adding, "When I left, he was getting ready to use a pair of gas pliers on her."

"You touch her and I'll kill you," Lassiter shouted.

Fellows laughed again. His radio crackled and a voice said, "Unit two to Captain Fellows. We've checked them all, sir," the voice on the radio said, when he answered. "Nobody left alive except one man believed to be Señor De la Noval."

"Bring him up," Fellows said.

Lassiter knew this would buy him a few extra minutes. His mind raced. The interior charges were still set. If he could somehow lead them all into the loading bay, he might be able to set off the remaining Claymores and IEDs. He wouldn't mind taking himself out in the process, but what would that mean for Ellen? If they really had her.

"How do I know you've got Ellen?" he asked, twisting his head so he could look up at Fellows.

The other man gazed down at him. "Want me to tell you what she was wearing? What kind of car she was driving? Or how about I just mention that real nice light blue blouse she used to have on? With that sexy, flowery bra underneath."

The mention of the color of the blouse cinched it. The pricks had her, all right. He had to somehow get free. He couldn't let her die. He couldn't.

Four men with rifles marched up the slight incline pushing a man in a dark suit, his hands on his head, in front of them. They stopped about twelve feet from Fellows.

The man in the suit was Jesús De la Noval. Lassiter recognized him from the photos he'd seen. The drug lord had a smile on his face, his white teeth shining distinctly, surrounded by his black goatee and mustache.

"I don't know who you work for," he said, "or how much they pay you, but I will double it if you let me go."

"That's very tempting," Fellows said, motioning with his left hand for his men to step aside.

De la Noval's grin grew wider and he lowered his hands. "That is more like it. How much do you want to drive me to the border?"

Fellows smiled and then turned toward Lassiter. "How much was this man supposed to pay you?"

"A million," Lassiter said. Perhaps if Fellows thought he could make some extra money in a deal with De la Noval, it would buy some time.

"Find any dough in the vans?" Fellows asked.

"Nothing," one of the men said. The security chief shook his head. "Looks like Señor De la Noval was planning on ripping you off, Johnny boy."

"No, no," the Mexican said. "I have the money. I did not bring it with me here." He started to speak rapidly in Spanish, almost none of which Lassiter could understand, except for the few stray words he recognized as "money" and "payment."

"*Lo siento, pero no hablo,*" Fellows said, and raised the Beretta, pointing it directly at De la Noval's face.

"But if you weren't going to pay him, why would I think you'd pay me?"

A second later a flash accompanied by a cracking roar pierced the night, and De la Noval twisted to the ground like a limp dishrag. Lassiter could see the round hole in the center of the dead man's forehead, a trickle of blood dripping out of it, his dark eyes glazed over, the lids half-closed.

Fellows stepped over Lassiter and pressed the barrel of the pistol to the side of his face. It felt hot.

"Time for our conversation to start, Johnny boy," he said. "Tell me where the stuff is or I'll start taking you apart, piece by piece."

Not good, Lassiter thought. Not good for Ellen.

BOLAN FLIPPED DOWN the charging handle, arming his Heckler & Koch MP-5 submachine gun. Grimaldi did the same. They'd tied black handkerchiefs over the lower portions of their faces to make their covert advance toward the group less visible. As they approached through the weeds, eight gunmen appeared in flat, green translucence through the night-vision goggles. The men seemed to be totally focused on the two prisoners.

When the man who was apparently in charge shot one of the prisoners, Bolan knew it was time to act. He and Grimaldi communicated with gestures, Bolan pointing to himself and then at the four men on the left. Grimaldi nodded and pointed right. Each of them knew that combat wasn't always governed by Marquis of Queensbury Rules, and while neither of them shot to kill without justification, both knew that engaging a numerically superior and more heavily armed group required deft action. Bolan and Grimaldi wore Kevlar vests under their black BDUs, but their vests were only threat level threes. A round from an AK-47 or an M-4 would go right through them. The soldier didn't know what kind of body armor the eight men below wore, but he had to assume it was of the highest level quality, certainly capable of stopping the 9 mm rounds from his MP-5. That meant selective fire and head shots. Bolan tapped the ceramic plate on the front of his vest once to get Grimaldi's attention, then pointed to his weapon and then toward his head. The Stony Man pilot nodded. Bolan raised his MP-5 and fired a 3-round burst into each of the standing gunmen. Grimaldi did the same to those on the left. The man in the center, who was standing over the prone individual, whirled and began firing his handgun. The Executioner centered the front sight on the man's chest and fired. His target fell backward.

Bolan and Grimaldi felt comfortable enough to advance cautiously. When they reached the fallen men, they quickly checked to see if any were alive, and gathered their rifles and sidearms. The prisoner on the ground was writhing in pain. Grimaldi knelt to check him. Bolan stepped around and looked at the last man he'd shot. It was Artie Fellows, staring up at him with sightless eyes. Bolan saw something else: the weapon Fellows had been using was the Executioner's missing Beretta 93R. A hint of a smile ghosted over his lips as he picked it up.

"Well, what do you know?" Grimaldi said. "Don't tell me you got your baby back."

"Looks like it," Bolan said. He removed the Beretta 92F from his tactical holster and replaced it with the 93R. He stuck the 92F in the left side of his pistol belt.

"Just like King Arthur pulling Excalibur out of the stone," Grimaldi commented.

The prone man grunted. "Thanks for taking him out. I owe you one."

Bolan looked down at him. It was John Lassiter. "No, we're even."

Lassiter gritted his teeth in pain and looked up. "Huh?"

"I owed you one," Bolan said. "About five years ago in Colombia. Operation Cat's Cradle."

Lassiter closed his eyes and shuddered. "Operation Cat's…" He paused. "Oh yeah. I remember. Jesús's brother, Vincente, right?"

Bolan squatted by Lassiter and removed the man's tactical helmet to make him more comfortable. Then he took out his knife and cut away the man's shirt so he could check the wound. "You're hit. How bad?"

Lassiter shrugged. "A through-and-through. Bad enough to hurt like hell, but that's the least of my problems."

"We'll call an ambulance," Bolan said, motioning to Grimaldi, who started dialing his cell phone. "Where's the arms shipment?"

Lassiter said nothing for a solid ten seconds. Grimaldi finished giving their location and paused.

"Valdez says the troops are on the way now," he said. "Plus an ambulance for our buddy here."

"I don't want an ambulance," Lassiter said. "But I need something else."

Bolan rolled him over, used his Espada knife to slice off Lassiter's BDU blouse and checked the wound site. "Looks like more of a graze. The bullet must have hit on an angle," he said, taking out a ballistic bandage. He stuck it in place. "Try not to move."

"Listen to me," Lassiter said. "I need to get to the GDF Industries compound. Fast."

"And I need you to tell me where that arms shipment is," Bolan said.

He stood and turned to Grimaldi. "What's the ETA for Valdez and his team?"

Grimaldi spoke into the cell phone, listened and then said, "He's on the way. Should be here inside of twenty."

"That'll be too late, damn it," Lassiter said. "They're holding Dr. Ellen Campbell at the compound. They'll kill her to cover all this up. We've got to get her out of there."

"Who's Ellen Campbell?" Bolan asked.

"She's…she's a doctor involved with the GEM program," Lassiter said. "She found out what they were doing and decided to help me bring them down."

"The GEM program?"

Lassiter managed to curl into a sitting position, his right hand clutching his left shoulder. "Genetically Enhanced Male," he said. "I was the prototype. They'd shoot us full of special drugs and we'd be like super MVPs playing in the big leagues. Me and two other guys. They didn't make it through."

Rodriguez and Paris, Bolan thought, remembering the names from the slides Brognola had shown him. This was all starting to come together. "How did killing Greg Benedict in D.C. fit in?"

"He was my boss in black ops," Lassiter said. "For years. Then the prick sent a wet team to kill me. They missed, so I decided to hit him back."

"Who's holding Dr. Campbell prisoner?"

"Godfrey," Lassiter said. "He's the one behind all this. He's been peddling arms to the De la Noval cartel in exchange for money and drugs to get rich and finance his buddy Hutchcraft's run for president."

Bolan said nothing.

"There was an undercover federal agent that infiltrated De la Noval's group," Lassiter said. "He found out about Godfrey and was gonna spill the beans. Godfrey sent my team down there to grab him and bring him back here."

Bolan's mind flashed back to the empty tiger cage. "And you did?"

Lassiter grimaced and nodded. "Yeah, but that was before I knew the whole story. I didn't know who he was." He stopped and coughed. "I found out the stuff they gave me is killing me. Ellen was trying to help. We got…involved."

Everything fell into place for Bolan—the tip-off about their raid, the betrayal of Chris Avelia, the disappearing arms deal. "Tell Callahan we're en route back to her location."

Grimaldi spoke into his radio.

Bolan reached down and helped Lassiter to his feet. "Think you can make it back to that copter?"

"Don't worry," Lassiter said, grunting in pain as he moved. "I'll make it. But first, I got something we might want to take along."

CHAPTER TWENTY

Against his better judgment, Bolan agreed to let Callahan come along. His attempt to try to get her to remain at the "massive crime scene" at Wally's Waterworld met with strong resistance.

"Bullshit," she said. "I'm going with you. From what I overheard, this sounds like a kidnapping, which, may I remind you, is a federal offense."

"Hey, Callahan," Grimaldi chimed in as he prepped the helicopter for takeoff, "we're talking beaucoup danger. Plus you still have your prisoner to worry about."

Callahan marched to the trussed-up security guard and dragged him over to the cyclone fence. She bent, secured his feet together with another pair of riot cuffs, and then used a pair of metal handcuffs to secure him to the fence wire. "Call Valdez and tell him the prisoner will be waiting for him up here," she said, slipping the nylon sling of the MP-5 over her head and left arm so that it hung in front of her.

"Better tell him to bring an ordnance team, too," Lassiter said. "The trailer with the goodies is in the loading bay of the old Montgomery Ward store, and I've got the place rigged to blow. Claymores and IEDs. The rest of the detonators are in that nylon bag."

Bolan punched in the number on his cell phone and told Valdez. When he'd finished he looked at Lassiter and said, "Thanks for the info."

The wounded man nodded. "I don't want any more good guys getting hurt, if I can help it."

"Neither do I," Bolan said, holding his hands in front of his waist. "Put your wrists like this."

"What for?"

"Just do it," Bolan said, holding up a pair of the heavy-duty riot cuffs.

Lassiter shook his head and sighed. "Come on, I'm not going to try anything. We've got to rescue Ellen."

His face was still twisted with pain, but he managed a quick smile as he held out his arms. Bolan slipped the heavy plastic cuffs over both his hands and cinched them tight. The man's movements would be limited, but not incapacitated this way, but with the shoulder wound Bolan figured putting Lassiter's hand behind his back would cause more damage. Besides, the guy's main concern now wasn't escape, but the rescue mission. Bolan let him keep the ballistic vest on.

"Too bad you didn't feel that way in D.C.," the soldier said. "When you hit me with that flying kick that knocked me off my motorcycle."

"I kind of figured that was you." Lassiter grinned. "Sorry about that. I saw Jackie Chan do that in a movie once, and always wanted to try it."

"I'm more of a Bruce Lee guy myself." Bolan helped him into the chopper and pointed to the center seat in the passenger compartment. "Now sit."

Lassiter edged forward slowly, like an old man who was stiff and barely able to move. He fell onto the seat, his breath coming in short, quick gasps.

"You all right?" Bolan asked.

Lassiter nodded and pulled his legs in close to the seat, hunching forward. "We ready to go?"

"Almost," Grimaldi said, doing his last equipment run-through.

Bolan waited while Callahan got in and sat in back of Lassiter, then he loaded in the four LAWs and the Stinger missile launcher with the three rockets into the area behind the seats. Lassiter had said that the GDF compound had a well-trained security force and some of their backups were apparently Russian *Mafiya* goons. That might make the entry and assault a bit tricky. Bolan glanced at his watch: 1:15 a.m. Valdez should be pulling up to Wally's Waterworld shortly, and Bolan wanted to be gone before that. It was time to finish this one. He got into the copilot's seat and nodded to Grimaldi.

The helicopter's rotors started turning, faster and faster, and Bolan felt the familiar feeling of liftoff. He flipped down his night-vision goggles and did a final survey of Wally's World as they swooped upward and in a semicircle back in the direction of South Tucson. He glanced over at Grimaldi, who was grinning ear to ear as he did every time he got behind the controls of an aircraft, and then back at the solemn-looking Special Agent Callahan and the shaking, taciturn Lassiter.

It was time for the final chapter. It was time to end this one.

GODFREY LOOKED DOWN at Ellen Campbell and wondered how she was holding up so well, under the circumstances. She lay on the floor, holding her left arm and moaning, her face extremely pale. He wondered if she was going into shock. Hutchcraft looked pale as well, almost sick to his stomach.

Fine presidential material, Godfrey thought. All show and very little substance. Still, that could be dealt with.

Chakhkiev and his stoic bodyguard looked unimpressed. With all the brutality they'd probably witnessed and perpetrated, watching the interrogation of a female was nothing out of the ordinary for them. They'd probably done a lot worse.

Lawrence was a weak link, sitting at the other end of the room and not even looking this way. Trang, on the other hand, appeared fascinated by the amount of pain Campbell seemed able to endure. And as if he was regretting not causing some of it himself.

Maybe I'll have him take over, Godfrey thought. It'll be a good test for him. See how much of the sadist is in him.

Campbell moaned again, practically delirious now, and he decided to back off a bit. He'd probably gotten everything he was going to get from her, anyway.

Godfrey straightened and slipped the pliers into his pants pocket. His face felt sweaty, and he pulled out his handkerchief to pat himself dry as he glanced at his watch.

It was 1:24 a.m. Why the hell hadn't that idiot Fellows called yet? Surely, with all the help he had, he'd been able to take out one man. A walking dead man, at that. Campbell had admitted she'd gone there earlier to give him some medication. Godfrey had quickly switched the topic, not wanting Trang to hear about his predecessor's medical problems and perhaps put two and two together.

Maybe Fellows was having trouble locating the shipment, Godfrey thought. The woman had admitted it was at the park. He took out his cell phone and dialed the security chief's number again. It rang several times and then went to voice mail. Godfrey punched the button and compressed his lips, feeling the rage still burning inside him..

"Maybe Lassiter was too good for them," Hutchcraft said. "He took out that wet team before. Maybe he took Fellows out, too."

Christ, he's falling apart, Godfrey thought. Presidential material, my ass.

But he had to remain calm.

"Fellows is a pro," Godfrey said. "Plus he had Dimitri's ex-Spetsnaz men to help him."

"You cannot get better men than Spetsnaz," Chakhkiev said.

"Spetsnaz, Spetsnaz, Spetsnaz," Hutchcraft said. "Oh, bullshit."

Chakhkiev perked up and looked at him. "What did you say?"

"I said *bullshit*!" The senator's face was reddening.

"Shut up, both of you." Godfrey took a deep breath, walked over to the wet bar, and thought about breaking his no-drinking-during-an-operation rule and pouring himself one. Then he heard the faint, syncopated sound. Helicopter rotors? He cocked his head. Yes, that's what it was. He turned.

"Do you hear that?" he said. "It's the helicopter returning. Fellows is back." He took out his cell phone and punched in a number. "Light up the helipad. They're coming."

He put his cell phone back into his pocket and smiled broadly.

"LOOKS LIKE THEY'RE all set to welcome us home," Grimaldi said, pointing to the now illuminated helipad.

Bolan glanced at the massive facility stretching over

almost as much real estate as a General Motors, then turned back toward Lassiter.

"Where do you think they've got her?" he asked.

Lassiter raised his head. His face was covered with sweat and he looked like hell. "That white, three-story building over there," he said. "The lab's on the third floor. The command center's on the top floor. See those windows all lit up?"

Bolan noted the huge, glowing windows lining the top floor of the four-story brick building.

"That's it," Lassiter said. "Elevators are in the center, but I don't think you'll want to be taking those. Stairwells are at either end of the hallway."

The Executioner looked the building over. "Jack, any chance you could set this baby down on the roof? That way we'd only have to go down one floor."

Grimaldi shook his head. "Doesn't look like it. Too many big air-conditioning units and other clutter on top." He continued to scan the landing pad. "Looks like they've got a welcoming committee waiting for us, too."

Bolan checked out the helipad. At least a dozen men with rifles waited alongside an armored Hummer.

The soldier considered their options. This was an official GDF helicopter, and there was a chance Godfrey didn't know Fellows had been taken out. Maybe they could use that to their advantage to gain entry into the facility.

He turned toward Callahan. "Call Valdez back and give him a sitrep. Tell him to get us some backup over here pronto. We'll go in and find her."

"What's our game plan?" Grimaldi asked, keeping the helicopter hovering about a hundred feet over the helipad. "Those guys aren't exactly going to be handing us the keys to the city once they see who we really are."

"I've got my FBI credentials," Callahan said. "I can tell them we're duly authorized federal agents investigating the report of a crime."

Lassiter coughed and then laughed. "You'll be dead federal agents about two seconds after that. These guys don't play."

Callahan started to say something, but Bolan cut her off.

"Are there any female security guards at this place?" he asked.

Lassiter shook his head. "None that I've seen."

"All right, here's the plan," Bolan said. "Land it so this door is facing away from the welcoming party. Callahan, you stay in the chopper, out of sight, until I get outside with Lassiter. Once we're on the ground, exit on the other side and get out of the way."

"What are you going to do?" she asked.

"I'm going to use those LAWs," Bolan said. "Now hand them to me."

"But—"

He silenced her with a look that said, *"Don't argue. It's not open for discussion."*

She compressed her lips, nodded and handed him the three missiles.

"You can advise them of their rights afterward," Grimaldi said with a grin.

"I'll aim for the Hummer," Bolan said, slinging two of the LAWs over his left shoulder and pulling the cotter pin out of the third. The circular metal covers fell off the ends of the launch tube. Bolan extended it and the front and rear sights popped up.

"Jack, I'll be depending on you to take out anybody on this other side with your MP-5."

Grimaldi nodded. "I've got your six."

"Once I hit them with this rocket," Bolan continued, "we'll move across that expanse toward the entrance. I'm assuming it'll be locked due to restricted access?" He looked at Lassiter, who nodded.

"About halfway there I'll use my second LAW to blast it open, so give me a wide berth as you're running. Once we get inside, we'll have to work our way up the stairwells. You two go up the closest one," he said to Grimaldi and Callahan. "I'll go down the hallway and take the one at the opposite end. We'll keep in communication by our radios."

"What about me?" Lassiter asked. He still looked as weak as a kitten.

"Make your way over to whatever cover you can find and wait for us," Bolan said. "Backup's on the way. You up to a little escape and evasion?"

"More than that, if you let me," Lassiter said. His hands were still secured by the thick plastic cuffs and he slipped them over his knees, leaning forward.

"Hey, you gonna be sick or something?" Grimaldi asked, shaking his head. "What's he doing?" Callahan asked.

Bolan looked back at them just as Callahan yelled again. "Cooper, he's reaching for something inside his boot!"

Bolan's hand went for his Beretta and he pulled it out, pointing it at Lassiter.

"Hold it," he said.

Lassiter's head leaned back and he flashed a weak smile. "Ah, take it easy, Cooper. It's just my epinephrine." He was moving with easy deliberation now as he held up an auto-injector syrette. He straightened slowly and stuck the end of it on top of his thigh. "You wouldn't want me to go into anaphylactic shock, would you?" His thumb pressed the button on the side and he jerked, his head lolling to the side. He took three deep breaths.

They watched as Lassiter said, "Oh, wow, it's cold… but it feels so good."

Before Bolan could react, the muscles in Lassiter's arms pumped up like steel cables raising a bridge. The riot cuffs split in two, and he grabbed the door handle. He glanced over at Bolan and their eyes locked.

"Don't worry," Lassiter said. "I'll keep my hands together until we get off this bird. But how about giving me a gun? I can help."

Bolan said nothing. Lassiter looked fully recovered now. The drugs had to have had the desired effect. The MVP of black ops was back, at least for the moment.

"Please, Cooper." His eyes were pleading. "I've got to try and save her. She means everything to me."

Bolan waited a split second more, then reached for the Beretta 92F, and handed it, butt first, to Lassiter. "Afterward, I'm still bringing you in to answer for your part in Chris Avelia's murder."

"I won't resist," Lassiter said as he took the pistol and shoved it into his waistband. "You got my word."

"What did you do that for?" Callahan asked.

"Just evening the odds a bit," Bolan said. "Help Jack take out the guys behind us."

"Sounds like a plan," Lassiter said. "But then I'm coming up that second stairwell with you."

Bolan looked at him, then nodded.

"How can you be sure we can trust him?" Callahan said.

"He's a real good judge of character," Grimaldi said. "If we get through this, I'll tell you a couple of stories. Over dinner, of course."

"Yeah, right." She frowned and ducked.

Grimaldi banked the helicopter and began lowering it slowly toward the landing pad. In less than thirty seconds he'd set the chopper onto the concrete with the precision of a professional race car driver pulling into the pit. The Hummer and about ten men were on one side of the chopper. Another five or so were on the other. They were all about thirty feet away, shielding their eyes from the rotor wash. "It's party time," he said, grabbing the MP-5.

Bolan opened the copilot's door and jumped onto the helipad, keeping the extended LAW as much out of sight as he could. His MP-5 was hanging in its normal slung position, in front of his chest. He grabbed the handle of the passenger door on his side and slid it back. Lassiter, his hands held in front of him as if they were still secured, jumped out. Bolan pulled the arming hammer forward, releasing the safety on the LAW.

"Now," Bolan yelled to Callahan. The FBI agent grabbed the handle, twisted it and shoved open her door. Bolan raised the LAW onto his shoulder, aimed at the Hummer and depressed the trigger. The back-blast thrust a cloud of heat and smoke toward the men behind him as the rocket shot forward. It struck the front end of the vehicle and exploded in a yellowish-red fireball, sending a concussive wave of flame and heat in all directions. A split-second later Grimaldi leaned over the seat and opened up with his MP-5, spraying a group of surprised guards. Lassiter reached into his belt, drew the Beretta and began firing.

Bolan brought his MP-5 into play, firing three quick bursts at the guards who were still standing. He aimed low, for their legs, then brought his aim upward. The guards twisted and fell to the ground.

"Let's go," Bolan yelled. Grimaldi and Callahan

scrambled out of the chopper. Bolan sent another volley of bullets over the decimated group in front of him. No one moved. Lassiter ran over and grabbed an M-4 rifle from one of the fallen guards. He pulled back the charging handle slightly, verified there was a round in the chamber, and tapped the bottom of the magazine. He tossed the rifle to Bolan, who caught it with his left hand. Lassiter took three more rifles, tossing one to Grimaldi, one to Callahan, and keeping one for himself.

Bolan motioned them toward the white building. As they ran, a few rounds zipped by them. Three new guards were firing off to the left. Lassiter twisted as he ran, taking out the three gunners with a controlled burst from his captured M-4.

They were about fifty feet from the entrance now, and Bolan slowed slightly as he brought up the second LAW and pulled out the cotter pin. Working as he ran, the Executioner stripped off the covers and extended the launch tube. The area had scattered building and parking lot lights, but was primarily dark.

"Wide berth," he yelled as he angled to his left to give himself a clear field of fire. The others strayed to the right as Bolan pulled out the arming hammer. He slowed his forward motion and after three more steps was stopped and in a firing stance with the LAW ready to go. The soldier lined up the front and rear sights on the doorway and pressed the trigger. The dark space around him lit up in a profusion of smoke and brightness. The rocket streaked through the night toward the entrance and exploded a second later. The upper half of the door hung in place for a moment above a vacant lower half, then fell.

Lassiter and the others were at the door now. Bolan followed as Grimaldi took a quick peek, then slipped inside. The soldier didn't hear the sound of any rounds going off, and assumed the hallway was clear, at least for the moment.

Lassiter went inside next, followed by Callahan. Bolan wondered how she'd do under fire for what most possibly was the first time. He knew combat either made you or broke you, and he hoped she'd be all right.

He ducked through the smoldering opening and into the bright hallway.

They were all inside. Now they just had to go up and find Lassiter's girlfriend without getting shot.

GODFREY'S FACE FELT hot and wet as he looked out the big window at the burning carnage in the parking lot. What the hell was going on? Had the helicopter crashed?

No, that's not it, he thought, when he saw the copter on the helipad, its rotors still, its doors standing open.

Where the hell was that damn idiot Fellows? he wondered.

The answer occurred to him as soon as he heard the gunshots and felt the reverberations of the explosions. Lassiter. He had to have managed to take out Fellows and his team and was now coming for him.

Godfrey felt as if a pair of big, cold hands had grabbed hold of his bowels. That man-monster's coming here, he thought. And he's coming after me.

He ran back to his desk and grabbed the television remote, quickly calling up the various camera views into a collage on the screen. Several angles showed four figures, one of them a woman, moving across the parking lot, firing a bazooka of some sort, and then disappearing in the smoke and flash. Another view showed them entering the first floor hallway. Godfrey recognized one as Lassiter, and he didn't look weak or sick at all. Just angry and determined. That stupid, worthless piece of shit Fellows. He couldn't even take out one man with the small army he had? Godfrey swallowed hard. One man...Lassiter.

"What is happening?" Chakhkiev asked, as he stood. His bodyguard was at Godfrey's side, looking out the window.

"Yes," Hutchcraft said. "What is going on, Tony?"

Godfrey ignored them. This wasn't the time to deal with idiots and morons. He glanced toward Campbell, who was still lying on the floor, semiconscious. She could be his bargaining chip, if it came to that, but what would Lassiter do once he'd seen what kind of shape she was in?

"Get some water and clean her up," he said to Lawrence. The man's face had a pale, grayish cast, and he looked half-dead. The idiot seemed frozen. "Get moving, damn it," Godfrey shouted at him. "You're a doctor, for Christ's sake, aren't you?"

Lawrence blinked twice, then nodded. He licked his lips and walked over to the wet bar, but instead of grabbing some water and a rag, the son of a bitch grabbed a bottle of whiskey, splashed some in a glass and tossed it down.

"What the hell are you doing?" Godfrey yelled. He'd picked up the phone now, the inner-compound line, and dialed Security. It rang several times before the harried dispatcher answered. "The lab and office building has been breached," Godfrey yelled. "Get me some damn protection over here fast."

"We know, sir," the dispatcher said. "But we have men down in the parking lot."

It took Godfrey a second to realize that "men down"

meant "injured" and not their location, but what did he care about them? They weren't important.

"I don't care," he shouted into the phone. "Get as many personnel over here as you have, at once!" He slammed down the phone and glanced back at Lawrence, who had a wet cloth and a glass of ice, and was heading toward Campbell. The idiot was still moving as if he was in a partial trance. Godfrey stepped forward and grabbed his arm.

The doctor gazed at him, startled. "Lassiter's on his way up here," Godfrey said.

"I know," Lawrence answered. He looked toward Campbell.

Godfrey reached up and slapped him across the face. Lawrence appeared shocked.

"Pull yourself together," Godfrey ordered.

He gestured toward Trang. "Can you amp him up? Like he was before?"

The big Asian was standing there with a snarl on his face. "I don't need nothing else. I can take him."

"In a pig's eye," Godfrey said. "I need you in top form. Roid him up. Now."

Lawrence nodded.

Godfrey took the glass of ice and the rag from the doctor's hands. "Then go do it. Now. He's our only safeguard against Lassiter."

Lawrence nodded again, his jaw slack, his mouth forming an O. He looked at Trang, then back to Godfrey.

"Move, you freaking idiot," Godfrey yelled.

Lawrence walked to Trang, put his hand on the bigger man's shoulder and ushered him toward the door.

"Don't you touch me," Trang said.

Great, Godfrey thought. We're losing control of this one, too.

Trang went to the door and yanked it open, almost pulling it off its hinges. Lawrence followed, seeming to gain momentum as he tried to catch up. By the time he got into the hallway he was practically trotting toward the elevators.

Chakhkiev had been standing by the window, watching. Now he took out a cigarette and stuck it in his mouth. His big bodyguard produced a lighter and flicked it on for him. After sticking the end of the cigarette in the flame, Chakhkiev leaned back, exhaling a cloud of smoke.

"Put that damn thing out, would you?" Godfrey said. "The smell's making me sick."

Chakhkiev smirked and took a long drag, exhaling more smoke. "With all that is going on, I am not surprised." He nodded to the man beside him, who drew a huge, semiautomatic pistol and held it down by his leg.

"But," Chakhkiev said, "I think you are in a poor position to dictate to me your personal whims." He motioned with his head toward the door, and he and his bodyguard left.

"To hell with them," Godfrey said. "Let them die." He glanced at Hutchcraft, who looked petrified.

Godfrey turned away from him in disgust. He hurried over to Campbell. She was still unconscious, with her left arm in a grotesque, unnatural position. Perhaps he shouldn't have twisted it quite so hard.

Hutchcraft was beside him now, panting as if he'd just run around the block. "What are we going to do?"

"Pick her up and put her in that chair," Godfrey said. "Be careful of her arm."

"You shouldn't have hurt her like that," Hutchcraft said, squatting and working his hands under her back and legs.

"Just watch her arm, you idiot." Godfrey looked around the room. Lawrence and Trang had gone down in the elevator. Chakhkiev and his goon must have taken the stairs. There was nothing to do but wait now, and hope that the security forces or Trang stopped Lassiter.

Godfrey glanced at the television screen and saw that a few of the camera views had gone blank, leaving a patchwork of pictures and black squares. Hutchcraft was dabbing the woman's forehead with the wet cloth. Godfrey walked over to his desk, opened the center drawer and took out a Glock pistol. He wished he had more than just thirteen shots. He wasn't sure that would be enough.

THE FIRST THING Bolan did, once they were inside and had determined there were no immediate targets, was to quickly take out the little plastic PTZ camera shells on the ceilings and walls. He shot them to pieces.

"What are you doing?" Callahan asked.

"Taking out their eyes," he said. He would have preferred to work from the roof down, but there was no choice this time.

He glanced along the hallway, which was still empty, and motioned for Grimaldi to push open the stairway door. Callahan stood behind the pilot. Lassiter had already moved to the far end of the hallway and stood by the other stairwell. Apparently, he was waiting for Bolan, at least for the moment.

Grimaldi shoved the door hard, and it moved back against an obvious pneumatic spring return. Bolan held his M-4 at the ready, but saw nothing inside. He checked the space between the door and the jamb, a determined it was clear and nodded for Grimaldi and Callahan to go in.

"See you on the fourth floor," Grimaldi said.

Bolan tapped one of the radios Valdez had given them and said, "Watch yourselves and keep in touch."

Grimaldi and Callahan slipped through and let the door swing shut behind them.

Bolan jogged down the hallway toward Lassiter, who suddenly made a palm-down gesture to drop. Bolan flattened as the wounded man opened up with his M-4, firing 3-round bursts over Bolan's prone body. The Executioner rolled on his side and glanced back. Four security guards, all armed with rifles, were twisting and falling to the floor. The soldier sprayed the group with his M-4 as he got to his feet, his back pressed against the wall. When no return fire came from the downed guards, Bolan ran to Lassiter's position. They both knew they had to get out of this hallway. It was the perfect kill zone.

Bolan nodded, and Lassiter pushed open the stairwell door and moved to the side.

Going from one kill zone into another, Bolan thought.

This time a flash of rounds zipped through the open door and ricocheted off the wall behind them. Lassiter stuck the muzzle of his M-4 on the other side of the doorjamb and fired. Bolan did the same after transferring the weapon to his left hand.

Suddenly, the door at the other end of the corridor burst open and a new contingent of security guards burst through, tripping over the twisted array of bodies that already littered the hallway. Just in time, Bolan and Lassiter managed to edge inside the stairwell. Lassiter kept firing upward, until the bolt on his M-4 locked back, signaling it was empty. Bolan handed his rifle to his companion and slipped the third, and last, LAW off his shoulder.

Lassiter fired more rounds upward. Several men

screamed. Bolan took a moment to stick the MP-5 back out around the doorjamb one-handed, and fired a quick burst. He knew he'd used up almost all the ammo in the 30-round magazine. He released the weapon, letting the sling catch it so that it hung downward in front of his chest again, and popped open the LAW. In two quick pulls he'd armed the weapon, then squatted, holding the LAW in the doorway and canting it so that the missile would travel down the hallway. He pressed the trigger and felt the ignition inside the tube. The hallway filled with a plume of smoke, followed a split-second later by a resounding explosion.

Lassiter gave him a thumbs-up and dashed up the first set of stairs, firing on the run. By the time Bolan joined him, they were both stepping over dead bodies. Three men rushed out the stairwell door at the second level. Bolan motioned for Lassiter to secure the next set of steps, and went after them, knowing it would be suicide to leave a known hostile force below them as they advanced upward. He pulled open the door, holding his MP-5 in his right hand and his radio in his left.

"Jack, where are you?"

"Second level," Grimaldi said. "Inside the stairwell."

Bolan took a quick look and saw the three men rushing along the corridor. "Bad guys coming your way now. Second floor hallway." He fired a short burst with his MP-5. The three gunners stopped, spun around and began to fire in Bolan's direction. They twisted and fell as Grimaldi opened up on them from behind. He grinned at Bolan and disappeared back into the stairwell.

Bolan checked his MP-5. Empty. He slid the sling over his head. With no extra magazines on his person, and no hope of finding any, it was just deadweight.

Lassiter was standing on the stairs leading up to the

next level. He glanced down as Bolan dumped the submachine gun and shook his head. Lassiter nodded. The Executioner unsnapped the Beretta 93R and almost smiled at the feeling of the familiar grip in his hand. He pressed the radio to his lips and said, "Jack, low ammo alert."

"Roger that," Grimaldi said. "Us, too. Almost totally out."

"Going up to three now," Bolan said.

"Roger—" Grimaldi's transmission stopped abruptly and Bolan heard more gunfire.

GODFREY SAT AT his desk and used the mouse to click on whatever camera views he had left. They popped up on the big flat screen in patchwork fashion, showing more black spaces between fewer pictures. The ones on the first floor had been taken out, and some kind of explosion had then rattled the entire side of the building. Who the hell were these three people with Lassiter?

Godfrey clicked on the second floor hallway and saw three black-outfitted security guards lying in a heap. How many more men did he have available? Lassiter and his buddies were going through them like a lawn mower.

He clicked on the third level, and as the images of the lab popped on, Godfrey saw something equally disturbing: Lawrence and Trang seemed to be engaged in some kind of argument. The supersoldier was shirtless, his muscle rippling, as he gestured at the doctor.

Godfrey clicked on the audio feed but could hear only snippets of the conversation.

"You don't give…about… Nobody does. You think I don't know?"

The big Asian began moving through the lab area, picking up beakers and microscopes and throwing them against the walls. He grabbed a high, curved metal faucet and snapped it off its base, then tossed that away, too. A steam of water gurgled from the broken pipe.

Lawrence moved forward, making placating gestures and saying something that sounded calming. Words to soothe the savage breast, Godfrey thought. I hope.

Trang grabbed one of the heavy laboratory tables, lifted it and threw it against a wall. Those things had to weigh a couple hundred pounds each, Godfrey realized. It was Trang on a rant. Obviously this whole GEM program was starting to turn into more trouble than it was worth. First Lassiter and now Trang. No wonder the military was gravitating toward drones. At least they could be controlled.

Godfrey picked up the phone, debating whether to send whatever men he had left to the lab to try to gain control of that fiasco, or try to locate and destroy the more immediate threat of Lassiter. More gunfire echoing from outside the room decided for him. It sounded closer this time. Lassiter and his friends were working their way up. If Godfrey could pinpoint the group, maybe he could have Lawrence send Trang after them. If he could take out Lassiter, and maybe that other big guy dressed in black, the third guy and the woman could probably be handled by the remaining security forces.

Godfrey dialed the central dispatch number and yelled into the phone, "They're coming up the stairwells now. Where are those extra men?"

"I've got a squad of six men on the way, sir," the dispatcher said. He sheepishly added, "And that's all we have on hand."

"What?" Godfrey yelled. He slammed the phone down.

Hutchcraft ran over to the desk and crouched beside it, his face was white. "What's wrong?"

"Everything."

"Where are they now?" he asked. He sounded almost breathless.

Godfrey shot him a look of disgust, but refrained from yelling at him, afraid it might send this "future president" completely over the edge.

Future president, my ass, he thought. Then his concerns turned more to the present situation. Six men… Maybe it was time to try to find a way out of here. He still had Ellen Campbell to use as a bargaining chip. Hopefully, she was still alive.

"What are we going to do?" Hutchcraft asked. He was just a scared little man now. A very scared little man.

But before Godfrey could think of what to say, Hutchcraft recoiled in shock and pointed to the screen. "Oh, my God," he said. "What's he doing?"

Godfrey looked back to the screen and saw two men struggling.

Trang and Lawrence.

What the hell? Godfrey clicked on the image to enlarge it, and saw the terrified expression on Lawrence's face as he struggled to get out of Trang's grasp. The big supersoldier had him by the collar and the hair. The old fool always kept it long, sometimes pulling it back into a small ponytail. Trang's right hand doubled up a fistful of the gray hair and twisted. His left hand closed over Lawrence's neck. The big fingers spread over the top of the doctor's head, turning it slowly to the left. Lawrence was grimacing, screaming. Bits of his voice were picked up by the audio.

"Trang, no…"

Godfrey saw the expression on the supersoldier's

face, his eyes wide open, his lips pulled back over his teeth in a manic grin.

Lawrence's head continued to rotate to the left until all Godfrey could see was his profile, and then the back portion of his long gray hair. The gurgling scream abruptly ceased and Lawrence's body slumped like a dishrag. Trang looked around, still holding the doctor's limp form by the neck, and then up at the PTZ lens on the ceiling, the smile still plastered across his face. The sound was intermittent, but Godfrey could make it out: "I'm coming for you next, asshole."

Oh, shit, Godfrey thought. Frankenstein's monster had just reached the point of no return.

BOLAN HEARD GRIMALDI'S voice coming over the radio, interspersed with gunshots. "We got bogies above us on the third level stairwell."

The Executioner turned to Lassiter. "Hold up here. I've got to give Jack a hand."

He pulled open the door, did a quick combat survey and saw no immediate threats. He went through, his Beretta 93R held in front of him as he quickly advanced down the hallway. Grimaldi and Callahan were in trouble, and almost out of ammo from the sound of it, with guards on this level firing down at them. Bolan figured if he could flank this group, he could solve the problem. The hallway ahead was long, running past a bank of elevators in the center, which were directly across from a series of floor-to-ceiling windows. A perpendicular plastic sign stuck out above the windows with Laboratory Facilities printed in black letters.

The soldier stopped and scanned the interior of the laboratory through the glass. The place was in shambles, with overturned tables and a sink overflowing with water.

Three more shots rang out from the stairwell, and he moved forward. His peripheral vision caught something dark moving at the last second, just before the window on his right exploded into myriad shards of glass. A man's body tumbled through the frame and slammed into him. The force knocked Bolan into the elevator doors, and they both fell to the floor, the Beretta slipping from the Executioner's grasp.

The man who'd come through the window didn't move. He was slender, with longish gray hair, and was wearing a white lab coat. Bolan caught a glimpse of half-closed, glazed over eyes, and knew in an instant that the man was dead.

He pushed off the body as he worked to get to his feet and recover his weapon. But a large shape appeared in front of him: a half-naked, sweat-drenched, muscular man rushing through the broken window. Trang grabbed Bolan's combat blouse and twisted, throwing him against the adjacent window.

Bolan tried to relax his body as much as he could to lessen the impact as he felt the glass shatter around him. His adversary drew him back just as a large, hanging shard fell down, narrowly missing both of them. Bolan used the moment to slam his right forearm against his assailant's wrists, trying to break the man's grip. He turned his body at the same instant. Another slab of fractured glass fell, this time landing on top of them. Bolan felt his assailant's grip relax, and delivered another hard forearm blow. That loosened the other man's hand further, and Bolan stepped back and away, into the lab, trying to get his bearings.

The other man, a big Asian guy, had a maniacal

grin on his face as he advanced again. His upper body was layered with bulging muscles and showed numerous flecks of red where the glass had sliced his skin. The cuts looked superficial, and Bolan knew that the blood, mingled with the sweat, would make the Asian hard to grab and hold.

The Executioner backed up and almost lost his footing from bumping against an overturned chair. The Asian looked as if he had a substantial weight advantage, making wrestling a bad option.

Bolan touched his right pants pocket for his Espada knife, but the pocket was torn open, the knife gone. It had to have fallen out when he went through the window. He reached behind him and grabbed the leg of the overturned chair, whipping it around and sending it flying at the Asian.

The man danced out of the way, the weird grin still in place.

So the guy's fast as well as big, Bolan thought. He kept inching backward, between two long lab tables. Bolan knew he'd just limited his own area of movement, but had little choice. The other guy was cutting off his retreat.

But they were in a laboratory, not a boxing ring. As Trang started to stride forward, Bolan reached out and grabbed a glass beaker from the table top and threw it at his face. The Asian brought his fist up in a quick block and brushed the beaker away, but Bolan had already found two more and hurled those as well. One shattered against the side of Trang's head, and he automatically wiped away the shattered glass with his hand, leaving a trail of crimson.

That seemed to enrage him, and he stormed forward, arms outstretched, head down, emitting a primal scream. Instead of moving back, Bolan grabbed his adversary's extended left arm and pivoted, propelling his opponent around him and sending him crashing into an overturned table. He was up in an instant, looking more enraged than before, and ran at Bolan again.

The Executioner vaulted over a table to the next aisle. Trang did the same, landing a few feet away. As the other man came down on the balls of his feet, Bolan stepped forward and delivered a left jab, right cross, left hook to the Asian's face.

The blows seemed to have no effect, and Bolan knew he'd moved in too close. He tried to step back, but felt the Asian's fingers grab the right sleeve of his combat blouse. Trying to twist away, Bolan got caught by a hammerlike blow to the side of his head, then felt the stinging pain of a kick to his left thigh. He brought his arms into a V in front of his body to try to absorb any more strikes, but his adversary delivered a crushing blow to his left side.

The Stony Man warrior managed to twist at the last second to avoid a jab to his liver, which would have probably produced a temporary paralysis. Bolan whipped a left back-fist into the Asian's nose, which stunned the man for a brief second. Pivoting, Bolan lashed out with a kick to Trang's right knee, angling it onto the side to try to rupture the meniscus. That slowed his opponent only momentarily. His hands found Bolan's combat blouse and right pant leg, and the Executioner felt himself being lifted off the ground and swung over the adjacent table.

After sailing through the air for a few seconds, he landed hard on his side. The Asian leaped over the lab table, making it look effortless, and came down a few feet away. Still on his back, Bolan knew he had to react fast or the other man would straddle him. The thought of a ground-and-pound, with his heavier opponent on top of him, spurred him to action. He lashed out with his legs, positioning the instep of his right foot firmly against the outside of the Asian's left shoe. Bolan then pivoted, slamming his other foot against the inner area of the big man's left knee, causing him to topple. He reached out, trying to prevent the fall, but only knocked hard against the thick, protruding edge of the lab table.

Bolan jumped to his feet and delivered a pair of uppercuts to Trang's jaw. The blows knocked the bigger man backward, but he rolled over and was back on his feet in a matter of seconds.

This time he paused slightly before surging forward again, his mouth a gaping maw, his face twisted with rage and hate.

This guy fights with his heart, Bolan thought. Not his head.

Bolan danced back, sweeping some titration tubes off the table and into the Asian's way. He blocked the glass tubes, which shattered, causing him to shut his eyes and sputter. As he ducked forward a second later, Bolan smashed a snapping front kick into the man's forehead. The kick sent the guy reeling against the table on the opposite side, but he used the momentum to bounce off, swinging back toward Bolan, whose fingers closed over a long, graduated cylinder.

Grabbing it around its base, the soldier swung it in an arching motion toward his adversary's head. The glass shattered, leaving deep lacerations over the Asian's cheekbone. He lashed out with a hooking punch that hit Bolan in the left side, causing him to feel as if his guts were on fire. Trang followed up with a quick front kick, his foot smashing into Bolan's chest and knocking him backward.

The Executioner couldn't breathe for a split second, with the wind knocked out of his lungs, but he knew he had to keep moving, stay on his feet. Otherwise, it would be all over. He lashed out with the jagged, broken glass tube and sliced open a swath of skin along the Asian's left deltoid. This stopped the man's advance for a moment. But then Trang rammed his massive fist against the Executioner's temple.

Bolan felt his knees buckle from the blow, but a lifetime of training and combat helped him to recover quickly. He retaliated with a left jab, then right, still holding the remnants of the shattered cylinder. The glass cut into the Asian's face, but Bolan's hand as well. He instinctively dropped the rest of the glass and shook his fingers. Red droplets flew outward.

The Asian was too close, and managed to reach out and grab him. They tumbled back, falling on the floor with a heavy thump, the big man on top and Bolan on the bottom—just where he didn't want to be. He tried to use his legs to get a scissors hold around his opponent's midsection.

But Trang was too quick, working his knees over Bolan's waist and pinning him to the floor. He sent his right fist streaking down at Bolan's face, but the Executioner managed to deflect it. A second blow from the Asian's left fist creased his cheek, and his head jerked to the side. He raised his forearms again, trying to ward off the blows, but the Asian grabbed his left upper arm and pushed it to the side. He then grabbed a fallen microscope the size of a cinder block and cocked his arm, ready to deliver a final, crushing blow.

Bolan's fingers brushed the floor next to his head,

then closed over the saucerlike bottom of the broken graduated cylinder. He grabbed it and swung upward, twisting his body with all his remaining strength, as the microscope smashed against the floor next to his head. The jagged edge of the glass zipped under Trang's jutting chin and sank into the soft tissue beneath. The soldier followed through with the blow, feeling a sudden dappling of warmth as the Asian's blood gushed from his throat. The supersoldier's eyes rolled back, and he grabbed his throat with both hands, trying to hold in the bloody flow. His weight shifted, and Bolan was able to grab his opponent's hips and shove him off, scrambling to the side and then back to his feet.

The Asian sat on his knees a few feet away, the cascade of blood pouring around, over and through his fingers. He glanced up, catching Bolan's gaze for a moment, then slumped forward onto the tiled floor, the crimson puddle expanding under his head. Bolan staggered over to the broken windows, every part of his body aching. He glanced both ways. Nothing. No sounds, either. He stepped through the gap and stooped to retrieve his Beretta, then felt his belt for his radio. It was gone. After taking a couple shallow breaths, each feeling as if someone were sticking a thousand needles into his chest, he looked around for the radio. It was nowhere in sight.

He hoped Grimaldi had overcome whatever adversaries had been firing at him. Bolan stumbled toward the door that led to the stairwell, holding the Beretta close to his chest this time. Pausing at the door, he took a few more deep breaths. The needles of pain had given way to a dull ache, but he was starting to get his legs back.

One more level to go, he thought.

LASSITER HEARD THE sound of footsteps rushing up the stairs from below. He opened the door to check on Bolan, but saw nothing except a body in a white lab coat lying in the hallway among a sea of broken glass. He turned back to the stairwell in time to catch a glimpse of black-clad security uniforms rushing up the stairs. Six of them. He set the M-4 on full-auto and stepped down to the middle of the stairs, holding the rifle over the banister and firing a series of quick bursts. Several of the men fell, yelling and twisting as they dropped. Lassiter pulled the trigger again, but realized the magazine was empty. He dropped the M-4 and pulled the Beretta 92F from his belt. Suddenly he felt the all-too-familiar twinge in his gut. It was starting again. The weakness. The auto-injector dose was wearing off.

He took a couple quick breaths.

Ellen was one floor up and he couldn't wait for the others. He had to find her, save her.

Lassiter ran up the rest of the stairs, worried that he was using too much of his remaining energy, but not knowing how much he had left. He prayed he'd have enough to save Ellen. Nothing else mattered.

His stride had slowed considerably as he neared the fourth level, his feet feeling as if fifty-pound weights were attached to his legs. Three more steps. One… two…three.

He was there. Lassiter pulled the door open and glanced down the hallway. Two men, one dressed in a blue suit and the other in some kind of camouflage BDU, like the ones he'd seen at the water park, stood in the middle of the corridor. Beyond them Lassiter could see the command center.

I can't stop now, he thought, stepping into the hallway. He marched forward on unsteady legs, holding the Beretta out in front of him.

The man in the suit pointed at him and yelled something in what he thought was Russian. The other man raised a big pistol and fired. Lassiter heard the bullet zip by his head. He pulled the trigger of the Beretta. The man in camouflage jerked, fired again. This time Lassiter felt the bullet strike his chest, but he still wore his body armor. He fired the Beretta once more. The man in the suit was pointing a gun now, and a yellow flame burst from the barrel. This round hit Lassiter in the left thigh. He kept advancing, adjusting his sight picture to bring the man into target acquisition. He squeezed the trigger. Blue Suit jerked and backed up several steps, looking down and grabbing the side of his chest. His lower lip curled into a snarl and he lurched drunkenly, bumping into the wall.

The camouflage man's pistol spewed a muzzle-flash and this time Lassiter felt the bullet penetrate his gut, below the body armor. It felt as if a giant clamp had seized his entire lower body, but he kept walking, kept squeezing the trigger on the Beretta until the slide locked back. The man in the blue suit, still leaning against the wall, sank to a sitting position and tumbled forward. The camouflage man fell, curling on the floor, his pistol's slide also locked back.

Beyond them was the command center...and Ellen. Lassiter forced his legs to work.

The stairway door burst open and Lassiter's heart sank for a second, until he saw it was Cooper's partner, the pilot, and the FBI woman. They sprinted down the hallway toward him.

Lassiter kept his focus on the door to the command center. Ellen had to be in there. She just had to be.

He stepped over the bodies of the camouflage guy and the man in the suit, not stopping to check them. They were dead, or near enough. Finding Ellen was all that mattered.

Grimaldi and Callahan were with him now, holding his arms, trying to get him to stop, but he couldn't. Not now. Not being this close.

The door of the command center opened and Ellen stood there. A man's arm curled around her from behind, snaking up between her breasts, his fingers digging into the soft flesh of her jawline. Godfrey was behind her, and his other hand held a Glock pistol at her temple.

"I've been waiting for you," he said. "Freeze where you are, or you'll watch her die."

Lassiter's eyes widened in horror.

No, he thought, I can't let it end like this.

BOLAN FELT AS IF he barely had the strength to make it up the stairs, but somehow he managed, and pulled the door to the fourth level, opening a tight sliver of visibility. In a flash he took in the scene unfolding down the corridor: the frozen figures of Grimaldi, Callahan and Lassiter, all staring in horror at the two people backing toward Boland. A man and a woman… He had a Glock pressed against her temple and was babbling something. It was Godfrey.

Calculating that the industrialist wouldn't reflexively squeeze the trigger and kill the woman, the Executioner brought up the Beretta, swung the door wide and fired into the back of the man's skull. Godfrey dropped to the floor like a discarded marionette.

That's justice for Chris Avelia, Bolan thought.

He stepped from the doorway to see the woman running down the hall. She went straight to Lassiter, who was on his knees, and pressed his head to her breast. The area below Lassiter's body armor was a dark crimson and his left leg was completely red from the thigh on down. Even from this faraway vantage point, Bolan could tell by the grayish color of Lassiter's skin that he didn't have long.

A warrior's death, Bolan thought. And it looked as if they'd saved Dr. Campbell.

The Executioner strode down the hallway, his Beretta still held at the ready. He heard movement to his left, whirled and pushed open the door to the command center. A haggard looking man in a blue polo shirt and tan slacks was stumbliing about in the middle of the room.

"Hands up," Bolan said, aiming the Beretta at Brent Hutchcraft. "Step out here."

Hutchcraft raised his hands and slowly moved toward the doorway.

"Listen, I'm a U.S. senator," he said. "Don't shoot. I surrender."

Grimaldi was next to Bolan now, pointing a Walther PPK .380 at the senator's chest.

"Where'd you get that?" Bolan asked.

Grimaldi shrugged. "From our dead buddy Dimitri over there. Mine are all out of ammo."

Hutchcraft stepped through the doorway, and Grimaldi grabbed him and placed him none too gently, face-first, against the wall.

"My, my," Grimaldi said, "I think we know this guy."

"Yeah, we do."

"Who are you men?" the senator yelled. "I demand you escort me safely out of here. Immediately."

"Shut up," Grimaldi said, and slipped past him to clear the command center area.

Bolan shoved the senator against the wall, did a pat-down search and twisted the man's hands behind his back.

Grimaldi exited the command center a minute later and said, "The room's clear, but the cleaning crew's going to have their hands full."

Callahan joined them now and handed Bolan a pair of riot cuffs, which he fastened over the senator's wrists.

"Valdez is on scene with a contingent of men and FBI SWAT," she said.

"Well, hell's bells," Grimaldi told her. "I feel safer already."

"Tell them to come up here and take charge of the prisoner," Bolan said.

"You can't do this to me," Hutchcraft protested. "I'm a member of Congress. I'm running for president."

"We know, Senator Hutchcraft," Bolan said. "And my friend here wants one of your eight-by-ten autographed campaign pictures."

"Yeah," Grimaldi added, "for the bottom of my bird-cage."

EPILOGUE

Arlington National Cemetery, Arlington, Virginia

Mack Bolan stood looking out over the sea of white headstones. He and Dr. Ellen Campbell weren't far from the Tomb of the Unknown Soldier, where the Army Honor Guard marched in endless duty and dedication.

Not a bad place to end up, Bolan thought.

He looked at the seven-member honor guard, which stood at attention around the flag-draped coffin in their full military dress uniforms. It was a small service, with only them, the bugler, Campbell and Bolan in attendance. No minister or priest was present, pursuant to her wishes. She was dressed in black, her left arm still in the cast.

The bugler raised the golden horn to his lips and began playing "Taps."

Bolan snapped to attention and saluted, even though he was wearing a blue suit with a navy tie. Once a soldier, always a soldier.

Visions of the many men he'd served with flashed through his memory—their dedication, their service, and now their much deserved rest. The bugler hit every note with practiced perfection. Bolan held his salute until the officer stepped forward and gave the command to prepare the flag.

The six other members of the honor guard moved

in, grasped the edges with a firm, yet respectful hold and stepped away from the coffin. They made the first, lengthwise fold with a crisp exactness, each subsequent one with rote precision. When they'd finished the second lengthwise fold, the two men at the back stood at attention as the final triangular folds advanced toward the field of blue with the white stars. The sergeant of arms finished and saluted, then clasped the folded flag. He did an about-face and marched to the officer in command, who made his salute, a slow, exacting motion, before accepting it. He then did a left-face and marched to Campbell, who was standing next to Bolan.

"On behalf of the President of the United States," he said, "and with the thanks of a grateful nation, I present to you this flag as a symbol of your loved one's service."

Tears ran down Campbell's cheeks as she took the flag and murmured, "Thank you."

The officer made his final salute, turned away, and the honor guard followed.

They marched off in formation as Bolan watched the sunlight dappling their shoulders and making their gold buttons gleam. He turned to Campbell. She was still clutching the flag to her breast as she gazed at the coffin.

"John would have liked it here," she said. "He talked about this place a lot."

"All soldiers do," Bolan replied. "It's as close to heaven as we can imagine."

She looked up at him. "Thank you so much for arranging it."

"Actually, a friend of mine deserves the credit," he said, thinking of the favors Hal Brognola had called in, cutting through ribbons of red tape to make the interment possible. "John will get an anonymous star on the wall at Langley, too."

She smiled and wiped her cheek with a handkerchief. "What's going to happen now?" she asked, dabbing at her eyes. "I'm scheduled to testify before a congressional committee, but do you think it'll do any good? Will it really make any difference?"

Bolan had his doubts, but he kept them to himself. "Give the system a chance to work. It might surprise you."

Campbell smiled up at him as another tear slid down her cheek. "And then what?"

"After you testify at the committee, we'll make sure you get placed in the witness protection program," he said. "With all the players involved in the conspiracy, you could end up a target of any of the survivors—friends of De la Noval, Chakhkiev, the Aryan Wolves.... It'll be a new start for the rest of your life."

"With lots of baggage from the old one," she said. "Do you think Senator Hutchcraft will be punished sufficiently?"

"He resigned from the senate and dropped out of the presidential campaign," Bolan said with a shrug. "I'm sure he'll plead to any and all charges that the attorney general brings. And if he doesn't, he knows there's my way."

She smiled. "Just before he died John whispered for me to trust you. He really respected you, even though he didn't know you that well."

"The feeling was mutual."

Another tear squeezed out of the corner of her eye and ran down her cheek. She turned back to look at the coffin.

Bolan looked at it, too. Duty, honor, country… All that a warrior could ask for. He silently wished John Lassiter peace.

Rest long and well, brother, he thought. You earned it.

* * * * *

The Executioner®
Don Pendleton's
MAXIMUM CHAOS

The mob will stop at nothing to free a ruthless killer

Desperate to escape conviction, the head of a powerful mob orders the kidnapping of a federal prosecutor's daughter. If the mobster isn't freed, if anyone contacts the authorities, the girl will be killed. Backed into a corner, her father must rely on the one man who can help: Mack Bolan.

Finding the girl won't be easy. Plus, with an innocent life at stake, going in guns blazing is a risk Bolan can't take. His only choice is to pit the crime syndicate against their rivals. The mob is about to get a visit from the Executioner. And this time he's handing out death penalties.

Available October wherever books and ebooks are sold.

Don Pendleton's Mack Bolan.

CHAIN REACTION

An old adversary's illicit plot threatens global security...

When a Stony Man Farm nemesis is suspected in the death of two FBI agents, Mack Bolan gets called into action. The last time Bolan crossed paths with the shadowy criminal organization, he annihilated their operations in North Korea. Now the group has brokered a deal that would send weapons-grade uranium to Iran in exchange for a cache of stolen diamonds. Joining forces with a field operative, Bolan sets off on a shattering cross-continental firefight. Bolan has no choice: he must destroy the criminal conspiracy behind the threat. Once and for all.

Available October wherever books and ebooks are sold.

JAMES AXLER

DEATH LANDS

POLESTAR OMEGA

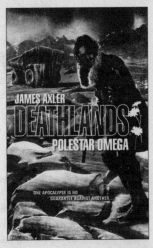

One apocalypse is no guarantee against another...

Ryan and his crew become the subjects in a deadly experiment when they're taken captive inside a redoubt at the South Pole. A team of scientists is convinced the earth must be purified of mutants, and now they have the perfect lab rats to test their powerful bioweapon. Filled with toxic chemicals and faced with Antarctica's harsh and unstable conditions, the companions must fight the odds and take down the whitecoats before millions are killed. But in this uncompromising landscape, defeating the enemy may be just another step toward a different kind of death....

Available November wherever books and ebooks are sold.

GOLD EAGLE®

GDL119

AleX Archer
THE PRETENDER'S GAMBIT

With one small chess piece, the game begins...

For archaeologist Annja Creed, a call from the NYPD means one thing: there's been a murder and they need her expertise. The only link between a dead body and the killer is a small missing elephant of white jade.

One misstep could mean the end...

ROGUE ANGEL
AleX Archer
THE PRETENDER'S GAMBIT

Once belonging to Catherine the Great, the elephant was key in a risky political gambit, but there is another story attached to the artifact—a rumor of hidden treasures. And for a cruel mogul with a penchant for tomb-raiding, the elephant is nothing short of priceless.

Annja must move quickly. It's a deadly battle of wits, and one wrong move could mean game over.

Available November wherever books and ebooks are sold.

GOLD EAGLE®